For Joan with

tion

—

2014

RCA

Echo by Dana Johnson, 2014 (see p.113).

Peter Blegvad

Kew. Rhone.

Uniformbooks 2014

First published 2014
Uniformbooks in association with Amateur Enterprises
www.amateur.org.uk

ISBN 978-0-9568559-8-5

Uniformbooks
7 Hillhead Terrace, Axminster, Devon EX13 5JL
www.uniformbooks.co.uk

Printed and bound by T J International, Padstow, Cornwall

By Peter Blegvad

Side One

1) Good Evening

2) Twenty-Two Proverbs

3) Seven Scenes from the Painting "Exhuming the First American Mastodon" by C.W. Peale

4) Kew. Rhone.

5) Pipeline

6) Catalogue of Fifteen Objects and Their Titles

Side Two

1) One Footnote (to Kew. Rhone.)

2) Three Tenses Onanism

3) Nine Mineral Emblems

4) Apricot

5) gegenstand

1

Eleven Thoughts re *Kew. Rhone.*

1. Opposite is the track list from the cover of *Kew. Rhone.*, an album of songs (mostly) by John Greaves (music) and myself (words and pictures) released first in 1977 and a few times since. Reviewing it on the BBC Experimental Music homepage,[1] Peter Marsh describes it as "Ludicrous, serious and (if the truth be known) much more seditious than the [Sex] Pistols ever were." American poet Andrew Joron says it's "...one of the few rock albums I'd consider genuinely surrealist in spirit and composition."

2. "Rock"? Maybe. Sort of. Critics have discerned evidence in the music of influences ranging from Soft Machine and the Art Ensemble of Chicago, to Kurt Weill and Leonard Bernstein.[2] A high point of the record is free-jazz maestro Andrew Cyrille's drumming. On his first day with us in the studio, Andrew was at a loss to come up with an approach until he managed to identify the genre—"it's *show* music!" To quote Peter Marsh again, the music is "...every inch the equal of the texts in their complexity; tidily anarchic, stuffed with blunt, vaguely jazzy harmonies and melodies that wander unpredictably. *Twenty-Two Proverbs* could almost be from a Bernstein musical. Sort of."

3. That qualifying "sort of" is the key. *Kew. Rhone.* is *sui generis*, slippery, it doesn't want to be defined. The parts—the music, the words, the illustrations and the performances—all work against each other yet somehow the whole coheres. In other words, *Kew. Rhone.* was very much a collaborative achievement.

---

1 www.bbc.co.uk/music/reviews/wd8c (accessed Sept. 2014)

2 I asked John Greaves about that list. He replied: "I actually think the influences cited are pretty accurate in terms of where the composer was coming from. Kurt Weill certainly. Funny time signatures came from the Softs exploded by Henry Cow. American free jazz is all Andrew, who called it 'show music'. Hence Bernstein. And we've always recognised the seamless incongruity of those lyrics and Lisa's Broadway delivery. There are bits that must have come from my early years playing danceband music with my father who also took me to see Ellington, Basie, Stan Kenton and Woody Herman. I'd like to think some of that seeped through on to *Kew. Rhone.* A major influence on me though is the bird in whose house we recorded it." (He means Carla Bley.)

4. As is this book. When publisher Colin Sackett and I began assembling material for it we had no idea that our invitation to contribute would elicit such a generous response from the individuals gathered here (most of them in the section starting on p.131). We're mighty grateful to them all.

5. We've used *Kew. Rhone.*'s track list as the organising principle for the first half of the book. A list seems appropriate, given that most of these songs involve lists of one sort or another.[3] Each track is treated in turn: the lyric being followed by a selection of related materials—texts, images and documents from the archives.

6. As exegesis this method is deliberately oblique. The aim being to illuminate without dispelling the mystery of a work designed to resist interpretation even as it invites it.

7. Suffice it to say, the songs engage lyrically with three interrelated themes: *Omen* (the reading/interpretation of signs), *Nomen* (the power of names, the pros and cons of identity) and *Numen* (the spirit in matter, the numinous).

8. This book likewise engages with those themes, being an experimental reading/interpretation of *Kew. Rhone.*, an attempt to name and identify some of its sources, and to imaginatively invest the material with something like a 'spirit'.

9. The book is also a memoir of sorts. Although it's almost 40 years ago, I remember the *Sturm und Drang*, but also the euphoric sense I had while working on these songs that everything I read or saw or heard seemed relevant or a potential part of the project.

---

3 "Lists are used as a formally alienating device, a dehumanizing agent, that is nonetheless entirely wrapped up in human life. How do we describe the fact of human existence? At a certain point, perhaps, style fails us. Language, even and in particular at its most evocative, becomes less of an aid and more of a difficulty. In these circumstances, a certain kind of writer has, again and again, reverted to the list—perhaps as the simplest proof of existence in the first place. It's no accident that these lists often delineate material objects, the physical evidence of a life." —Katie Kitamura, 'Literary lists: Proof of our existence', *Guardian Review*, 16 February 2013

[In a list] "proximity creates meaning, however uncertain we are of the combinations or the methods by which they were combined." www.artfagcity.com/2009/10/22/img-mgmt-teen-image/ (accessed Sept. 2014)

In the introduction to *An Elizabethan Song Book* (1955), W. H. Auden quotes Rossini's remark, "Give me a laundry-list and I will set it", and adds that "a laundry-list, or any list for that matter, has a poetic value, and one which is exceptionally translatable into musical terms."

In *The Writing Problems of Visual Thinkers* (1991), author Gerald Grow includes "*Aesthetic indiscrimination*—All details are equally important. Everything is everything else. Author does not take a position. Everything hangs in a mesh of undefined relationships. Bland, even, one-level quality to [text]. No main point. Reads like a list." *Kew. Rhone.* embraces these 'problems' as opportunities.

10. I felt like Robert Walser as described by William Gass: "To his eye, everything is equal; to his heart, everything is fresh and astonishing; to his mind, everything presents a pleasant puzzle."[4]

11. A pleasant puzzle and a story, of sorts. Susan Hiller: "I take it that any conscious configuration of objects tells a story."[5] The objects (texts and images) presented here offer various tellings of *Kew. Rhone.* The ancient Hindu TOE ('Theory of Everything') is embodied in the metaphor of a net with a jewel at every node. In every facet of every jewel all the others are reflected. It's known as 'Indra's net' and might be a model of the mind or of the internet. *Kew. Rhone.*, in its modest analogue way, was interactive *avant la lettre*, and I think I'm at least half-serious when I say that these bits and pieces aim to evoke a unified whole that points beyond itself to a vast, nebulous, unstated revelation of universal correspondence.

Peter Blegvad
Roquebrune Village, April 2014

---

4 William Gass, *Finding a Form* (1996).

5 Susan Hiller, Barbara Einzig, Lucy Lippard, *Thinking About Art: Conversations with Susan Hiller* (1996).

Good Evening

(*comp.* John Greaves)

Twenty-Two International Proverbs

1. Would ye both eat your cake and have your cake? *(English)*
2. Would ye brak a butterfly upon the wheel? *(English)*
3. He who sows wind will reap a tempest. *(Portuguese)*
4. Milk the mosquito to serve your king. *(Bulgarian)*
5. To cut into another man's ear is like cutting into a felt hat. *(Danish)*
6. She is neither fish nor flesh nor good red herring. *(English)*
7. Names are not the pledge for things, but things for names. *(Romanian)*
8. One should write bad things on running water. *(Romanian)*
9. A drowning man would catch at razors. *(Italian)*
10. Coupled sheep drown one another. *(Dutch)*
11. One may well be too young to marry, but one is never too old to love. *(Finnish)*
12. Treat your friend as if he will one day be your enemy and your enemy as if he will one day become your friend. *(from Laberius)*
13. Herring in the land, the doctor at a stand. *(Dutch)*
14. Dead as a doornail. *(From 'Piers Plowman')*
15. A single hair casts its shadow on the ground. *(Spanish)*
16. What have I to do with Bradshaw's windmill? *(English)*
17. Better to live one day as a lion than live a hundred years as a sheep. *(Motto on Italian 50-lire coin)*
18. The stone that the builders rejected has become the corner stone. (*Paraphrase of* Psalms *CXVIII, 22;* Luke *XX, 17*)
19. The stone that everybody spits upon will be wet at last. *(Danish)*
20. A cat may look at a king. *(English)*
21. By night all cats are grey. *(French)*
22. The pen of the tongue should be dipped in the inkwell of the heart. *(Italian)*

2

Proverbs, Perverbs, Emblems, *Koans*

> *"The age-old and persistent links made between omen, nomen, and numen surely reveal both an inveterate leaning towards playing with words, and a proper deference towards mystery and the ineffable."*
> —Walter Redfern, *Puns* (1984)

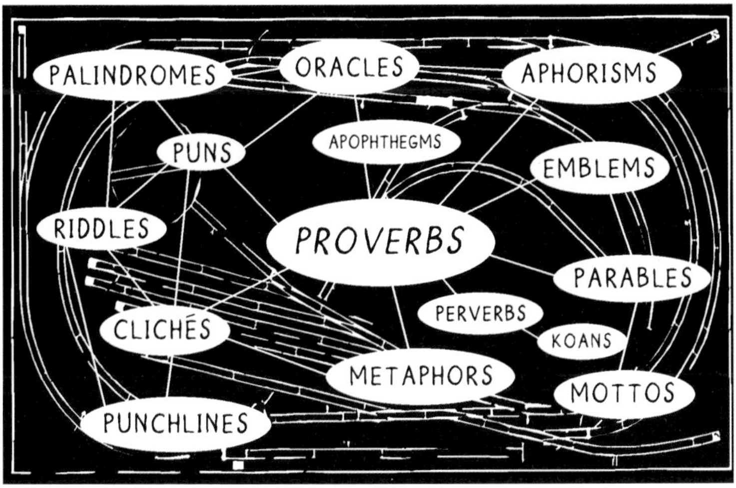

Paroemiological Diagram, showing proverbs in a constellation with other related forms.

The proverb is a repository of folk wisdom, the plebeian cousin of the aphorism, which is more the expression of individual wit or sagacity. The proverb expresses the experience of the collective. In that sense this is a political song.

Thematic repetition is used in lieu of linear narrative to give a sense of structure. Repetition—of cats, herrings, drowning, couples, writing—sets up a net of correspondences while vectors of association connect individual proverbs with other songs on the album.

Proverbs lose their power over time, they become clichés. But a proverb new to us packs a poetic charge. Proverbs are also related to metaphors, mottos, riddles, puns, and to oracles: "to cut into another man's ear is like cutting into a felt hat", for instance, or “a single hair casts its shadow on the ground”—such formulae have the ominous ambiguity of something a sibyl might utter through a cleft in the rock. Like oracles, proverbs require engagement, decipherment, interpretation to see whether or not or how they might apply.[1]

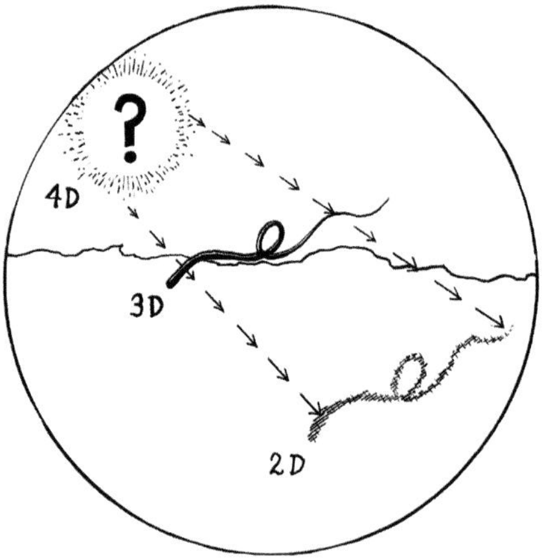

In 1985 I sent a copy of *Kew. Rhone.* to Harry Mathews whose writings influenced and inspired me. He responded positively, saying he would “present” the record to the Oulipo.

Several years later, invited to contribute to *Kew. ROM.*[2] the author of *Tlooth*, *Cigarettes*, *Armenian Papers* and other experimental works[3] diced and spliced the proverbs in the song to produce 20 ‘perverbs’. His operations boosted their poetic charge, revealed new meanings, emotions and truths. They still express a kind of collective wisdom, though now the collective might be the collective unconscious.

Rue Cone (Wide Son): Twenty Perverbs

1. Would ye both eat your cake and its shadow on the ground?
2. Would ye brak a butterfly on Bradshaw’s windmill?
3. He who sows wind would catch at razors.
4. Milk the mosquito and live a hundred years as a sheep.
5. To cut into another man’s ear will reap a tempest.
6. She is neither fish nor flesh nor too old to love.
7. One should not write bad things to serve your king.
8. A drowning man will be wet at last.
9. Coupled sheep should be dipped in the inkwell of the heart.
10. One may well be too young to marry and drown one another.

1 Apropos the relationship between oracles and puns, cf. Jean Cocteau: “*L’ami Zamore de Madame du Barry* is a fact. *La Mise à Mort de Madame du Barry* is an oracle.” When reproached for his use of puns in his poetry, Cocteau declared “Metaphors are badly finished puns”. From ‘Giorgio di Chirico’ in *My Contemporaries* (1967).

2 An edition of the album released in 1997 on the Voiceprint label which contained a substantial ROM extension created by a Belgian team under the direction of François Ducat, programmed by Denis Thiriar and designed by Serge Gutwirth.

3 “Everything that happens in these books —the least details of their vicissitudes, their erudite digressions, their *langoureux vertiges* —are nothing more than the ghostly, frail delineations of the legendary wrestling match in which from the beginning of time we have been engaged with the world of words, signs, meanings and dreams, which we call fiction.” —Georges Perec, *Avez-Vous Lu Harry Mathews?* (1981).

11. Treat your friend as if he will one day be your enemy and have your cake.
12. Herring in the land, good red herring.
13. Dead as a corner stone.
14. A single hair may look at a king.
15. What have I to do with the doctor at a stand?
16. Better to live one day as a lion than one day become your friend.
17. The stone that everybody spits upon will be grey.
18. A cat may look like cutting into a felt hat.
19. By night all cats are but things for names.
20. The pen of the tongue should be dipped in running water.

—Harry Mathews, Paris, 17 September 1997

A visual relative of the proverb is the Emblem.

> "Emblem Books were popular compendia featuring page after page of epigrammatic texts, normally with illustrations. A reader coaxed meaning out of the combination of picture and text. Sometimes it seems as if the text was generated to explain the picture, and with others it's the reverse. One notorious emblem remained long unillustrated, for it described the act of literally shitting where one eats: 'This act stands for all offenses exceeding the canonic measure of sacred law…'"
> —www.artfagcity.com/2009/10/22/img-mgmt-teen-image/
> (accessed Sept. 2014)

A helmet used as a beehive was the emblem of conflict-resolution, of peace. A winged figure (Inspiration) blowing a trumpet riding on a turtle's back represented the idea *Festina Lente* (hurry slowly). An airborne hand with an eye in its palm conveyed prudence, and might be paraphrased as "don't strike out blindly". Is this one (an ass? with masks) something to do with cunning, duplicity etc.? Not sure. Breughel painted a range of proverbs, e.g. Pissing against the moon, emblem of hopeless ambition, useless effort.

A QUO TREPIDABO (Whom shall I fear?)—From the first, perhaps only, emblem book to be compiled by a woman (Georgette de Montenay), this shows Faith lending assurance to a youth ascending to a higher stratum (cf. John Masten frozen on his ladder in the song *Mastodon*). *Emblèmes ou devises chrétiennes* (1571).

The perverb is closer than the proverb is to the Zen *koan*, defined by Nancy Wilson Ross as "a formulation in words not soluble by the intellect alone—indeed, often quite senseless to the rational mind, a veritable 'riddle.' *Koans* are meant to be directly experienced. They are formulations on which to practice that famous 'law of reversed effort' by which results are often mysteriously obtained in the hidden, unconscious depths of one's being."

In *The World of Zen, An East-West Anthology* (1962) Ross quotes a few of Paul Eluard's *Proverbs*: "Make two o'clock with one o'clock," "I came, I sat, I departed," "A crab by any other name would not forget the sea," "Who hears but me hears all." She compares these to *koans*: "'When Tom drinks, Dick gets tipsy,' 'Last night a wooden horse neighed and a stone man cut capers,' 'Lo, a cloud of dust is rising from the ocean, and the roaring of waves is heard over the land.'"

Opposite: *Would ye both eat your cake and have your cake?*
"A common source of confusion about this idiom stems from the verb *to have* which in this case indicates that once eaten, keeping possession of the cake is no longer possible, seeing that it is in your stomach (and no longer exists as a cake). Alternatively, the two verbs can be understood to represent a sequence of actions, so one can indeed 'have' one's cake and then 'eat' it."—Wikipedia

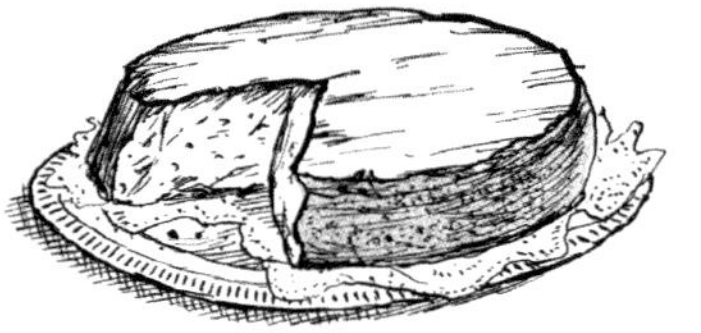

RICE & APPLE CAKE

SIMNEL CAKE

CAKES OBSERVED

RICE & APPLE CAKE

SIMNEL CAKE

CAKES DEVOURED

RICE & APPLE CAKE

SIMNEL CAKE

CAKES (MENTAL PROJECTIONS)
RECOLLECTED IN TRANQUILITY

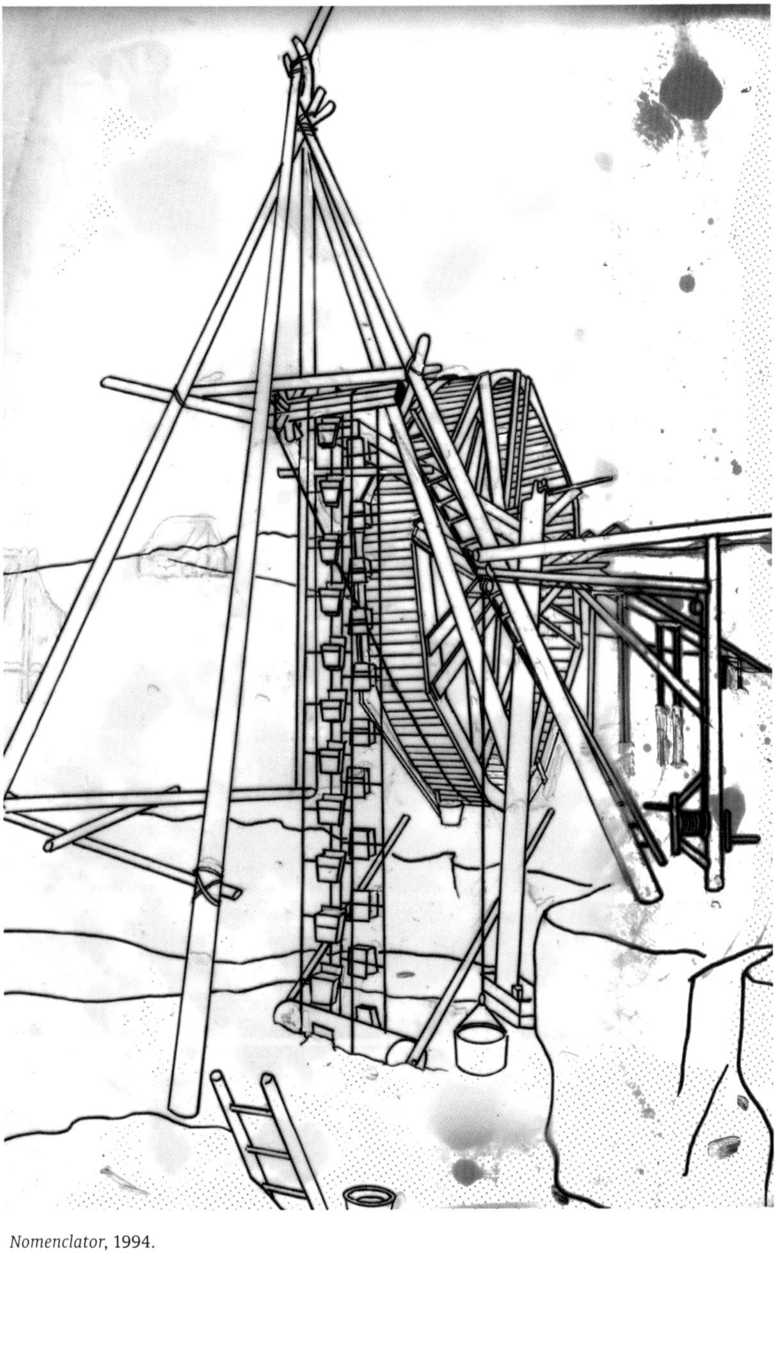

Nomenclator, 1994.

Seven Scenes From the Painting 'Exhuming the First American Mastodon' by C. W. Peale

I. Youth with no name cuts out of the frame
with an axe.

II. Those who extol a bone on a scroll
turn their backs, sanction his escape.

III. Attached to his toe, shackles
below the surface hold a neophyte fast who
ogles aghast a bone of gold emblazoned
with his name.

IV. Three green umbrellas are shown in all.
These denote degrees by which a fall
(a fall from grace) may be measured
as virtual, potential or as actual.

1. the first has been dropped,
2. the second picked up, but not untied,
3. the third has been spread high overhead to
   hide the sky.

V. Nourished by the two syringes shown,

VI. the wheel 'Nomenclator' (better known
to the world as The High Priestess) names (i.e. defines)
her victims forever.

VII. John Masten has hung so long
from a rung he now depends on it as much as from it
for such a vantage lends itself
    to one who proudly claims
    to be amphibious though actually allergic
    to the
    two predicaments
    to which his ladder leads.

Exhuming the First American Mastodon by C. W. Peale.

After *Exhuming the First American Mastodon* by C. W. Peale. (Version by François Ducat for *Kew. ROM.* 1997.)

3

On Charles Willson Peale

A scientific expedition that took place in 1801 in Newburgh, New York, is the subject of a history painting of uncommon interest not only in itself but because the artist who painted it is also the scientist who engineered and directed the event. The talented and versatile painter, inventor, and natural historian Charles Willson Peale built up a natural history museum, which housed stuffed and preserved creatures set with skillfully reproduced bits of their natural habitats, all carefully labeled. The skeleton of the mastodon that Peale reconstructed from the bones he himself helped dig up in the expedition depicted in his 'Exhuming the First American Mastodon', of 1806–8, became the prime attraction of his museum. Of the many figures in the scene, only three had in fact taken part in the digging: Peale himself, who holds up the drawing of a bone and gestures toward the marl pit; his eldest son, Rembrandt, who stands beside him and helps him hold the drawing; and the farmer on whose land the excavation took place, John Masten, in the foreground climbing out of the pit on a ladder. The other figures are mostly members of Peale's large family and friends of his, some deceased—all posed as in a great family portrait. The idea of combining all these elements, representing the many eventful changes in Peale's own life (including his three marriages and his seventeen children), may have been linked in his mind with the momentous changes in geological history suggested by the extinct mastodon.

—Abraham A. Davidson, *The Story of American Painting* (1974)

These words accompanied a fuzzy reproduction of *Exhuming the First American Mastodon*, in a book I came across at my in-laws' home in Ithaca, New York, *c.*1975. I remember poring over the picture in their backyard, trying to puzzle out the details. The crowded scene dominated by the jerry-built contraption under a threatening sky, the division of the composition into upper and lower strata, and the dreamy self-absorption of the figures suggested an allegory which wanted interpretation. It summoned me to dredge meanings up from the depths to 'explain' various figures in the tableau.

Loath to disturb or dilute the mystery of the painting by any more facts than Mr Davidson had already provided, I protected my ignorance about its author until *Kew. Rhone.* was finished. In the years since, I've read about Peale and the dynasty he founded (his sons Rembrandt, Rubens, Titian and Raphaelle were all celebrated painters) with mounting curiosity and delight. I've learned that he carved a set of wooden teeth for George Washington, that he might have deliberately hastened Raphaelle's demise by arsenic and mercury poisoning,[1] that not one mastodon but two were exhumed, that their discovery was a first proof of the then contentious theory of species extinction, that Peale thought of his museum as an American 'ark' and sold it, after 40 years, to another resourceful Yankee maverick—P. T. Barnum.

The portraits he painted look a bit wooden compared to works by his English mentor, Benjamin West, or those by his contemporary, Gilbert Stuart. Peale's technique lacked *finesse*. The word that comes to my mind is 'clunky'. Clunkiness is a quality I associate with American design, which tends to prize function above beauty (the grace and subtlety of Shaker furniture and many other exceptions to this blatant generalisation notwithstanding). The gradual evolution of America's pride in (and the concomitant erosion of its shame of) the clunkiness of its products, particularly in comparison to European models, is the history of American culture, a culture that dominated the globe from the end of World War Two until the close of the Millennium by which time its cultural credit seemed to be exhausted. At the roots of that awesome arborescence, fertilising it with his bones, lie the remains of an extraordinary individual, Charles Willson Peale.

---

1 "Telling a tale of parental envy and murderous spite, two scholars say they have found evidence that Charles Willson Peale, one of the founders of American art, induced his eldest son, Raphaelle, also an accomplished artist, to poison himself... [The scholars, Phoebe Lloyd and Gordon Bendersky] maintain, first of all, that the death of Raphaelle Peale was caused by poisoning rather than by alcoholism, as is generally believed by historians. They also say that the poisoning can be traced to the elder Peale because, besides painting... Charles Willson Peale was a pioneer taxidermist who developed compounds of arsenic and mercury that enabled him to preserve bird and other animal skins for display on stuffed models.

[...] The elder Peale, Lloyd and Bendersky write, knew of the toxicity of the preservative chemicals... knew the symptoms of arsenic and mercury poisoning, knew and used the presumptive antidote, and yet insisted that Raphaelle perform taxidermy at the family museum without warning him of the danger involved.

While Raphaelle was experiencing delirium, tremors, headaches, loss of hair and teeth, and bone necrosis of the upper jaw, all of which are characteristic symptoms of arsenic and mercury poisoning, the authors say, Peale did not provide his son with what he believed to be the antidote and dismissed his complaints as the effects of gout and high living.

'If you feel disease, do you not know that you are deserving of pain?' Peale wrote to his son in 1818, by which time Raphaelle had become emaciated."

—From 'Arsenic and Old Paintings, a Who-dunit', by William H. Honan, *International Herald Tribune*, 7 July 1993

THE PEALE MUSEUM

225 Holliday Street — Baltimore, Maryland 21202

The Municipal Museum of the City of Baltimore 1931

April 1, 1977

Mr. Peter Blegved, Room 1506
29 John Street
New York, New York 10038

Dear Mr. Blegved:

Pursuant to our telephone conversation back in January, I have billed Virgin Records Ltd. relative to the use of the Mastodon painting.

As far as I know, this is the first time that our famous painting has been used on a record cover. I'm anxious to see the finished product and look forward to receiving the two copies we agreed upon. Please send them to my attention so that I may make the proper notation on the forms.

Very sincerely yours,

Paul A. Amelia

Paul A. Amelia,
Archivist

Built in 1814 as Rembrandt Peale's "Museum and Gallery of the Fine Arts"
A Registered National Historic Landmark

Top: Photograph from the Peale Museum in its original glassine envelope.
Bottom: Letter from the museum, 1977.

4

Excavating *Mastodon*

> "Humanity is a well with two buckets,—said Wylie, "one going down to be filled; the other coming up to be emptied."
> —Samuel Beckett, *Murphy* (1938)

> "One has already to know (or be able to do) something in order to be capable of asking a thing's name. But what does one have to know?"
> —Ludwig Wittgenstein, *Philosophical Investigations* (30) (1953)

From my first glimpse of Peale's painting, *Exhuming the First American Mastodon*, I felt it was an allegory which required interpretation. The experience was akin to an 'apophany', a sense of abnormal significance in something. It seemed to be a portrait of the state of my psyche, using symbols only I could decipher, personal, while at the same time being somehow universal or archetypal. In his book *Why Are Our Pictures Puzzles?* (1999) James Elkins writes:

> "...there is a form of the desire for interpretation that specifically pertains to pictures." He calls it a kind of illness. As to why we feel this desire, he suggests it "...may be a response to the apparently unstable ontology of pictures, in that pictures may be understood as objects that appear 'lost' and make us think of returning them to words and to the world. ...Or else—and this is my favorite hypothesis, the one that I think goes farthest toward making sense of our behavior—pictures are bewildering because they present us with the most powerful examples that we can know of the absolute lack of meaning. ...we behave so strangely because we sense a very simple, unanswerable property that pictures have always had: in the end, after all the interpretations have failed, they reveal themselves to be utterly meaningless."

When I say *nomen* is one of the themes of *Kew. Rhone.*—I mean names and their slippery relationship to identity. On *Kew. Rhone.* names are often seen as reducing and restricting the phenomena they designate (as in the sinister baptism ritual described in my story 'Nomenclator'[1]).

---

1 "The ritual always began pleasantly enough, with a feast and gifts but, at a signal from Dr Ark, the congregation commenced to moan and cut themselves with shards. The neophyte was thrown naked into the river where the current was swiftest. Swept towards the mill, he'd be dragged under by the inexorable Wheel, boiled in thunder awhile, and borne up, gasping for air, with all that had once burned in him extinguished. In him or in her—it happened to girls as well as boys, and they usually paired off after the Wheel had named them. Soon the cycle began again with their children the victims."

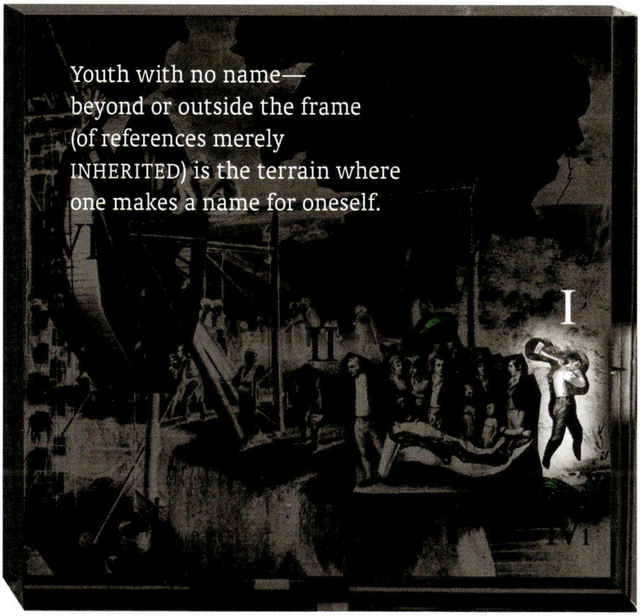

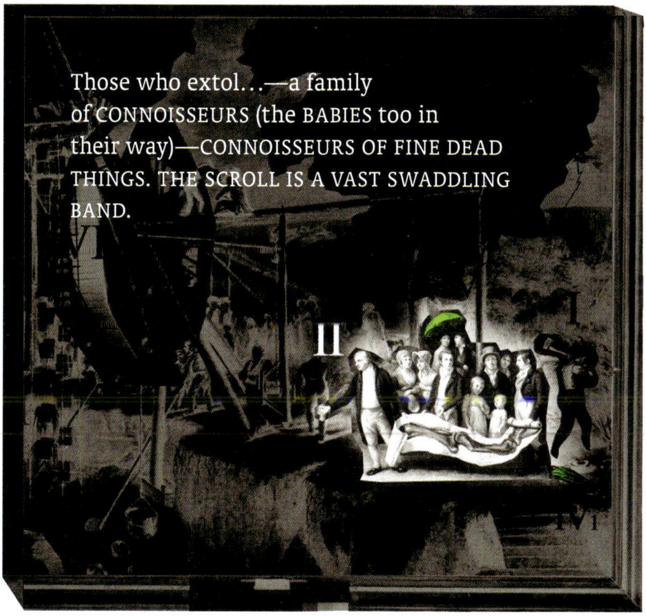

Texts (above and over) from an early attempt to interpret Peale's picture (1976).

The Mastodon was not named until some years after the exhumation of its bones. Dr George Graham in his report [1801] refers to it as "The Great American Incognitum". From the *Kew. Rhone.* perspective, that may have been the tusker's apotheosis.

From the *Kew. Rhone.* perspective, when Adam named the animals in Eden he set the clockwork of the Fall in motion.

> "Names are not the pledge for things, but things for names."
> —*Proverbs*[2]

cf. old art school admonition: "draw what you see, not what you know". If you don't know what it is you're drawing, chances are you'll see and draw it better. It takes practice and effort to resist the impulse to label rather than look.

> "To see is to forget the name of the thing one sees."—Paul Valéry

To be unlabelled, anonymous, is to be free. ANON and NEMO. Odysseus saves himself and his men by giving his name to the Cyclops as "no one".

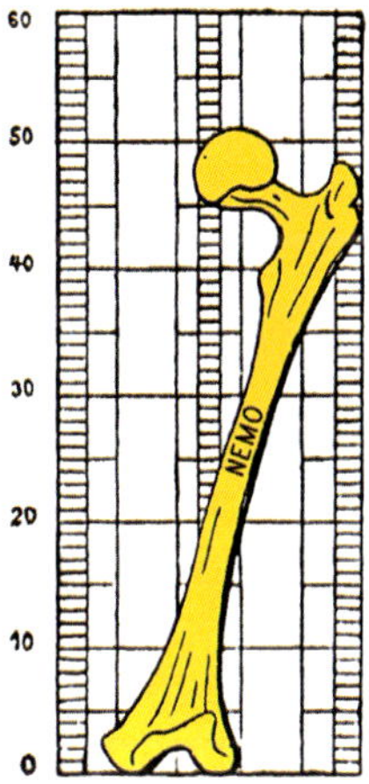

In my teens and twenties I went through what psychiatrists in those days referred to as an 'identity crisis'. I was morbidly aware of my own non-entity, transparent even to my own interrogations. I remember a girlfriend saying "I'm lonelier with you than when I'm by myself." I was a phantom, a figment, a fume.

Fear and trembling and the sickness unto death. (Kierkegaard identifies three green umbrellas, three kinds of despair: being unconscious in despair of having a self, not wanting in despair to be oneself, and wanting in despair to be oneself.) I could relate to them all.

> "I confess it, why should I repress it? Unless it's wrestled through, it grows on you..."—PB, 'Strayed', on the album *Desperate Straights* (1975)

When it came to writing the words for *Kew. Rhone.* I was determined to resist the confessional mode, to suppress the subjective and be as objective as possible. Well, everyone knows what happens to repressed content. It grows monstrous down there in the depths and finds devious backdoor means of expression.

This song is a case in point. If the intention was to deny or disguise my mental dis-ease, *Mastodon* did not succeed.

'Youth with no name' (I)—in order to make a name for himself he has to cut out of the frame that contains/confines him.[3] He's going

2 cf. Alfred Korzybski's dictum: "the map is not the territory."

3 An alternative view of the frame the Youth finds so confining: "You argue that the frame provides coherence only through repression and exclusion. But the trick is to discover Everything within the frame."—Chris Kraus, *I Love Dick* (1997)

through the painful process of waking up from what Whitman calls "contemptible dreams":

> "Long enough have you dream'd contemptible dreams,
> Now I wash the gum from your eyes,
> You must habit yourself to the dazzle of the light
> and of every moment of your life"
> —*Leaves of Grass* (1855)

Should he stay or should he grow? John Masten (VII) clinging to his ladder, is 'allergic' to climbing or descending; like Buridan's ass, he's stuck. The Youth isn't. He's hacking his way out. But, like any ephebe in transition from childhood to "the fierce order of virility",[4] he both dreads and desires what he'll have to do 'off the map', beyond the frame, and what it will do to him. No longer nameless, he'll be known, his cover blown...

cf. *Gunslinger* (1968), the epic poem by Ed Dorn: "it is dangerous to be named / and makes you mortal." That's it. That's what will happen to him. He'll *die*. As we all will. His exemption will be withdrawn.[5]

> "We realise our freedom in the dizziness that is dread,
> and make our choice in fear and trembling."—Kierkegaard

The neophyte in toe-shackles (III) is aghast at his name, i.e. the definition imposed on him by the wheel Nomenclator.[6] He represents everything the Youth is keen to avoid, from blinkered thinking to the living death of a nine-to-five job.

The wheel (VI) has another name: "The High Priestess". The only female in the song. Related to the Great Mother? cf. the song *Kew. Rhone.*—same theme of slaves in thrall to an autocratic matriarch?

---

4 Michel Leiris, *Manhood* (1946).

5 One thing I've learned in the years since *Kew. Rhone.*: in many cases pessimism is mere laziness which in turn is only (only!) fear. These days I'd be inclined to interpret Peale's painting as a project not to impose death on the living but to reverse time's arrow, to bring the dead back to life.

6 cf. "To him that overcometh will I give to eat of the hidden manna, and will give him a white stone, and in the stone a new name written, which no man knoweth saving he that receiveth it."—*Revelation* II, 17

cf. "...you'll know what to do, after the Holocaust, after the Aliens come and give us all those GIANT PILLS, and all them machines that'll run our lives and that BIG WHITE STONE that everybody's gonna know PERSONALLY in their very own living rooms. That's the stone that you think you might know and you think might HELP YOU, but BY GOBBS, that's the stone that's gonna ruin your VERY LIFE!" —Dr Philo Drummond, *The Book of the Sub Genius, The Sacred Teachings of J. R. "Bob" Dobbs* (1983)

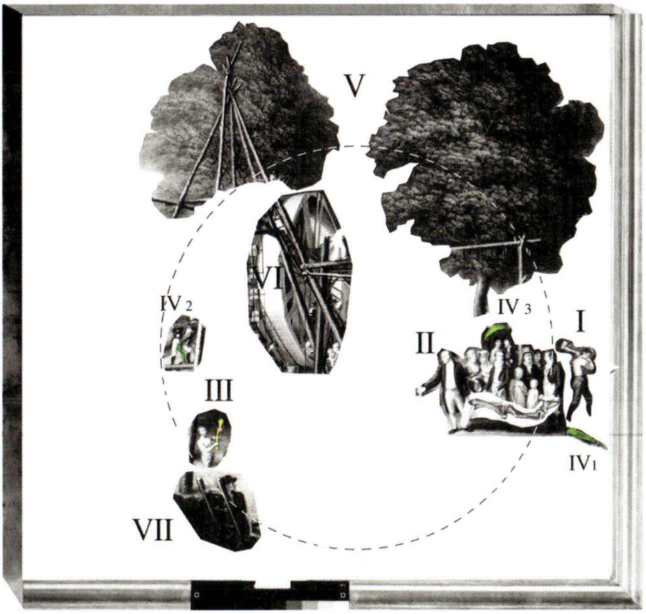

By performing a few simple operations on the image we can expose the symbolism, render it more legible. Cropping, encasing, desaturating it, reversing polarities, spotlighting details—reducing it to something more like a map or blueprint.

I'd forgotten, but reading Alain Robbe-Grillet's *Ghosts in the Mirror* (1988) it came back to me how, in 1975, his theories of the *nouveau roman* had led to Edmund Husserl and phenomenology. R-G was trying to write with a phenomenological eye. He alludes to a protagonist (in his first novel, *Un Régicide*), an "...unhappy soul who was pretending—doubtless for obscure moral reasons—to be nothing but a pure Husserlian consciousness."

I had my reasons for wanting to be dispassionate and phenomenological too. I wanted to avoid emotional confession partly because it wasn't fashionable, but also because I was an unhappy soul that summer.

> "One may well be too young to marry, but one is never too old to love."—*Proverbs*

I could relate to that. The unforeseen result of trying (pretending) not to write about my feelings, in songs like *Mastodon*, *Kew. Rhone.* and *Nine Mineral Emblems*, was to compress those emotions into unlikely, and therefore, perhaps, more effective metaphors.

The trees are referred to as two syringes, a reference to the twin pillars in Solomon's temple, Jachin and Boaz. Sketch by PB, 1976.

5

Excerpt from 'Nomenclator or The Big Wheel'

Bratt was a community of wattle huts and farms not found on any map. The people who eked out a subsistence there worshipped a wooden wheel they called Nomenclator, the one who names. Nomenclator was a water wheel, part of a ruined mill a mile outside of town.

The mill, the only such marvel ever attempted in Bratt, had been built in another time by Outsiders. Its destruction by fire a century ago had occasioned much comment. Comment had become lore, and lore had petrified into a grim religion. Nomenclator was its autocratic deity. Five storeys high, turning with slow majesty like a planet in space, the Wheel's glazed flanks drooled foam and water-diamonds like a hydrophobic maw. Around it crackled a nimbus of telepathic heat-lightning. Unquestioning obeisance to the Wheel, and connivance in its dark designs upon the world improved a person's chances in the here and now, and secured them a place in a better world hereafter. Nomenclator's head priest and mouthpiece, Dr Ark, stressed this in his sermons. In many ways, the grovelling peasants of Bratt were grateful to the Wheel for providing them with a binding focus, a hub of shared feeling in the purposeless monotony of their lives. It almost didn't matter that the feeling shared was fear.

Dr Ark could pass for human, but he had grown from a mandrake root into a tall lithe figure with breasts, a penis and a little beard. He went everywhere naked, even in midwinter, displaying these attributes with pride. He told his congregation that Nomenclator was in the process of redefining the Universe and everything in it—everything would be given a new name. Outwardly, he said, things would not appear to change, but inwardly, the instant they got their new names, they would be "gone"—a term he used to mean purged, spiritualised, absorbed into the energy field which fed the ravenous Wheel. When the process of renaming was complete, the world would be "gone" entirely. Then a marvellous new world would arise in its place, with Bratt its capital.

Dr Ark decreed that children should be given temporary names at birth. When they reached puberty the Wheel would name them permanently in a baptism ritual that was not for the squeamish. The Wheel named them and they were “gone”—“for death is in their new name like fire is in a log”—as the head priest put it. Few actually died, but after baptism, the youths became cowed zombies like everyone else in Bratt, shambling from one appointed task to the next, usually at the telepathic behest of the doctor.

Excerpt and illustration from ‘Nomenclator or The Big Wheel’, short story in the collection *Head Cheese*, Atlas Press (1994).

AMATEUR

First that a wheel[1] like a mill wheel turns between two trees. Then that the trees store a substance in their foliage. Then that they broadcast this substance in installments to the wheel. Then that this substance nourishes and lubricates the wheel and makes it turn. Then that the foliage blows green. Then that the nourishment broadcast is envy, that if the wheel had what it wanted it wouldn't turn[2]. Then that even turning slowly wheel is emblem of a kind of frenzy. Then that a space extends to either side of trees & wheel & recedes to a horizon behind them. Then that much of this space is peopled. Then that the space advances to constitute a foreground & that this foreground encompasses a pit. Then that certain people in the pit are holding objects. Then that, in a space like this one an object is the attribute of whoever bears it much as saints in icons bear as attributes the implements which killed them. Then that in a space like this one even a wheel like a mill-wheel has its attribute: the continuous chain of buckets which it drives. Then that when the wheel turns, buckets rise from the pit full of rocks & mud, empty themselves down the chute at the top of the chain & return down the other side bottoms up for more. Then that a bucket descending empty is emblem of residual frenzy. Then that a bucket coming up full is emblem of potential frenzy. Then that a bucket as it empties is ~~image~~ emblem of actual frenzy.

1 "Thus there are the seven forms of the mother of all beings, from whence all whatever is in this world is generated; & moreover the Most High has, according to this mother, introduced & created such properties as this mother is in her wrestling forms (understand, as she brings herself with the wrestling into properties) into a wheel, which is as a mind of the mother, from whence she continually creates & works." Signatura Rerum, Jacob Boehme

2 "Everything that moves, moves for the sake of something which it has not & wch is the goal of its motion; ... everything that moves, then, has some defect, & does not grasp the whole of its being at once." Letter 26 to Can Grande, Dante

Original paste-up of handwritten one-page pamphlet, an issue of *Amateur* (1978). The text describes Peale's painting and was set to music by John Greaves for broadcast on John Peel's BBC radio show, *Top Gear*, 1977.

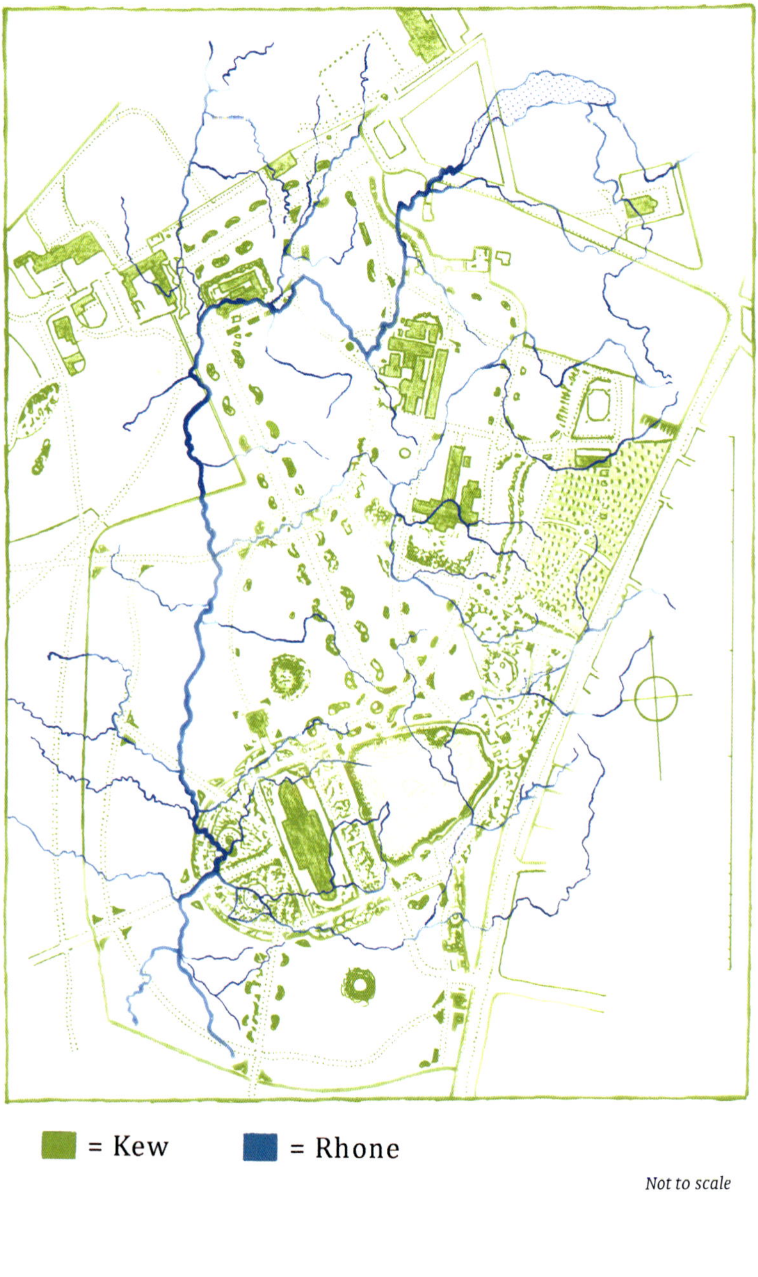

Not to scale

Kew. Rhone.

(who?) we who knew no woe
we who were her hero

(when?) when we were on her knee
when we knew her
when we were one

where?
Kew. Rhone.

we won renown

(how?) we were her worker

we won honor enow
when we knew her
when we were one

where?
Kew. Rhone.

not a set animal,
not a set animal, laminates
laminates a tone of
a set animal,
animal, laminates
a set animal,
animal, laminates
laminates a tone of sleep.
a tone of sleep.
Peel's foe, not a set animal, laminates a tone of sleep.

Three views—Imagined, Observed, Remembered—looking down from the top of the South Tower, World Trade Center, NYC, 1978.

6

Spiritual Skyscraper

> *"The lights are much brighter there,*
> *you can forget all your tables, forget all your chairs*
> *and go DOWNTOWN..."*

Kew. Rhone. is a phantom or spiritual skyscraper which is only visible to specific individuals, briefly, at a specific time and from a specific vantage, though these coordinates are never the same twice. Its appearances are not confined to a single city. The first recorded sighting was in Chicago, in 1919. Since then, materialisations have been reported in Lisbon, Buenos Aires, Stockholm, Toronto, Marseilles, Delhi, Durban and Hong Kong. *Kew. Rhone.* is a city thing. There is no record of a sighting in a non-urban setting. John Greaves, Lisa Herman and I were not ourselves privileged to catch a glimpse of this marvel, but in the summer of 1976, in downtown Manhattan, the three of us met a person who claimed to have seen *Kew. Rhone.* with her own eyes.

Because she prefers to remain anonymous I'll call her X. When we met her, all those years ago, X was in her 60s. John, Lisa and I were in our early 20s. X's husband had died the year before and X was glad to have company. We made her welcome at our table in the backroom of the Blarney Stone on Fulton Street where we held court each night.

X described how, 25 years before, she and her husband had watched *Kew. Rhone.* materialise from the 15th-floor window of an office building on John Street, between Broadway and Nassau. It was summer. It was the 'golden hour', when ("the City's fiery parcels all undone"[1]) the setting sun reflects off the myriad windows of the financial district. X told us all this and described how a kind of memory or ghost of the reflected rays imprinted on the air converged like laser beams in a hologram to form the image of a soaring edifice the baroque glory of which eclipsed all gross material skyscrapers. The façade she said was of beaten gold and silver, ornately worked and studded with sequins, lamps and twinkling gems. She closed her eyes as she described the numberless windows leaded with patterned and variegated panes in constant kaleidoscopic motion, the beams of

1 Hart Crane, 'To Brooklyn Bridge' (1930).

spiritual light and glinting clouds of gold dust that enveloped its base which she compared to a rocket on the launch-pad moments after ignition. X told us of the rapture she and her husband felt witnessing this apparition, how time was suspended… how they'd both cried out when *Kew. Rhone.* began to fade, how desperate they were to prolong the epiphany even for a moment! But the sun had sunk by a critical few degrees and where *Kew. Rhone.* had stood there was now nothing but air polluted by car exhaust.

Seeing how moved we were, X concluded by reciting a poem she declared to be "the fairest flower of the English tongue":

Life is Butter, Life is Butter
Melancholy Flower, Melancholy Flower;
Life is but a Melon, Life is but a Melon
Cauliflower, Cauliflower.

H.M.S. *Kew. Rhone.* in dry dock, lower Manhattan visible in the distance.

7

Anagrams and Palindromes

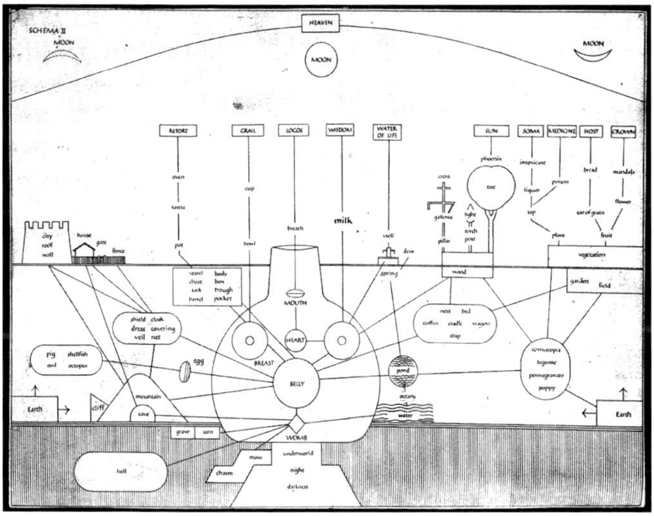

Diagram from *The Great Mother*, by Erich Neumann (1955). "...a poetic diagram is not simply a drawing. It must find a way to integrate the hesitations and ambiguities which alone can free us from realism, allow us to dream."—Gaston Bachelard, *The Psychoanalysis of Fire* (1938), trans. Alan C. M. Ross (1964)

Constraints liberate—Michel Leiris re Raymond Roussel: "...his voluntary submission to a complicated, difficult rule (...having to focus his attention on solving a problem whose givens are as foreign, detached, futile as possible) is accompanied, as a corollary, by a *distraction* from all the rest, which results, through this indirect method, in a much more effective lifting of censorship than a process such as automatic writing can achieve.

"...*pure* poetry, that is, the creation of interplay among concrete elements beyond any sentimental or didactic preoccupation..." but which nonetheless "expressed as clearly as possible the author's deep layers of emotion...".[1]

"Limits are / what any of us / are inside of."—Charles Olson[2]

---

1 Michel Leiris, review of Raymond Roussel's *Comment j'ai écrit certains de mes livres*, in *La Nouvelle Revue française* 24, 1936, trans. Lydia Davis (1989).

2 Letter 17 of the *Maximus Poems* (1953). For an alternative view, cf. Redell Olsen, Letter 4 of *The Minimaus Poems* (2004): "what is aware is / that anything is I, more than that / is called for. Limits / suggest confines for / revolt from within."

In 1975, an unbalanced youth struggling to write, I fell under the spell of Raymond Roussel and Harry Mathews. Their use of constraints to force inspiration inspired me to try.

My first inkling of Oulipo—the workshop for potential literature—was gleaned from one of Martin Gardner's 'Mathematical Games' columns in *Scientific American* magazine. As I recall, palindromes figured. Magical word-objects, they seemed to embody both innocence and experience, play and labour. Their symmetry made me think of Jung's work with mandalas—the palindrome as a kind of verbal mandala. A device designed to generate equilibrium.

In his poetry class at the New School, Gilbert Sorrentino told us about Louis Zukofsky's long poem *"A"* which Hugh Kenner called "a sequence of word games, of which we are not told the rules." We were told enough to be boggled. For instance, in the first half of part '9' phrases from *Das Kapital* are set to the rhyme scheme from Cavalcanti's *Donna mi prega* with the 'n' and 'r' sounds distributed according to the formula for a conic section.

Did voluntary submission to the use of constraints (anagrams and palindromes) free me to tap into "deep layers of emotion" as Leiris says in the quote above? Affirmative. Emotions similar (unsurprisingly) to those which inform *Mastodon*. William Empson (he of *Seven Types of Ambiguity*) puts his finger on it:

> "I remember believing I should have to die in order to grow up, and thinking the prospect very disagreeable."
> —*Alice in Wonderland: The Child as Swain* (1971)

The Great Mother diagram is here because the 'knee' we were on was 'hers'—i.e. it was the maternal knee. The song looks back nostalgically to a place identified as 'Kew. Rhone.', but it might be Never Never Land, the lost paradise of childhood. On one level, the song is an Oedipal regression fantasy. It also identifies us as 'her worker' which I interpret to mean her slave. It's not a healthy dependency.

Seventeenth-century Polish mystic, Jacob Boehme, described the Great Mother wrestling herself into the form of a wheel (an oracular passage which I found haunting though it resisted understanding):

> "Thus there are the seven forms of the mother of all beings, from whence all whatever is in this world is generated; and moreover the Most High has, according to this mother, introduced and created such properties as this mother is in her wrestling forms (understand, as she brings herself with the wrestling into properties) into a wheel, which is as a mind of the mother, from whence she continuously creates and works."—*Signatura rerum* (1651)

Sensing an oracular potential in the way they resisted understanding I made several attempts to link palindromes to various phrases in the song as it was evolving.

phrase I. ("when we were on her knee")
1) pilot to lip   dial laid
2) diamond I.D. did no maid
3) first little welt tilts rif/le

phrase II. ("work wore on")
1) a navaho o havana
2) due species net tense ice pseud
3) leg nave draw star rats ward evangel

phrase III. ("we were her hero")
1) one nut, pencil, rag, garlic, neptune, no
2) emit tacit ore, erotic at time
3) peed on a tuba, abut a node ep/hebe

phrase IV. ("we knew no woe")
1) an era lived, elapsed on node's pale devil arena
2) ten set are calcified, a lesion parts a strap. Noise,
"la deific", lacerates net

From these and other failed efforts the 'Peel's foe' palindrome evolved and the song finally found its form.

The Great Mother is a wheel. So is the rolling Rhone:

> The word 'Rhone' comes from Latin *Rhodanus*, which itself comes from Greek *Ροδανός*, *Rhodanos*, the Greek rendering of the Gaulish name of the river, as heard by Greeks living in the colony of *Massalia*. The Celtic name of the river was something like *Rodonos* or *Rotonos* (Great River) (*onos*/ *ona* is a suffix meaning Great). *Rodo/Roto*, literally 'that which rolls', or 'that which runs', is a frequent name of rivers in the ancient Celtic tongue. It was also the name of the lower Seine, as well as several other rivers of western Europe. The Celtic name comes from the Proto-Indo-European root **ret-* ('to run, roll'), which yielded the word *rota* ('wheel') in Latin, from which is derived 'rotate' and 'to roll' in English. Cognates in modern Celtic languages are Irish *rith* (in some dialects *ruth* or *ruith*), Scottish *ruith/rith* and Welsh *rhedeg*, both meaning 'to run', as well as the Gaelic noun *roth* ('wheel').

(Lisa Cunningham, *née* Herman, collected these etymologies for this book.)

> *kew*
> 1939, as a clipped form of *thank you*.
>
> *where (adv.)*
> Old English *hwær*, *hwar*, from Proto-Germanic **khwar* (cf. Old Saxon *hwar*, Old Norse *hvar*, Old Frisian *hwer*, Middle Dutch *waer*, Old High German *hwar*, German *wo*, Gothic *hvar* "where"), from PIE interrogative base **qwo-* (see *who*).
>
> *know (v.)*
> Old English *cnawan* (class VII strong verb; past tense *cneow*, past participle *cnawen*), "to know, perceive; acknowledge, declare", from Proto-Germanic **knew-* (cf. Old High German *bi-chnaan*, *ir-chnaan* "to know"), from PIE root **gno-* "to know" (cf. Old Persian *xšnasatiy* "he shall know"; Old Church Slavonic *znati*, Russian *znat* "to know". Meaning "to have sexual intercourse with" is attested from *c.*1200, from the Old Testament. To *not know one's ass from one's elbow* is from 1930. To *know better*, "to have learned from experience" is from 1704. *You know* as a parenthetical filler is from 1712, but it has roots in 14c. To *know too much* (to be allowed to live, escape etc.) is from 1872. As an expression of surprise, *what do you know* attested by 1914.

Losing and finding, a theme (covert) of *Kew. Rhone.* See *A Field Guide to Getting Lost* (2005) by Rebecca Solnit which inspired these ruminations:

There's a tradition out there—no matter how disaffected and unplugged in you feel when young—I was aware of it, wasn't sure how I might connect with it.

Fake it? Make the leap.

I'd picked up bits and pieces.

The piece you pick up, which proves decisive, can be anything.

Sages say "the commonest thing to be picked up anywhere" might turn out to be the Philosophers' Stone.

And the power that this has, what that is able to do, is to transform you. We want to be changed. Even if we don't know what lies on the other side.

Pipeline, *Catalogue of Fifteen Objects*, *Mastodon*—these songs are hopeful engines for change, for transformation. Transformation of myself, obviously—but mine would be the by-product (latent) of the target transformation (overt) which was that of the listener/reader.

Art—high and low—may be useless for anything else, but it does have the power to transform.

KEW RHONE—an anagram of KNOWHERE—cf. hippie adage: *Be here now.* To know where (and who) you are—the theme of identity and location, the construction/discovery of a stable self it might be bearable to be. (A luxury not everyone can afford.)

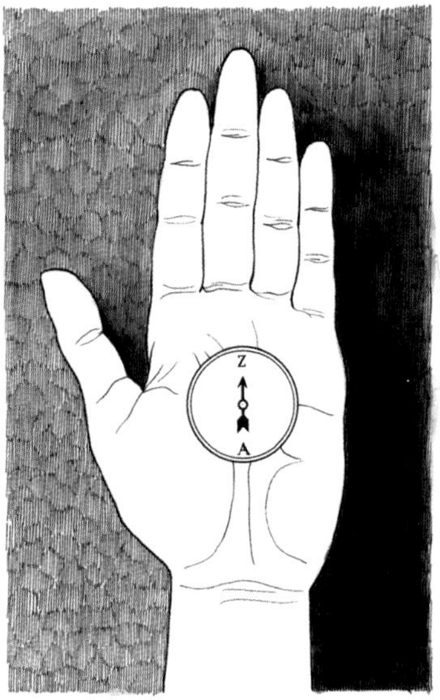

Slight nihilistic edge to it, no? What's the point in knowing where you are when, as Neil Young had it in title of 1969 album, *Everybody Knows This Is Nowhere?*[3]

cf. Samuel Butler's novel, *Erewhon* (1872). Wikipedia: "Butler meant the title to be read as the word Nowhere backwards, even though the letters 'h' and 'w' are transposed, therefore Erewhon is an anagram of nowhere."

cf. William Morris' novel *News from Nowhere* (1890).

> "There is a sense in which all we experience lies within the brain. And yet we see our bodies, of which the brain is a part, through the activity of the brain itself. So the brain seems to be dissolved into one of its own creations, to become a 'nowhere', in which nevertheless the whole of experience is somehow located—a 'little nowhere', in one of those phrases in which the logic of poetry defies and so enlarges the sense of the logician."
> —From *Tea with Walter de la Mare* by Walter Russell Brain (1957)

cf. *Nowhere in America—The Big Rock Candy Mountain and Other Comic Utopias* by Hal Rammel (1990)—begins with a composite of 'directions' on how to get there from a range of diverse fables and folktales: "Away off somewhere, on the other side of far, back of beyond on the bias toward the deep side near the gallows, up a straight crooked lane three miles beyond Christmas, far further than I can tell you tonight, tomorrow night, or any other night in this new year."

Rammel says "This place has been called the Land of Cockaigne, Schlaraffenland, Lubberland, and Topsy-turvey-dom in the European tradition and has a long history that can be traced back to at least

3 As Dr Faustroll says in his telepathic letter to Lord Kelvin, we're "simply NOWHERE, or SOMEWHERE, which is the same thing."—Alfred Jarry, *Exploits and Opinions of Doctor Faustroll Pataphysician*, trans. Simon Watson Taylor (1965)

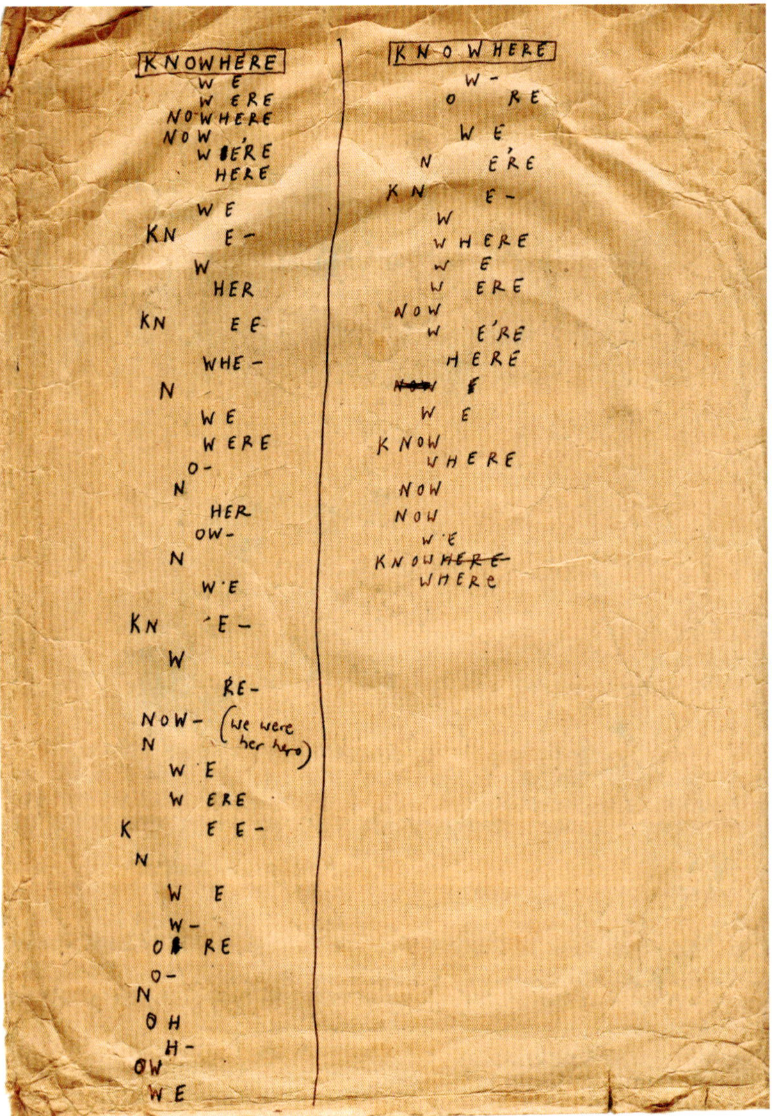

Original sketch for what became the lyric *Kew. Rhone.*, Paris, 1973.

440 BCE. The Big Rock Candy Mountain is part of this tradition, for when such stories reached America, that is how this place came to be known, along with other names such as Ditty Wah Ditty, Oleana, or, simply, Nowhere."

In the conclusion to his book *Deep Time of the Media* (2006), Siegfried Zielinski quotes from *The Republic of Dreams* (1936), by Bruno Schulz: "Schulz proclaimed the republic of dreams to be 'the sovereign territory of poetry,' where one could live 'a life of adventure, of perpetual dazzlement and amazement.' His personal paradise is not so different from the realm of flowing honey that Queen Kyris protected for Empedocles. Schulz conceives it as a haven and, especially, as a place of boundless hospitality. Anyone 'pursued by wolves and robbers' who manages to get there is in safety: 'His reception is triumphal, his dusty garments are removed. Festive, blissful, and happy, he steps out into the wafting Elysian winds, the sweet rose-scented air' that pervades the garden and its 'cells, refectories, dormitories, libraries, pavilions, balconies, and belvedere'."

The 'nowhere' *Kew. Rhone.* is 'at' is the centre of a labyrinth. Siegfried Zielinski: "The centre is a phantasm. In a true labyrinth the centre is never reached; it remains imaginary. Like a utopia the centre is a non-location."

cf. Helen Adam, last verse of her ballad, 'In and Out of the Horn-Beam Maze'[4] ("...in Scotland, there are still old mazes in sort of deserted gardens here and there, and some of them used to be called 'Troy-town', because it was something to do with the falling of the walls of Troy, and usually on May-day, the village people would run round and round, inside the maze, and there was something to do with circling inside a maze that always seemed to me very mysterious"[5]).

Flora ran into the maze, the maze,
Flora ran into the maze,
With a ring on her finger,
And a bow in her hair.
Her golden, glittering, new washed hair.
Light, and lovely, she danced along,
Singing a half forgotten song
In the Queen of Elfhame's praise.
When she reached the center nothing was there.
Nothing! Nothing! nowhere, nowhere!
Only silence, and radiant air.

---

4 From *Turn Again to Me and Other Poems* (1977).

5 ginsbergblog.blogspot.co.uk/2012/12/helen-adam-1909-1993.html (accessed Sept. 2014)

She never ran out of the maze.
This was the end of their mid-summer play.
They sought for Flora a year and a day,
In and out of the Horn-Beam maze.
They found her hair ribbon hung on a thorn.
Her silver ring at the center shone.
But although the children searched on and on,
Three hundred and sixty six days;
Through storms of snow, when the woods were bare,
When the rain blew wild, or the Weather was fair,
The huge, hot sun, stood high in the air
Shining down on the maze.
(Terrible splendor showering down
On the garden maze that was called 'Troy Town'.)
She never ran out of the maze.
Flora, Flora, gentle and fair,
She was always nowhere, nowhere,
Lost, long lost in the maze.
Nothing left for remembering
But a hair ribbon, and a silver ring.
Her bright hair loose, and her ring tossed down,
She never ran out of 'Troy Town'.
She never ran out of the maze because
She found the center where nothing was,
Far, far away, in the Horn-Beam maze.
She will never run out of the maze.

Room 1506, 29 John Street, lower Manhattan during work on *Kew. Rhone.* (1976).

Pipeline

(FIGURE A.)
Here are two gentlemen and a lady contemplating
a length of dug-up pipeline.

FIGURE B. illustrates the assertion—"ambiguity can't
be measured like a change in temperature"

FIGURE C. consists of a list of assorted equipage.
A gentleman imagines how the items on the list
would look if only part exhumed. (He thinks they
wouldn't look unlike a length of pipe.)

(The Lady's Assertion):
"When you remove a rung from a ladder, the whole
is suddenly part, the part is whole. But the hue and
temperature of a pipeline are ineluctably parts,
without the pipeline they would cease to be."

(Second Gentleman's Assertion):
"Anything you care to mention of three dimensions
(like a length of pipe) in a certain light may be seen
as the projection or the shadow of an entity of four
dimensions."—see FIGURE D.

(Words to be used in conjunction with illustrations, overleaf)

FIGURE A.

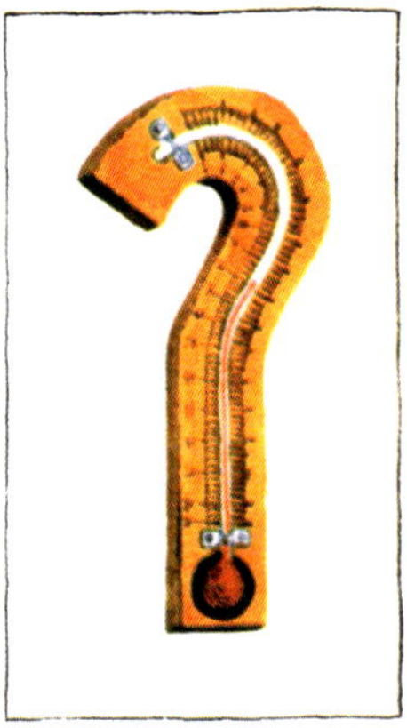

FIGURE B.

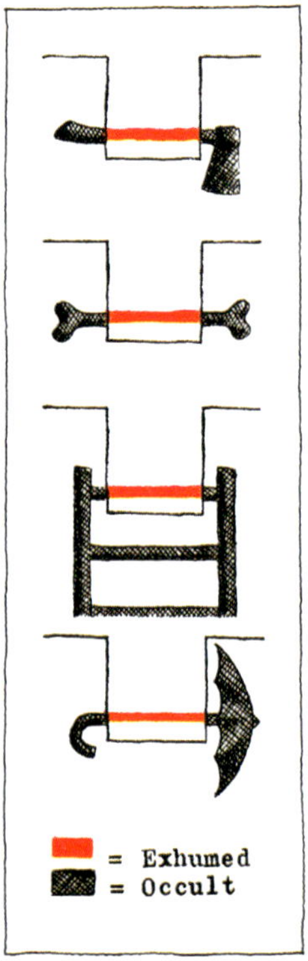

FIGURE C.

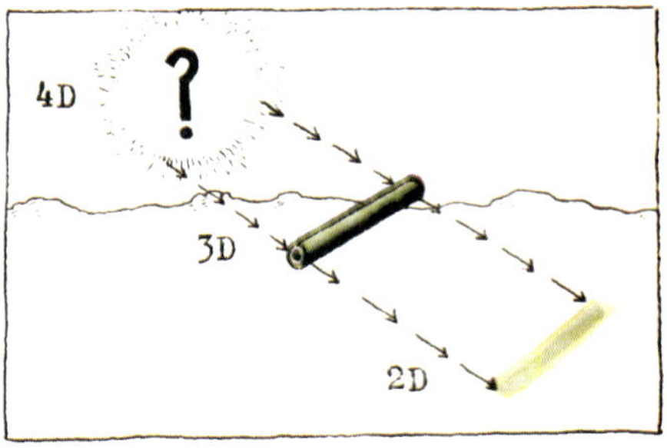

FIGURE D.

(Illustrations to be used in conjunction with words, overleaf)

8

"This is not a pipe"—on the vacancy of *Pipeline*

> "*Pipeline* is my favourite track on *Kew. Rhone.* Part of its appeal for me is that *Pipeline* is also the title of a 'surf' instrumental that was a hit for the Chantays in 1962."
> —PB, unpublished interview with Juan Deutsch (1978)

> "We seek the absolute everywhere, and only ever find things."
> —Novalis

A word is an intellectual object. A well-knit poem even more so. It's a THING with internal tensions, with resistance. If we set the poem to music the words which were a whole now become a part of a song. This extra dimension, the music, reinforces the poem's objecthood. Lyrics and music. Are they dependent or independent parts? In *Pipeline* the rung is an independent part of a ladder. I wanted the words and music of the songs on *Kew. Rhone.* to be independent parts. On most of the tracks I wrote the words to fit music John had already composed. Lapidary work. While the arrangement of the words would be dictated by his melodies, I wanted the lyrics to be able to stand on their own. Not alone only. In two cases their objecthood was further boosted by illustrations printed on the sleeve. The words were then locked in triangular tension with both audial and visual data. The songs were now, in a sense, 3D constructs. I was aiming to create a mental object with the presence and resistance of a physical thing. Further, like the *Pipeline*, the 3D construct can be seen as the projection of a hypothetical entity of four dimensions. But then all songs are the shadows—the echoes—of an 'ideal' song which can only be imagined.

Both lyrics and illustrations are conventionally regarded as 'parasite' or shadow forms, subservient to the music or the text they accompany. But a system of universal correspondence—e.g. Indra's net or *Kew. Rhone.*—in which everything is connected to everything else, obviates such hierarchical distinctions. The lyrics to both *Pipeline* and *Mastodon* are a kind of *ekphrasis*—writing based on an image.[1] Only in this case the illustrations and words require

1 cf. the Greek verb *ekphrazein*, to proclaim or call an inanimate object by name.

that both be simultaneously present, being mutually dependent, symbiotic.

A wand or dowel wouldn't have worked, while a pipeline had the necessary 'vacancy' to serve as a sign not just for something but for *anything*. A sign stands in an equivalence relation to other things. If the thing being used as a sign is truly 'vacant' it "can serve as a support for any intellectual or emotional value whatever."[2] cf. the jar which Wallace Stevens describes as "gray and bare" in his poem, 'Anecdote of the Jar' (1919). The pipeline is in an excavated pit, Stevens places his jar on a hill. Low or high, both objects are 'navels' being contemplated by ardent nombrilists. The ancient Greeks marked the navel (*omphalos*) of the world with a stone. *Pipeline*, jar and stone are all examples of 'vacant' signs made numinous by ardent contemplation.

> "No ideas but in things."
> —William Carlos Williams[3]

> "We don't know what a thing is."
> —Robin Blaser[4]

In Figure B. of *Pipeline* a thermometer in the form of a question mark "illustrates the assertion *'Ambiguity can't be measured like a change in temperature.'*" Our guesses won't get 'warmer' or 'colder' because the enigma is such that we can only imagine the answer. We'll never *know*, so we might as well embrace not-knowing.

"Man is a lookout marooned in strangeness."—John Weightman's translation of Paul Valéry: *"L'homme est un poste d'observation perdu dans l'étrange."*[5]

In his book *Why Are Our Pictures Puzzles? On the Modern Origins of Pictorial Complexity*, James Elkins refers to the 'monstrous ambiguity' of images like the Mona Lisa, or Giorgione's *La Tempesta*. What makes them 'monstrous' is the massive quantity of critical literature that has accrued around them. Isn't the literature that has accrued around an enigmatic object a measure of its ambiguity?[6]

Pipeline presents the idea of measuring ambiguity as an 'impossible survey', something Elkins finds 'helpful': "...not least because listing ambiguities helps us begin to understand the dimensions and possib-

---

2 Michel Leiris, 'The Arts and Sciences of Marcel Duchamp', in *Fontaine* 7, no. 54, 1946, trans. Lydia Davis (1989).

3 From *Paterson* (1927).

4 From a talk he gave at 'The Recovery of the Public World' Conference, University of British Columbia (1995).

5 Epigraph to Weightman's book, *The Cat Sat on the Mat, Language and the Absurd* (2002).

6 cf. Duchamp's *Large Glass*—an elaborate apparatus designed to produce, among other things, its own 'monstrous ambiguity'.

ilities of our own sense of uncertain meaning—a thing seldom studied." That's what the two gentlemen and the lady are students of, not the pipeline itself so much as their own uncertainties about it. They're listing the pipe's ambiguities, but their study is themselves, their own minds studying. They're connoisseurs of *aporia*, of doubt.[7] Their pleasure is to defer certainty indefinitely. It's a melancholy sport and, at the core, erotic (onanistic):

> "An unrequited love for something intangible sits at the core of melancholy, a desire to long for it but never achieve it, to imagine the desire that is at the heart of such a relationship."[8]

The pipeline is 'ambiguous' in the sense that it's only 'part exhumed'—i.e. it's simultaneously Virtual and Potential as well as Actual. The relative participation within it of these three states determines an object's level of ambiguity, suggesting that this could be calibrated, perhaps using the green umbrellas in *Mastodon* as units of measurement. The umbrellas denote degrees of a 'fall' from the 'grace' of pure possibility (100% ambiguity) into the state of necessity where everything is all too clear.

Another aspect of its ambiguity is that the pipeline under scrutiny is also a word. As Freud says: "Words, since they are the nodal points of numerous ideas, may be regarded as predestined to ambiguity. ...The advantages thus offered by words for purposes of condensation and disguise"[9] are made use of by neuroses, dreams and jokes. The songs on *Kew. Rhone.* make use of them too, none more so than *Pipeline*.

The trio[10] in the song are on a quest for ambiguity, that's their quarry. And they've found it. The pipeline is not a static object, it's unfixed, fluid, in flux, without clear limits. If this is taken as a metaphor for a kind of freedom it's also offered as a contrast to the object in *gegenstand* which, while never identified by name, is extolled, envied, and emulated as a model for its *lack* of ambiguity, for its unwobbling commitment to its own quiddity, holding its own against corrosion (coercion). The pipeline will not be fixed, the *gegenstand* will not be moved.[11] There are pros and cons to both situations.

---

7 An *aporia* is a philosophical puzzle or a seemingly insoluble impasse in an inquiry, often arising as a result of equally plausible yet inconsistent premises.

8 Jacky Bowring, from a blog entry entitled *The Eros of Melancholy*. Bowring is also the author of *A Field Guide to Melancholy* (2008).

9 *The Interpretation of Dreams* (1900).

10 On one level we might surmise that the configuration "two gentlemen and a lady" is a reference to the three people billed on the record as its principals: John Greaves, Peter Blegvad and Lisa Herman. Which suggests that "contemplating a length of dug-up pipeline" might be the symbolic equivalent of composing and recording *Kew. Rhone.*, of bringing it into being. Or it may represent the effort the record requires of the listener.

11 In this the pipeline has points in common with the nameless 'Youth' (I) in *Mastodon*, while the *gegenstand* is more like John Masten (VII).

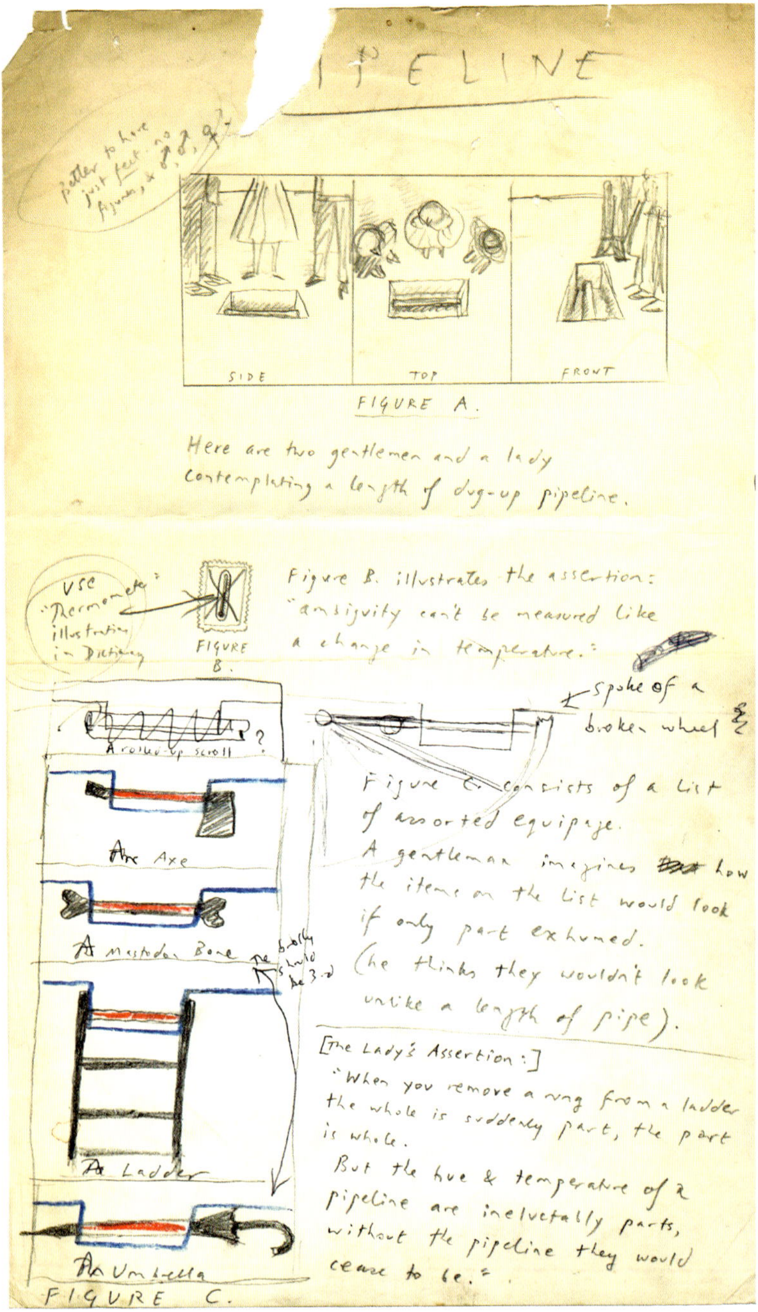

Pipeline, early sketch, 1976.

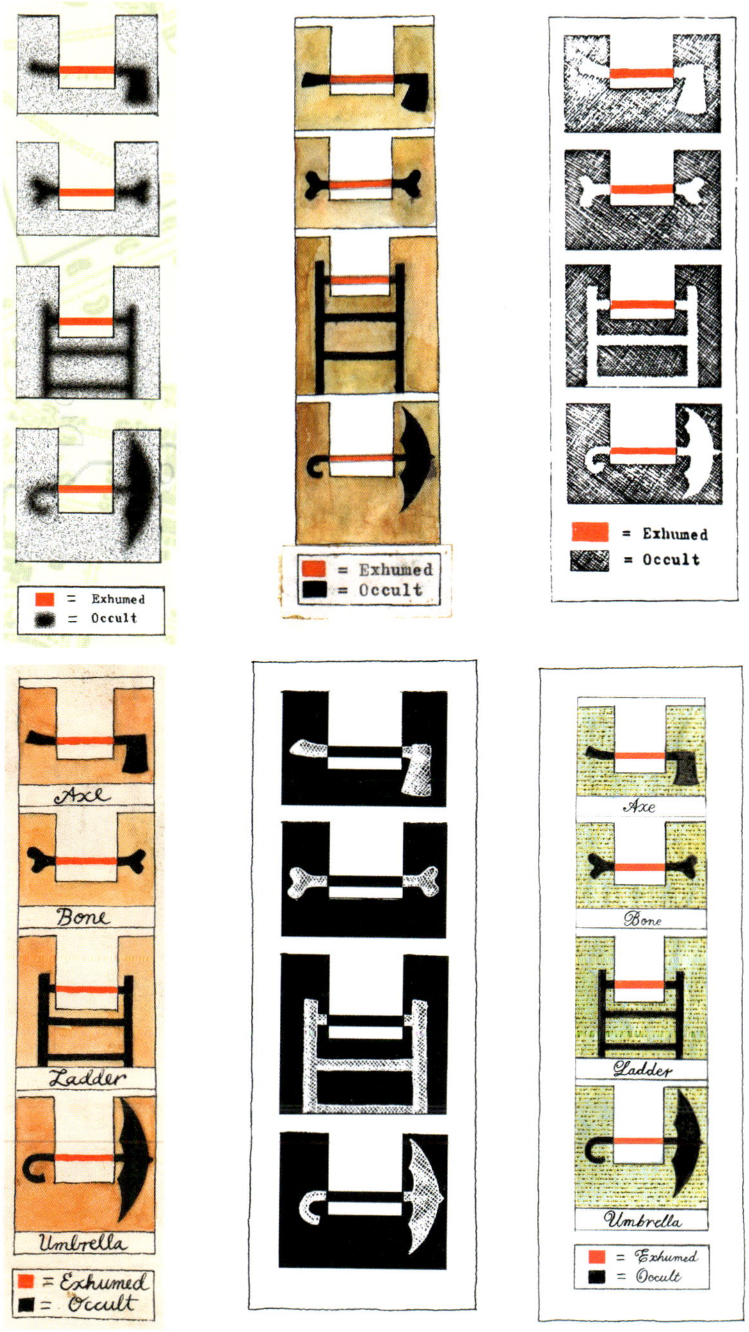

Various versions of *Figure C*, from 1977 to 2014.

A Prime Object, 1976.

9

On the lyrics to *Pipeline*

Excerpts from an interview with the author (1977)

Q: When is an object prime?
A: When it and the First Principle are the object's only factors.
Q: Not sure I'm with you. By 'First Principle' do you mean God?
A: I mean that to which nothing you applied would stick.
Q: Can you give us some examples of prime objects?
A: Certainly—this Wall Street night bell—(proffers photo). In actual confrontation the bell bears an uncanny resemblance to itself—the test of primacy. Another example is the glass of milk Cary Grant takes upstairs in *Suspicion*; Alfred Hitchcock made it prime by putting a light inside the glass. By the way, the song *Catalogue of Fifteen Objects and Their Titles* lists what you might call candidates for primacy. I've constructed a few of them but have to confess none quite qualify.

Kenneth Clark cites Piero della Francesca's "idea that the whole complex of appearances should be reducible to five shapes, which, because they were geometrically complete and regular, partook of divine perfection".[1] Perhaps by crossing what Clark calls this "magical hocus-pocus of Pythagoreanism", with a little 'pataphysics one might establish the theoretical basis for a similar set of prime objects.
Q: Of what use would they be to anyone?
A: A tantric cargo-cult might find them useful contemplative aids, as tantrikas do mandalas. The cult could affirm that while no object is the One, all point beyond themselves towards it.
Q: For your purposes in *Pipeline* a length of pipe in a pit was prime, while for instance a wand put there would not have been. Why?
A: A wand is not quite ordinary. What pit had in it had to be. I tested several cylinders—rods, dowels, wands. But all were wanting. Aesthetically, a wand's too slender. Pipe is squat, closer to the quiddity I sought.

---

1 *Piero della Francesca* (1951).

Q: Is the pipeline a fetish?

A: No it's not. But the 'gegenstand' could be. I'm not sure.

Q: What's 'gegenstand'?

A: Aside from being another song on the same album as *Pipeline*, it's German for object. But it translates literally as counter-stand or resistance. Marcel Jean refers to it in a definition of external object: "a complex of fantasy and restraint, of desire and resistance which possesses a material substance".[2] I'm very much interested in exploring that further. Interpreting the strangeness Heraclitus refers to in the fragment runs: "Though men associate with it most closely yet they are separated from it, and those things which they encounter daily seem to them strange."[3]

Q: What made you think a bossa-nova was the appropriate vehicle for such exploration or interpretation?

A: John (Greaves) and I felt stressing the gap between the words and the music would be interesting. We made it as incongruous a marriage as possible. To 'get' the words you almost have to stop the record and read them, you know, referring to the illustrations on the sleeve. Naturally, if your main concern is with the music, you won't want to be burdened by all that textual paraphernalia.

François Ducat's drawing of Edmund Husserl, spelunking, trapped, waiting for rescue, interrogating a pipeline.

Q: Who is Edmund Husserl?

A: 'Father of Phenomenology'. He starred in an early version of *Pipeline*, guessing wholes an object might be part of.

Q: As the First Gentleman now does?

A: Yes. Only Husserl was buried to his chin in rubble and guessing to kill time while awaiting rescue. Also he was intent on observing his own mind in the process of making guesses. It was this attempt to avoid the mind while using it, to get an objective view of how it views objects, which kept his faculties engaged and *ennui* at bay. All that's been cut out, but Husserl still informs the song. The Lady's assertion is culled entirely from a paragraph of his on simple and compound objects, dependent and independent parts.

---

2 Marcel Jean and Arpad Mezei, *The History of Surrealist Painting* (1960).

3 *Fragment 72* (c.5th century BCE).

Q: And the Second Gentleman's assertion?
A: Straight from Duchamp's notes on the Large Glass. It's something I think Jouffret[4] thought up: a 3D object casts a 2D shadow, but is itself the shadow of a 4D unknown. A statement Jasper Johns made relates well to all this. He said: "I think one is now able to question the object itself, whether it has any real body or any real use—what we call reality I guess. I think one wonders if one couldn't shift one's focus a bit in looking at a thing, and have the object be somewhere else, not be there at all."[5] For my own part, there's a kind of anger at the root of these concerns. Something like what André Breton suggested in the phrase "getting one's revenge on things".

Early sketch for Figure A.

Q: What did you mean by the line "ambiguity can't be measured like a change in temperature"?
A: Ah yes. I thought I'd coined a new Uncertainty Principle! But I screwed up. There are degrees of ambiguity after all, so that line which sounds so pregnant doesn't actually hold. I had the pinned man in mind, Husserl, trying to guess the identity of some hidden thing. What he can't measure is the accuracy of his guesses, whether they get 'warmer' or 'colder'. He's given nothing, not a clue, so there's no telling how close the world or guess he makes comes to being the 'real' or 'right' one. Pure subjectivity, a kind of despair. It's often from such a point that the heroes of legend set off. Eventually they learn to lose the vision of there being any finish-line. That's the only hope, that the quest itself become the goal.

Text first published in the *Ré Records Quarterly*, vol. 1, no. 1, 1 May 1985, on pages designed by Chris Gibbins and Graham Keatley.

---

4 Esprit Jouffret (1837–1904), author of *Traité élémentaire de géométrie à quatre dimensions* (Elementary Treatise on the Geometry of Four Dimensions, 1903), in which he described hypercubes and other complex polyhedra in four dimensions and projected them on to the two-dimensional page.

5 Interview with David Sylvester, *Jasper Johns: drawings* (1974).

Above: Pipelines, male and female.
Below: Collection of pipes, John St., 1977.

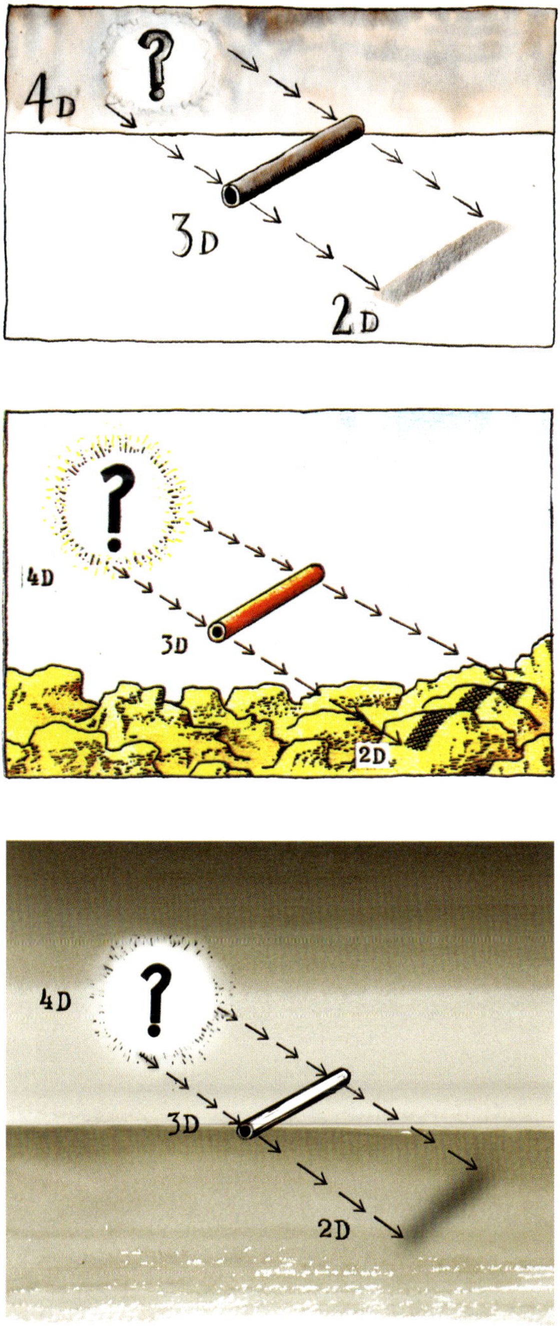

Versions of *Figure D*, 1976, 1984 and 2014.

1
2
3
4
5
6
7
8
9
10
11
12
13
14
15

Catalogue of Fifteen Objects…

1. Cylinder of dust
2. Salt cross with a crust of iodine
3. Plank of pine
4. Loaf of rust
5. Hollow cone of tobacco which contains a tin coin
6. Pillar of yeast in linoleum jacket
7. Circular puddle of yogurt and neon
8. Arrow of ice wrapped in surgical gauze
9. Coin stacks, several columns—voltaic piles of gold plated bamboo
10. Water in a bakelite box, and a box full of oil
11. A yolk of leather in a tobacco egg
12. Citronella spilled in a spiral upon a blanket of fat
13. Mixture of paregoric and dew in a creosote cone
14. A disc of wicker beside a pill of zinc
15. Figure made of two copper pyramids glued base to base with sap

...and Their Titles

1. "Silo"
2. "Referee"
3. "Threshold" (meant to be flat on the floor, part of a door none can see)
4. "Altar from a Metal Cathedral"
5. "Dunce's Trumpet" (for V.)
6. "Dry Cell"
7. "Lunatic Mirror"
8. "Signal From a Memory"
9. "Ladder of Kings"
10. "Ransom to Secure the Release of a Mother and Child"
11. "October Seventh"
12. "My Uncle's Monocle"
13. "Fuel for a Tiny Machine"
14. "Two Equivalent Forms"
15. Quote from Swedenborg to the effect that angels fucking shed light.[1]

---

1 In the first of his *Supernatural Songs* (1934) W. B. Yeats writes "...the intercourse of angels is a light." In *Per Amica Silentia Lunae, Anima Mundi* (1917) he wrote of the dead "I do not doubt that they make love in that union which Swedenborg has said is of the whole body and seems from far off an incandescence".

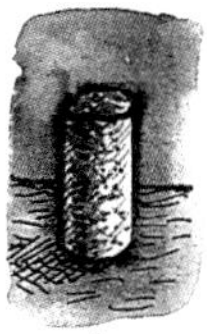

1

2

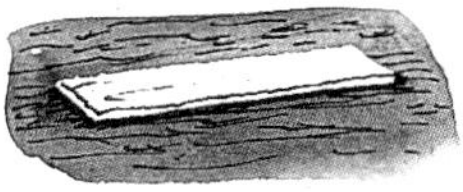

3

4

5

6

7

8

9

10

11

12

13

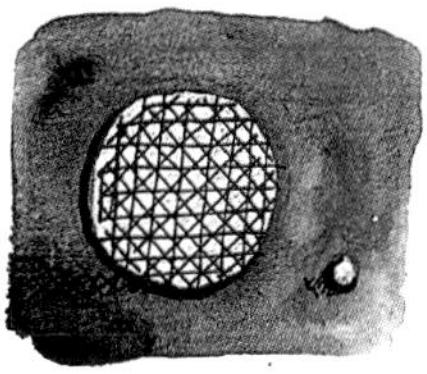

14

15

A Song in Two Halves

1. *One by one the fifteen objects are described (reference is made to their forms and to the materials of which they're compounded).*
2. *The list is repeated in the same order, but this time the objects are identified only by title.*[1]

"For it is in these things that we are most lost, as it is in these things alone that we must better be hidden."
—Ben Marcus, *The Age of Wire and String* (1995)

Objects are the subjects of several of these songs. The *Proverbs* are full of them—a felt hat, razors, a doornail, a stone, a pen. In *Pipeline* there's the eponymous conduit, plus the ladder, axe, bone and brolly that also appear in *Mastodon*. Then there are the specific *Minerals*, the singular *Apricot*, and so on. These are all named objects. There's also the incognitum, *gegenstand*. But the fifteen objects in *Catalogue* aren't just named, they're first described, in terms of morphology and material constituents, and then, as the melody repeats, they're given a title.

In fact, they couldn't be named the way we can say "doornail" or "umbrella" and be understood. Most of these objects are *sui generis*. Of no practical use, their purpose is to puzzle, to stimulate conjecture. They're metaphysical toys, *objets d'art*.[2]

"The object no longer has a function but a virtue: it is a sign."
—Jean Baudrillard, 'Subjective Discourse on the Non-Functional System of Objects', in *Revenge of the Crystal* (1983)

The fifteen objects are compounded of materials carefully chosen to

1 The idea of repeating the same inventory but from a different perspective was inspired by the two-part structure of Raymond Roussel's novel *Impressions of Africa* (1910).

2 They're all imaginary. But it's interesting to note that a real object, a sculpture compounded of brass and concrete by Carol Bove in 2013, has had *Peel's foe, not a set animal, laminates a tone of sleep* bestowed upon it as a title. And Nathan Coley made *Untitled (Threshold Sculpture)* in 2007, ten years after Cornelia Parker made *Ghost Town Threshold*, consisting of two 'thresholds' (old and young) which resemble the one (ageless) in the song.

generate in combination (and in that particular form, with that particular title) a charge, something like the way voltage is generated by the alternate layers of zinc and other stuffs stacked in a voltaic pile. The materials the song employs include water, one of four elements in the medieval system. Zinc is used, as well as copper and neon, elements in the periodic table. But the *Catalogue* suggests a taxonomic system in which *everything* is elemental. The diversity of these substances —water, copper, neon, zinc, ice, yogurt, iodine, creosote, gauze, dust, rust, citronella, pine, tobacco, sap, fat, salt, linoleum, leather, yeast and oil—is calculated to suggest universal reach.[3]

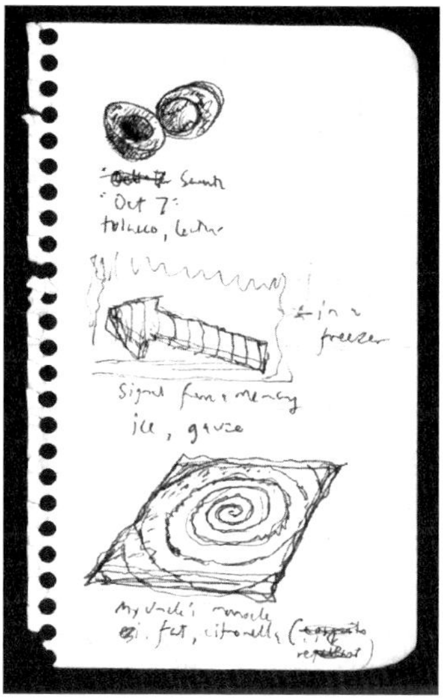

Notebook page, 1976.

The *Pipeline* generates a charge, too, but in a different way from the objects in *Catalogue*. It's a 'magnet for projection' by virtue of its partial occultation (ambiguity). We're not told what it's made of. Try boosting its ambiguity. Would it generate more psychic voltage if the pipeline was made of wood or glass, or from the near weightless solid which scientists have created from kelp?

Possibly. Because far from being inert, the antithesis of spirit, matter is the "mother substance" of poetry and dreams.[4] According to Giorgio de Chirico: "The discovery of the terrible void is nothing other than the truly senseless and tranquil beauty of matter."

The fifteen objects in *Catalogue* are attempts to generate numinosity, to make spirit matter and *vice versa*. The question they're designed to raise is one which has occupied both scientists and artists from ancient times to the present: how to 'animate' a material object, to invest it with something like a spirit or soul.

> "How to construct a vehicle of reverie, an object that would enrich the imagination of the viewer and keep him company forever."—Charles Simic, 'The Truth of Poetry', in *Dime-Store Alchemy, the Art of Joseph Cornell* (1992)

---

3 cf. Lewis Carroll's list in 'The Walrus and the Carpenter'—shoes and ships and sealing-wax, cabbages and kings—a "thumbnail sketch of *everything*". Francis Spufford, *The Chatto Book of Cabbages and Kings: Lists in Literature* (1989).

4 According to Gaston Bachelard (i.e. matter is an aspect of *mater*, the Great Mother).

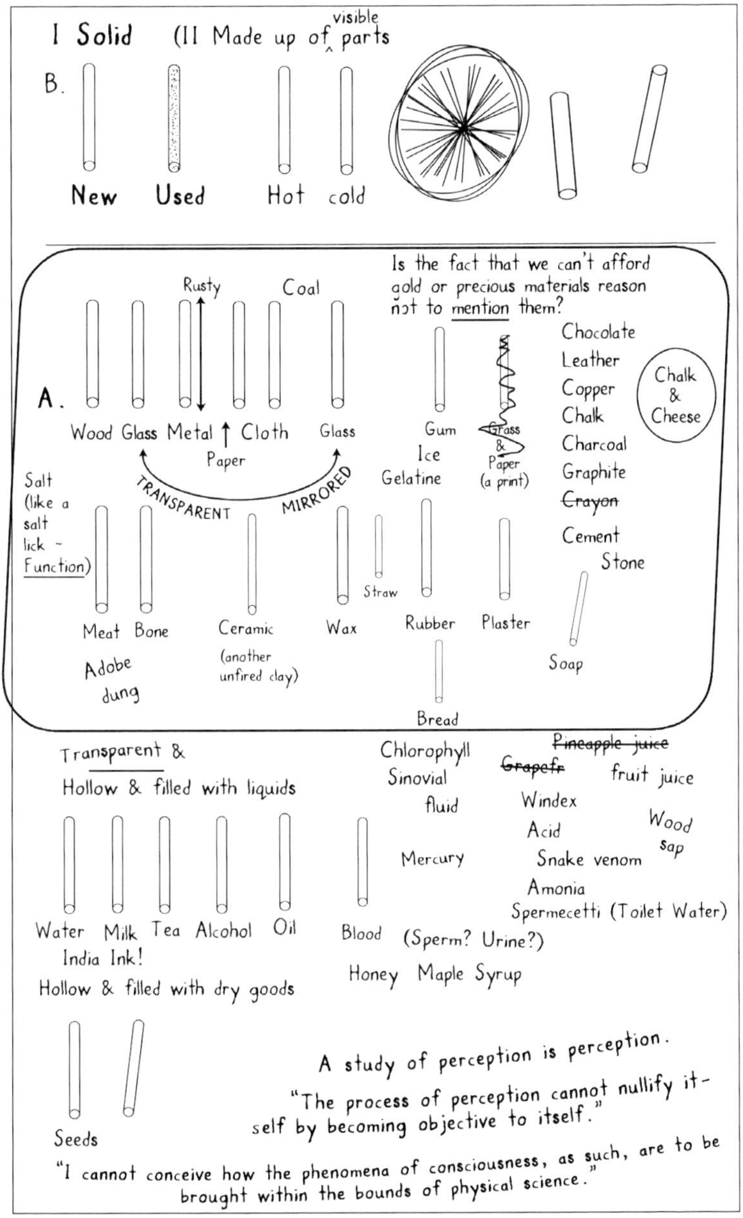

Imagining pipelines made of different materials. Transcription of notebook page (right).

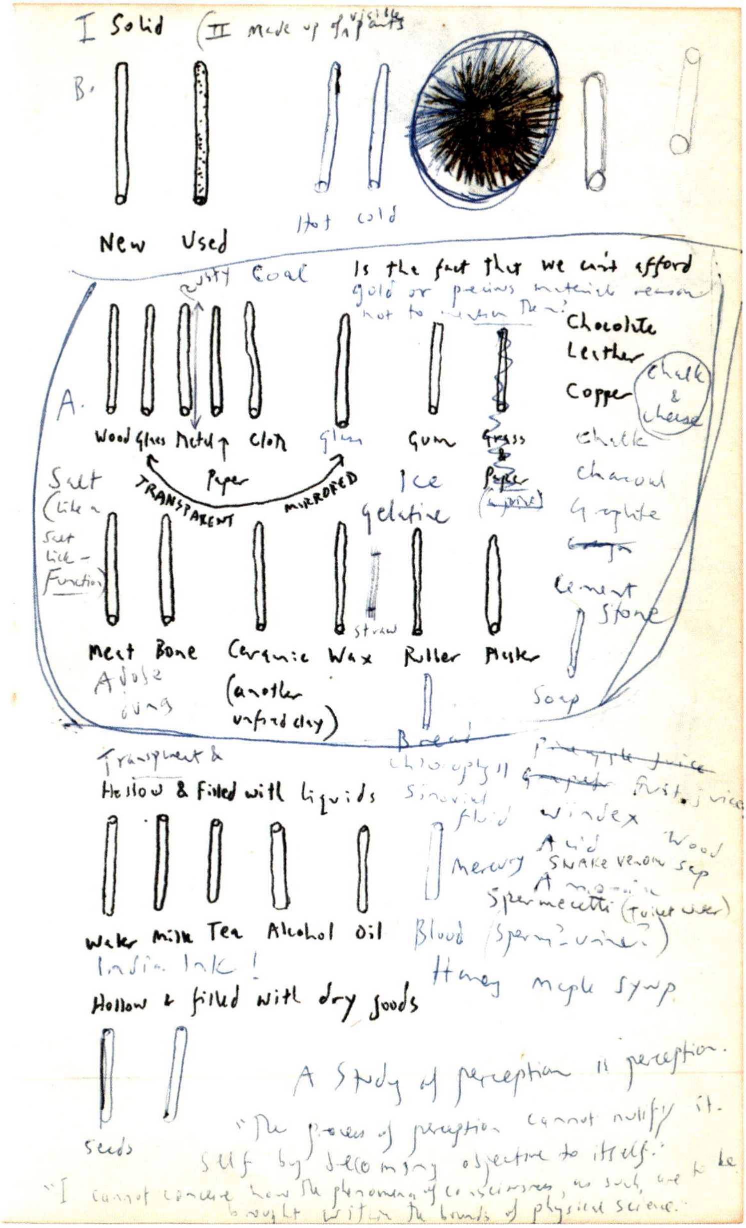

Notebook page (1976).

cf. the ironic shamanism of Joseph Beuys. His use of fat, hare's blood, honey, felt and iodine were attempts (often successful) to demonstrate the numinous potential in objects made of unlikely materials.

> "Things have a life of their own… It's simply a matter of waking up their souls. The gypsies do it with a magnet."
> —Gabriel Marquez, *One Hundred Years of Solitude* (1967)

> "We have to choose between the quick and the dead. The quick is God-flame, in everything. And the dead is dead. In this room where I write, there is a little table that is dead: it doesn't even weakly exist. And there is a ridiculous little iron stove, which for some unknown reason is quick. And there is an iron wardrobe trunk, which for some still more mysterious reason is quick. And there are several books, whose mere corpus is dead, utterly dead and non-existent. And there is a sleeping cat, very quick. And a glass lamp that, alas, is dead."
> —D. H. Lawrence, 'The Novel' (1925), in *Selected Critical Writings* (1998)

The taxonomical system the fifteen objects are elements in might be a kind of lexicon or vocabulary. One way to animate them, of bringing them to life, might be to interpret them as words, to translate them into language. (Language being neither dead nor alive but paradoxically both: "'dead' because it is a *given*, inherited from the past, and alive, because it is reanimated—but always with a halo of ambiguity—in the present."[5]) Giving them titles is a step in that direction.

Does our experience of the fifteen objects change when we're told their titles? How? Are they now more 'quick'? Or is their 'freedom' compromised, are their wings clipped by having titles imposed upon them? How arbitrary are these titles? What criteria might apply when judging for suitability or effectiveness the title of an object like "hollow cone of tobacco which contains a tin coin" (*Dunce's Trumpet [for V.]*)?

René Magritte: "An object is not so attached to its name that it cannot be found another that suits it better. There are objects that do without names."[6]

Magritte also said: "An object implies that there are others behind it." Do these objects imply that? (cf. the 4D incognitum of which the 3D pipeline is only the shadow.)

What other objects might be behind this lot?

---

5 John Weightman, *The Cat Sat on the Mat, Language and the Absurd* (2002).

6 *Les mots et les images* (1929).

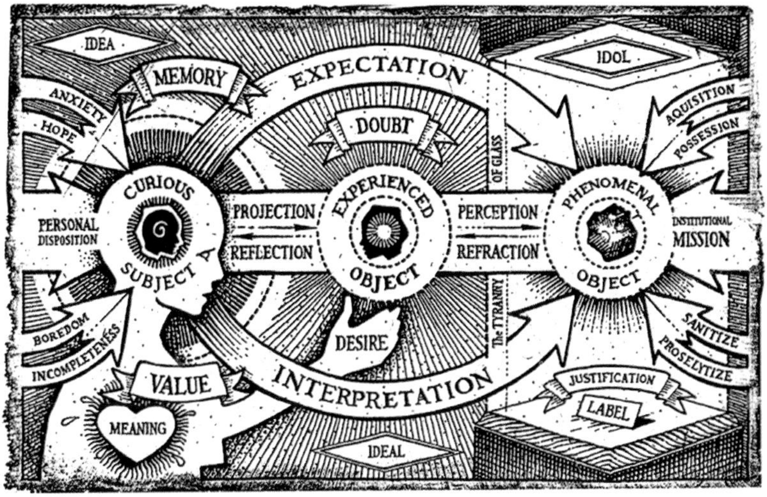

Diagram by Jeff Hoke, from *The Museum of Lost Wonder*, No. 3, Spring 1998.

Three ways of interrogating an object:

1. *Consideration*—the object *Observed* (Nomen)
2. *Association*—a magnet for *Memory* (things it resembles, or 'rhymes' with) (Omen)
3. *Fascination*—the object *Imagined* (Numen)

> "When any object is too delicate and minute to be examined by the sense of touch and sight, the Martian shuts his eyes and puts it against the pit of his stomach, and knows all about it, even its inside."—George Du Maurier, *The Martian* (1898)

cf. the science fiction story called 'Mimsy Were the Borogoves' by Lewis Padgett (1943) in which children arranging what look like toys and bits of junk on the nursery floor are actually constructing a portal into another dimension.

Consciously and unconsciously we invest objects with values and energies of one sort or another. The German word for object—*Gegenstand*—acknowledges the resistance we sense emanating from material things; the word recognises that objects attract and repel both physically and psychologically.

> "By studying objects, consciousness discovers its form. It haunts the world as the spirit of what the world might be, or what it might still become."—Tracy Daugherty, *Hiding Man, A Biography of Donald Barthelme* (2009)

Like a ladder and its rungs, a chain and its links[1] *may be used to illustrate the difference between 'dependent' and 'independent' parts. Remove a link from its chain and the whole becomes a part, the part a whole. A chain is only as strong as its weakest link, but its weakest link, considered separately, may be more powerfully numinous than the chain as a whole.*

---

1 The 'Great Chain' across the Hudson was cast at the Stirling Iron Works in Newburgh, New York, near where Peale exhumed the mastodon(s). 1,700 feet long, each link a 2½-inch iron bar, 30 inches long, it was stretched upon a boom from West Point to Constitution Island with the object of preventing ascent of British war vessels up the Hudson. Placing it in position began 16 April and on 30 April 1778 it was secured at the two ends.

11

Numinous Objects and Their Manufacture

> "The eagerness of objects to
> be what we are afraid to do
>
> Cannot help but move us Is
> this willingness to be a motive
>
> in us what we reject?"
>
> —from 'Interior (With Jane)', Frank O'Hara (1951)

Objects proliferate as never before, but they are mostly dead husks, the shells of things, wherein no *daemon*[2] resides. We own them merely, or covet them, we are not nourished. Meanwhile, the fundamental appetite for numinous[3] objects grows ravenous. Never mind that it remains unconscious in most citizens and unacknowledged by the authorities. Only *numinous objects* can make possible the communication between people and so-called 'dead matter'[4] which must be established if we wish to avert calamity.

I am not here referring to fetishes, which are a means to evoke a system of belief and not properly ends in themselves. Nor am I referring to fantasy-constructs like, for example, the ship made of fingernail parings described in Norse mythology. This ship is a fine thing, but it is only feebly numinous compared to a block of sodium in a meadow, its edges mollified by the tongues of cows into a lopsided loaf like snow. And, while my more sceptical readers may scoff, it is a fact that if this salt-lick be removed from the meadow and placed in a confined enclosure or, better still, sealed into a lead container, its numinous charge will be boosted many fold.[5]

---

2 Daemon—the animating spirit of a place or thing. cf. the painter Giorgio de Chirico's diktat: "One must discover the daemon in everything."

3 Numinous—invested with power or spirit.

4 Guy Davenport: "...science and poetry from the Renaissance forward have been trying to discover what is alive and what isn't. In science the discovery spanned three centuries, from Gassendi to Niels Bohr, and the answer is that everything is alive." Davenport also quotes Einstein: "...every clod of earth, every feather, every speck of dust is a prodigious reservoir of entrapped energy." From 'Olson', in *The Geography of the Imagination* (1981).

5 cf. Leonora Carrington: "The explosion... had momentarily dispersed the powers that always gathered around the Cup in enclosed areas. This is a magic law and true for nearly all charged objects." From *The Hearing Trumpet* (1976).

It may be, as some have theorised, that the object *au naturel* or in its 'accumulator'[6] is numinous to the degree that it functions as a mirror of the spirit, i.e. to the degree that you or I can imaginatively see something of ourselves, something we do not ordinarily have a name for or an image of, made objective in it. That salt can function as a mirror of anything, especially when sealed in lead, will smack of blatant hocus-pocus to the sceptics—but it is in such unlikely ways that the imagination actually works.

A numinous object is charged like a condenser. It distorts induction and resonates ambiguously. In Surrealist parlance, it is "convulsive", with the power to drain definition from its surroundings and become the solitary and radiant focus, the omphalos or navel, of an entire world. An object with sufficient numinous charge can stop time.

The numinous objects which already exist in our environment are easily overlooked by our harassed and addled species. Education is the remedy, teaching people of all ages to resist distraction and become sensitive to the subtle radiations emanating from these items (which often masquerade as common refuse on the street). I imagine students returning from expeditions bright-eyed and exultant with eclectic spoil. Objects would be tested, graded and catalogued before being made available to the public from a chain of lending libraries.

Besides numinous 'found objects', fresh numinous objects must be manufactured. To meet this need a new science is being evolved here at the offices of Amateur. The *Morphological Tables* illustrate the first phase of this work: discovering the morphologies or forms most conducive to numinosity. We're still compiling the list of materials of which these forms or objects might be compounded. The selection is vast, and the distinction is critical, in terms of numinosity, between a ball, let's say, of snow, and one the same size, made of, for example, soluble glass[7]—although both balls, viewed from a certain distance, might otherwise be twins.

How would an alchemist seeking the *lapis* or Philosophers' Stone picture it in his mind? (The *Tractatus aureus* says the precious Stone is "altogether vile", but aside from that…) Would he imagine an amorphous lump, a perfect sphere, or a brick? Would it be oily or dry, dull or polished, cold or warm to the touch? Would it be fused into a dense solid, or porous, ventilated like a honeycomb? Such grossly

---

6 cf. Wilhelm Reich and his 'accumulators' and 'boosters' (of orgone energy).

7 One reason the list of materials is potentially endless is that science keeps inventing new, potentially numinous matter. Dr Cyril Drake, for example, "accidentally made a glass that dissolved in water. …Without silicon, using phosphorus, calcium and sodium oxides", the ingredients in Dr Drake's soluble glass can be adjusted to make it dissolve as swiftly or as slowly as required, "from a few minutes up to ten years."

materialistic speculations demean the spiritual associations the stone evokes, no doubt, but in seeking the recipe for numinous objects we have found it useful to ask such questions…

To return to the morphologies—we have deliberately restricted the choice to basic forms and objects, at least for our first tentative experiments. If an object can be inserted into the phrase "the object is _______-shaped" (e.g. cigar-, bullet-, barrel- or teardrop-shaped), it will usually qualify for selection. Other objects qualify as nearly archetypal "signs for themselves" (e.g. gallows or gibbet, coffin, house etc.). It is a basic "building block" quality that we seek. Certain forms, by their inclusion, automatically disqualify others. Hourglass, for instance, renders dumbbell redundant, because the latter is too nearly the former on its side.

Forms and objects have been separated into three categories: those composed entirely of straight lines ("Straight"); those in whose lineaments curves and circles are involved ("Curved"); and lastly, those indefinite units of matter, the humble blob, chunk, chip, lump, heap, hill etc. which, while sometimes suggesting the quantity of matter involved, do not imply more than a very approximate form ("Amorphous"). The reader will notice that some two-dimensional figures have been included on the Tables, and even a few negative shapes (holes, cracks, crenellations). They are there because it seems certain that an aperture or apertures could contribute to the numinosity of an object, and that a two-dimensional tattoo or illustration might do likewise.

Many forms and objects are missing that should be included. Should more letter-shapes qualify? L, T, V, O, S, U, X and Z all seem to be basic forms, maybe the rest are too. Sometimes one wonders if a numinous object could not therefore be a word…

It may transpire that unless we find the appropriate context in which to place a finished object, it will not "convulse", its numinosity will remain dormant. Conventional gallery design would indicate that the aesthetic qualities of an art object are supposedly savoured best in an antiseptic interior and under electric lamplight. But an object such as we propose to manufacture, and which we do not think of simply as "art", might require a specific site, a specific hour of the day or night, specific support "props", weather conditions and so on before "its soul, its whatness, leaps to us from the vestment of its appearance"[8] and it becomes numinous.

First published in the *Ré Records Quarterly*, vol. 2, 1 September 1985

---

8 James Joyce, describing an 'epiphany' in *Stephen Hero* (1944).

Second Morphological Table (Straight)

1. Brick, Box, Rectangle
2. Ladder
3. Plank, Board, Rectangle
4. Line
5. 8-pointed Star
6. Pentagram
7. Seal of Solomon, Star of David
8. Envelope
9. Swastika
10. Asterisk
11. Trellis
12. 'L', Right Angle
13. Octagon
14. Hexagon
15. Cube
16. Square
17. Diamond
18. Parallelogram
19. Frustum
20. Sheet, Page, Leaf
21. 'T'
22. Prism
23. Zigzag
24. Cross
25. Saw-tooth
26. Crenellation
27. Pennant, Triangle

28. Obelisk
29. Arrow
30. Wedge
31. Triangle
32. ?
33. Ziggurat
34. Pyramid
35. Chevron, ‘A’ frame
36. Coffin

37. Grid
38. Trident, Fork
39. ‘Y’ fork
40. Tripod
41. Staircase
42. Gallows, Gibbet

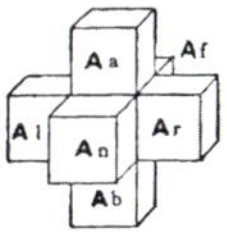

Missing: Hypercube
(Charles Howard Hinton, from *The Fourth Dimension*, 1912)

First Morphological Table (Curved)

1. Sphere, Ball, Globe, Orb
2. Crescent
3. Horn
4. Pillar, Column, Pole, Cylinder
5. Roll
6. Cylinder
7. Tube, Pipe, Hose (if flexible)
8. Hoop (a large Ring)
9. Rod, Wand, Dowel (if wood)
10. Pencil or Stick (as of chalk)
11. Straw (a thin Tube)
12. Needle
13. Drum or Cylinder
14. Bell
15. Crook
16. Cane
17. Coin (a small Disc)
18. Disc
19. Grommet (a small Ring)
20. Ring, Terret
21. Circlet
22. Hole
23. Hemisphere (a solid Cup)
24. Hemisphere (a solid Bowl)
25. Ellipsoid
26. Cone
27. Spine, Spike, Tang (a thin Cone)
28. Dot
29. Funnel
30. Arch
31. Wheel
32. Circle (bisected)
33. Oval
34. Barrel, Keg, Tun
35. Hourglass (a vertical Dumbbell)

36. Belt or Band
37. Spool (with cross-section)
38. Reel (with cross-section)
39. Fan
40. Coil
41. Spring, Coil, Gyre, Helix
42. Spiral, Coil, Helix, Whorl, Gyre
43. Heart
44. Kidney
45. Bean (a small Kidney)
46. Spoon, Paddle
47. Cigar
48. Pear
49. Noose
50. Scallop, Shell
51. Puck, Quoit
52. Curl, Loop
53. Teardrop
54. Bulb
55. Egg
56. Scroll
57. Lens (convex)
58. Lens (concave)
59. Pill
60. Bullet
61. Button
62. Mushroom
63. Almond
64. Serpent
65. Saucer (with cross-section)
66. Donut or Doughnut
67. Sausage
68. Magnet, Horseshoe

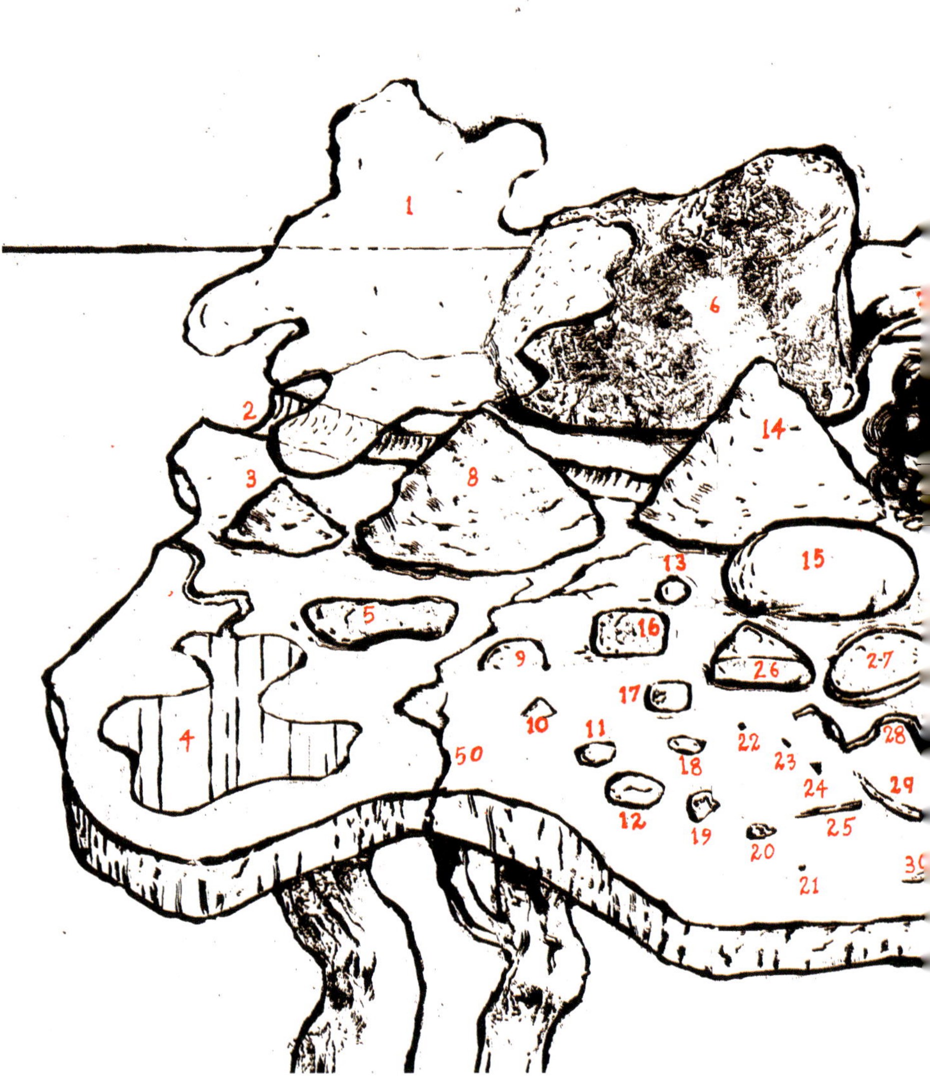

Third Morphological Table (Amorphous)

1. Cloud
2. Ditch, Trench
3. Pile
4. Puddle (with Rill or Runnel)
5. Batch
6. Mass
7. Flap
8. Mound
9. Lump
10. Papule
11. Nugget
12. Blob
13. Bolus
14. Heap
15. Loaf
16. Clod, Clump
17. Plug
18. Wad
19. Glob
20. Morsel
21. Crumb
22. Flake
23. Chip
24. Speck
25. Smear
26. Chunk
27. Slice, Flitch

28. Strip
29. Stroke
30. Strand
31. Mountain
32. Hill
33. Talus
34. Tangle
35. Block
36. Cudgel, Club
37. Swathe
38. Thong
39. Hunk
40. Streak
41. Scratch
42. Wodge
43. Scrap
44. Swatch
45. Shard
46. Seam
47. Slab
48. Patch
49. Floccule, Tuft
50. Crack

Missing: Nodule or Bump

12

On Numinosity

From 1929 to 1962, the French phenomenologist, Gaston Bachelard, wrote several books in which he analysed and elucidated the poetics of matter, revealing the subtle yet profound ways the properties and associations of various substances affect the imagination. He demonstrated that water, for instance, could be experienced as "dissolved girl". He psychoanalysed fire and spoke knowledgeably of the "hidden spirit" imprisoned in the solids, liquids and gases we usually take for granted. "Dreaming of the secret power of substances, we dream of our secret being. The greatest secrets of our being are hidden from ourselves."[1]

For some time, we at Amateur have been exploring a small branch of the tree he planted. A numinous object is one in which matter, form and situation combine to 'haunt' or otherwise fascinate the imagination. The objects we attempt to understand and hope to create are sometimes physically tangible, actual things. But literary objects are also an important part of our research.

> "I have always been haunted by objects that possess their own light: things and situations that cast peripheral illumination on known ideas, causing them to be viewed in a different configuration."
> —Brian Catling, sculptor, author, performer

An early experiment: Fifteen objects were created by choosing from a menu of thousands of possible forms and materials. The aim was to create things which would generate a numinous charge in any situation (though, obviously, the charge would be different on, say, a ship at sea or in, say, a mushroom-cellar). Using an instrument of our own invention—the numenometer[2]—we took calibrated readings. For "a yolk of leather in a tobacco egg", for instance, a reading of 63.7 nmns was recorded. While an "arrow of ice wrapped in surgical gauze" generated no more than 37 nmns. The figure in nmns is the average of many hundreds of individual readings made over several years, in some cases over several decades.

1 *On Poetic Imagination and Reverie, Selections from Gaston Bachelard*, trans. Colette Gaudin (1987).

2 Recipe for a numenometer: You cross a Geiger counter / with a divining rod, / and in case of trouble add / a touch of cattle prod.

That some of these objects bore more than a passing resemblance to the art of the day was noted. As an experiment, wondering if we weren't artists ourselves, we assigned titles at random to our models. This completely altered the readings we got. The cylinder of dust which had generated a modest 22.6 nmns when untitled, was now identified as "Silo" and registered an impressive 81.8 on the numenometer. Calling the yolk of leather in a tobacco egg, "October Seventh", on the other hand, diminished its charge from 63.7 nmns to a mere 7 nmns. Identification and analysis of the factors involved in such shifts will continue to absorb us for some time.

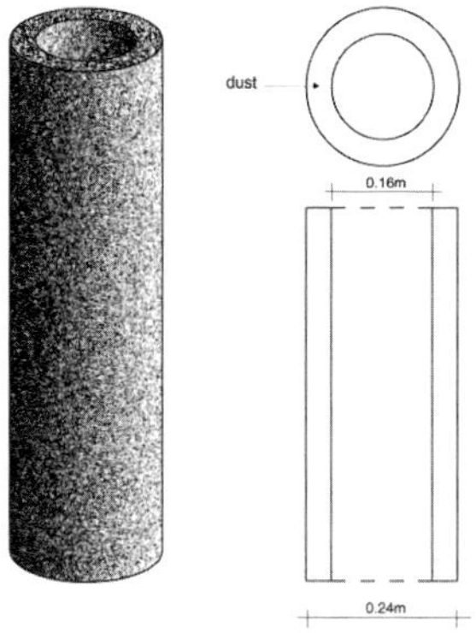

Silo by Simon Lucas.

More rapid has been our progress in techniques of Object Generation. Once a tedious process involving pages of documentation and cumbersome equipment, matter and form can now be combined automatically on a computer screen thanks to the object-generating engines developed by Simon Lucas for the Amateur Enterprises website: www.amateur.org.uk.[3]

3 See pp.166–169.

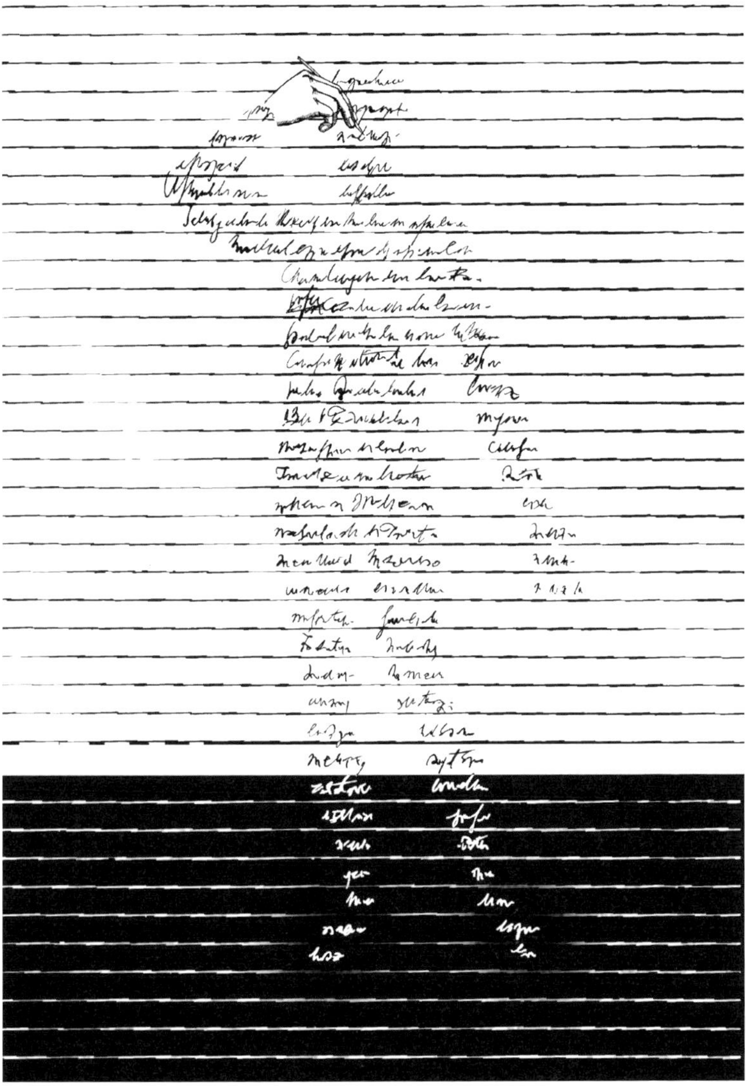

One Footnote (to Kew. Rhone.)

Other anagrams to be found in
the words Kew Rhone:
horn, honk, heron, hew, keener, hone,
owner, week, new, row, error, reek, whore.

You can no doubt eke out a couple more.

13

The Unconscious of the Text

> "It is said that the cabalists among the Jews were professed anagrammatists, the third part of their art called *themuru* (changing) being nothing more than finding the hidden and mystical meaning in names, by transposing and differently combining the letters…"
> —*Gleanings for the Curious from the Harvest-Fields of Literature*, C. C. Bombaugh (1874)

What does it tell us that *orchestra* is a rearrangement of the letters in *carthorse*? Or that *William Shakespeare* can be converted into *I am a weakish speller* on the one hand and *I'll make a wise phrase* on another? That *astronomer* yields *moon-starer*, that *funeral* converts into *real fun*? These are all on one level (the rational) mere coincidences, but they also irresistibly suggest the possibility that there are 'cabalistic innuendoes' in every word and secret meanings concealed beneath the surface of all things.[1]

Although it doesn't get very far, *Footnote* is an attempt to interrogate language as *Mastodon* interrogated a picture, and with the same aim: to reveal hidden meanings.[2]

The anagrams listed in the song include *keener*, not a 'perfect' anagram due to an extra 'e', and *error* (which self-reflexively describes itself) with its three 'r's. A list of further anagrams we can *eke* out includes: *wonk* (someone studious or hard-working), *wee*, *ewe*, *ewer*, *hoke* (an insincere, sentimental, or melodramatic act or actor—cf. 'hokey'), *hoe*, *krone*, *wren* and *woken*.

---

1 "As Francis Bacon said, 'Nature is God's second book.' It's a text—it needs to be interpreted. I mean, you get it in the Greeks, in Virgil—every flight path of a sparrow or movement of an ant over a tuft of ground is a message. It is a sign—it needs interpretation. In more modern literature you get this sensibility very much in the work of Thomas Pynchon or William Burroughs, the sense that we are living in a world of signs, that there's an order behind the visible that needs to be drawn out through interpretation."
—Tom McCarthy, interviewed by Mark Alizart in *The Believer*, June 2008.

2 The suspicion that there's more going on than meets the eye can be traced back to the watchfulness our ancestors needed in the wild, the ability to read 'signs' in order to recognise and avoid threat. As we developed we learned to apply this suspicion—a kind of paranoia—not only to matters of survival but to everything (and even to 'nothing' which of course is anything but), to all the beings and things outside as well as within us. Science and art both have their roots in our need to know what might lie behind or beneath the surface, our desire to lift the veil of appearances and reveal hidden truths.

The idea of a text having an occult subtext is figured in the nature of the footnote itself.

> "The footnote is the unconscious of the text"
> —Patricia Duncker

This quote comes from a typically engaging essay on the subject by Kevin Jackson[3] in which he also quotes Hugh Kenner declaring that the footnote "is a step in the direction of discontinuity: of organizing blocks of discourse simultaneously in space rather than consecutively in time".[4] The footnote is allied to the list in this—and to the 'constellation'—as strategies and structures of non-linear (dis)organisation.

Time machine based on *How to Construct a Time Machine* by Alfred Jarry (1899), originally drawn for the London Institute of 'Pataphysics in 2005.

If, as has been suggested,[5] *Kew. Rhone.* is a kind of time machine, it's one that's designed not to travel backwards and forwards along a continuum, but to so thicken time that the flow stops and the present becomes a miniature eternity.

Jackson quotes Nicholson Baker putting it succinctly: "footnotes really are a beautiful way of stopping time."

---

3 In *Invisible Forms, A Guide to Literary Curiosities* (1999).

4 From *The Stoic Comedians: Flaubert, Joyce and Beckett* (1962).
Jonathan Dunne's translation of *Bartleby & Co.* by Enrique Vila-Matas was published in 2004, too late for this quote from *Note senza testo* (Notes Without a Text) by Bobi Bazlen (1970) to make it into Jackson's book: "Virtually all books are no more than footnotes, inflated until they become volumes. That is why I write only footnotes."

5 See the end of Siegfried Zielinski's essay in this book, 'Getting Down from the Cross: The *Kew. Rhone.* Feeling'.

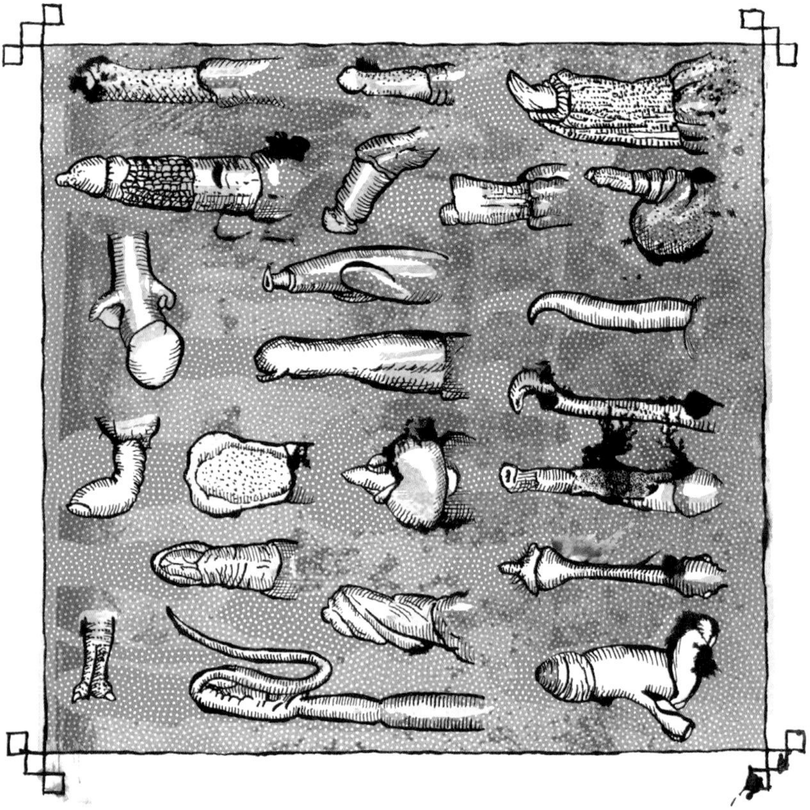

Mammalian penes (all flaccid and not to scale) from groups in which penis morphology is generally poorly known and has not been used to make taxonomic distinctions. Those in the top two rows are all primates.

Three Tenses Onanism

Frank sang a song began
“some guy clobbering a gong”
and further
“J. Arthur” (Rank)
“slang for wank”
(jack off)

Then slack will tense
and gong connect
(to arms!) hands
called will hence
incline to commence

Sun brass arising
some guy lies—
a raft,
as flat (mast
down) as that

Remembered

After a decade living in the UK and Europe, I'd lost my American accent. One of the pleasures of returning in 1974 to New York, city of my birth, was becoming reacquainted with the music of American vernacular speech. It 'spoke' to me like a mother tongue (which it was), although my own voice, as heard on this track, sounded British or at least mid-Atlantic.

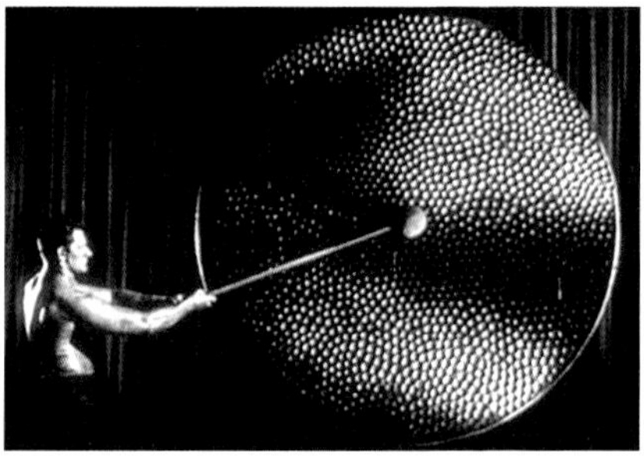

I remember that what sparked this lyric off was hearing Frank, an American, speak the phrase that became the second line. I loved the way he said it, the rhythm and sound of the words: *some guy, clobbering a gong*. It had a nice clunky American music, though the image it referred to was the 'Gongman logo', trademark of the Rank Organisation, a British entertainment conglomerate.[1]

The 'slang' referred to is Cockney rhyming slang.

The song is in three tenses: past, future and present, and depicts in turn the three phases of human sexual response:[2] desire, excitement and release.[3] Three Tenses on not just any ism. Onanism. A form of self-expression.

1 Research reveals that the 'guy' had a name: Ken Richmond, an Olympic wrestler, who died in 2006 aged 80. What's more, the gong he clobbered wasn't 'brass' but made of papier mâché.

2 As described by the psychologist, pioneer in sex therapy and advocate of sexual freedom in the 1960s, Helen Singer Kaplan.

3 Knud Jensen, quoted in 'Jensen's Shangri-La', an essay by Lawrence Weschler in the collection *A Wanderer in the Perfect City* (1998): "...one is lonesome, two is sterile, but three—ah, three is fertile, the number of possibility." cf. virtual, potential, actual; imagine, observe, remember; nothing, everything, something; transparent, translucent, opaque; reception, elimination, retention; thinking, willing, judging; posse, nosse, velle; past, present, future; apprentice, assistant, master; root, blossom, bole; art, literature, music; breakfast, lunch, dinner; animal, vegetable, mineral; thesis, antithesis, synthesis; physical, mental, spiritual; father, mother, child; veni, vidi, vici; certain, credible, possible; etc. etc. etc.

Wanking is a selfish act. Pure DIY. Forget romance or reproduction, its sole purpose is personal gratification. cf. the credo *art for art's sake* which affirms that artistic pursuits are their own justification, divorced from any didactic, moral, utilitarian or commercial function.

Uncoupled, a lonely man takes matters into his own hand. In this he is not alone.

> Animals do it, both male and female. "A variety of creative techniques are used, including genital stimulation using the hand or front paw (primates, Lions), foot (Vampire Bats, primates), flipper (Walruses), or tail (Savanna Baboons), sometimes accompanied by stimulation of the nipples (Rhesus Macaques, Bonobos); autofellating or licking, sucking and/or nuzzling by a male of his own penis (Common Chimpanzees, Savanna Bonobos, Vervet Monkeys, Squirrel Monkeys, Thinhorn Sheep, Bharal, Aoudad, Dwarf Cavies); stimulation of the penis by flipping or rubbing it against the belly or in its own sheath (White-tailed and Mule Deer, Zebras and Takhi); spontaneous ejaculations (Mountain Sheep, Warthogs, Spotted Hyenas); and stimulation of the genitals using inanimate objects (found in several primates and cetaceans)."
> —Bruce Bagemihl, *Biological Exuberance* (1999)

> "I remember when my father would say 'Keep your hands out from under the covers' as he said goodnight. But he said it in a nice way."
> —Joe Brainard, *I Remember* (1975)

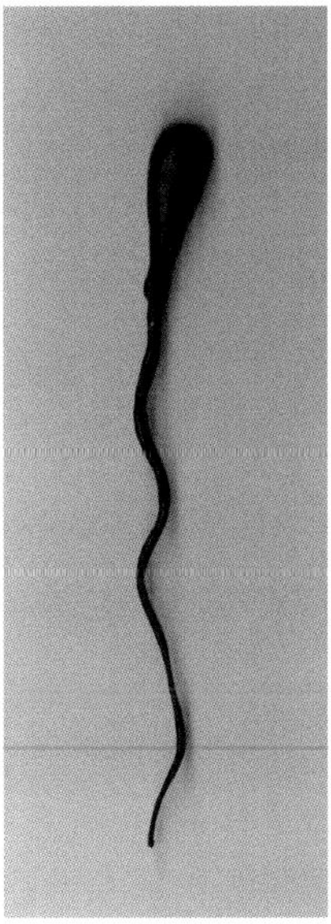

Model sperm, NYC, 1986.

I remember my father telling me that when *his* father caught him masturbating he warned "see that white stuff coming out of you? That's your *brain*."[4]

I remember *Singular Pleasures* (1983), by Harry Mathews, in which mention is made of MAID (Masturbation and Its Discontents) an organisation which invents obstacles (constraints) to overcome while selfloving.
I remember *Sex for One, the Joy of Selfloving* by Betty Dodson, Phd. (1986).

---

4 A belief that dates back to an ancient paleolithic *Ur-kultur.* "The skull, as the bone enclosing the most plentiful *muelos*-marrow in the body (the brain), is therefore the major repository of the generative life-stuff or semen."—Weston La Barre, *Muelos, A Stone Age Superstition About Sexuality* (1984).

I remember Diogenes, reprimanded for masturbating in public, replying "If only it were as easy to banish hunger by rubbing the belly." I remember that once upon a time every sperm was sacred and masturbation was considered a form of murder. The penalty for wanking could be death. I remember that Hans Christian Andersen was a chronic masturbator who suffered terrible guilt over it. He died a virgin. I remember Kellogg, the inventor of Corn Flakes, being obsessed with the dangers of onanism. I remember his advocacy of carbolic acid on the clitoris for girls, circumcision and a silver suture through the glans for boys, to dissuade them from 'self-pollution'. I remember photos from German police files of men auto-asphyxiated by their own 'bachelor machines'.

I remember sisters doing it for themselves. I remember that Dorothy Parker named her canary Onan because he spilled his seed. I remember the title of a book by Tuli Kupferberg: *I Say to Masturbate is Human, to Fuck Divine* (1966).

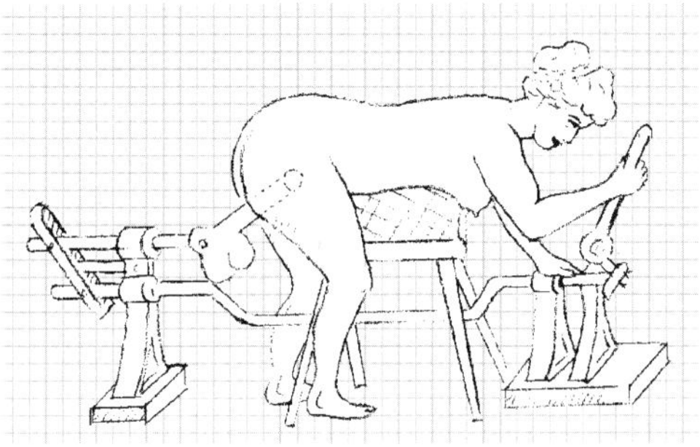

> "Ideas about masturbation have… undergone a radical change throughout the last 2–3,000 years: an activity thought valuable and necessary by physicians in the ancient world became a sin, then a physical and mental disorder, until finally, it has again become a healthy and necessary alternative to vaginal penetrative sex. Such is the life cycle of a sexual perversion."
> —Julie Peakman, *The Pleasure's All Mine, A History of Perverse Sex* (2013)

I remember that everyone's a critic and liable to condemn as 'wankers' people who commit acts or create works they consider pointless, self-indulgent or pretentious.

I remember Allen Ginsberg teaching that the rhythm of poetry wasn't metrical, it was the rhythm of the body: "jacking off under bridges".[5]

5 From a class on 'Spontaneous Poetics, William Carlos Williams and prosody', Naropa Institute, June 1976. Ginsberg described Williams, one of his early mentors, as hearing American vernacular speech "with raw ears. The sound, pure sound and rhythm—as it was spoken around him, and he was trying to adapt his poetry rhythms out of the actual talk-rhythms he heard rather than metronome or sing-song archaic literary rhythms."

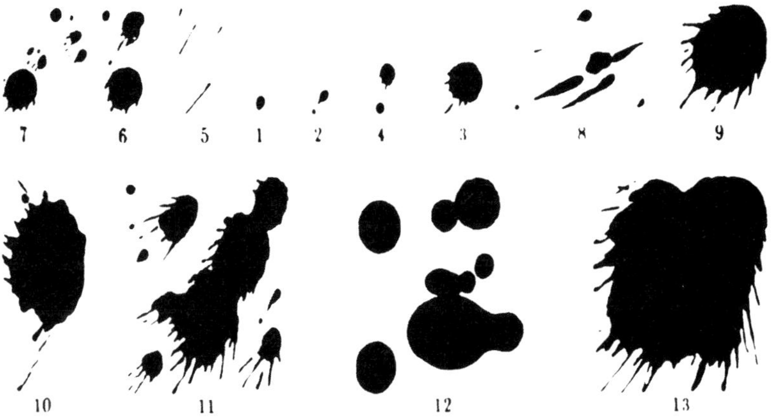

Ink Spots
(From *130 Alphabets & Other Signs*, ed. Julian Rothenstein and Mel Gooding, Redstone Press, 1991)

I remember that writing is a form of masturbation, that letters themselves have what Freud called a 'libidinous charge.' In *The Problem of Anxiety* (1936), he writes that what he's doing (writing) "consists of making a liquid flow from a tube onto a sheet of white paper". An act that Michel Thévoz says "...can be eroticised to the point of causing hysterical paralysis of the hands. The act of writing, in effect, brings into play all the libidinal impulses combined in the 'polymorphous perversity' of infancy: the urethral libidinal libido of flowing ink, the sado-anality of staining, the onanistic rhythms of the hand, the pen caressing the fecund paper 'defended by its whiteness,' etc. The alphabetical characters themselves have a libidinal charge going back to the time when the little child was enchanted by the intrinsic configurations of the letters when it began to draw."—'The Sorcery of Words in the Body of the Text', trans. Allen S. Weiss. *Art & Text* 27, 1988

I remember Freud's theory that dreams have manifest and latent content. If onanism is the manifest subject of this lyric, its latent subject could be writing, specifically 'experimental' writing using constraints etc.

Passion / Obsession / Jealousy

Nine Mineral Emblems

I am your quarry, your mine.
Mineral emblems define
sublunar love—here are nine:
    1. ADAMANT is a hard stone.
Harder is being alone, your whereabouts
unknown.
    2. I feel an attraction for you
just like certain metals feel
for LODE.
    3. Inconstant SELENITE waxes,
wanes. You are my delight despite
your tendency to do the same.
    4. As carbon will become
DIAMOND when pressured, so we come
through love to realise our maximum.
    5. When there is mirth you're
the SALT of my earth, the perfect condiment.
When there is strife you're the spice
of my life, a vital aliment.
    6. CLAY is an old cliché meaning flesh—
it all blows away, so let's enjoy the stuff
while it's still fresh.
    7. MICA reflects the light of another,
is in itself incapable of coruscation—
lovers beware!
    8. When heated, SCOLECITE lengthens,
squirms—not unlike the worm which looks
for lodgings in a pearly urn.
    9. Phosphor's citron glow
is barely bright enough to show
the MACLE of our love—
(two crystals grown together)

15

Lapidary Longings

> "The man who works at the silex loves the silex, and one does not love stones any differently than one loves women."
> —Gaston Bachelard, *The Psychoanalysis of Fire* (1938)

> "Strange sicknesses, curious customs, bell-tolling love, where have you led me? In these stones I find no trace of what I seek."
> —Robert Desnos, *Mourning for Mourning* (1924)

> "the rock is the least living of the
> forms man has fucked"
> —Frank O'Hara, *Odes* (1960)

Nine Mineral Emblems overlaps with *Three Tenses Onanism* in that both songs concern sexual love. In *Onanism* it's 'selfloving', while most of the *Mineral Emblems* depict aspects of love in which self and other—a couple or couples—are involved. Aspects depicted include desire, separation, dependency, fickleness, betrayal and lust. The list culminates with consummation—two becoming one.

Take it from the top:

I am your quarry, your mine.

'Quarry' flickers between two meanings here. The word usually signifies either an object of pursuit or an open pit from which minerals are extracted. Here it means both. Reinforced by the additional punning on 'mine', the line evokes on the one hand an image of predator and prey going round in circles, and on the other harks back to Novalis by investing geological excavation with a romantic/erotic charge.

The song is on one level a love letter, on another an exercise in animating matter, investing stone—the coldest, hardest, least responsive and most inanimate of matters—with something like a responsive soul or spirit. A material equivalent of "knocking on silence for an answering sound." (Archibald MacLeish)[1]

Mineral emblems define
sublunar love

There's an echo here of John Donne's 'A Valediction: Forbidding Mourning', specifically this verse:

> Dull sublunary lovers' love
>   (Whose soul is sense) cannot admit
> Absence, because it doth remove
>   Those things which elemented it.

'Sublunar' means earthly, the physical realm of material things which were thought to be 'elemented' (compounded) of fire and air (masculine) and water and earth (feminine) variously entwined. The four elements constituted all corporeal phenomena—animal, vegetable and, lowest of all—furthest from heaven (on the ladder or chain of being)—mineral.[2]

Donne's poem teasingly imagines an alternative to physical (animal) love, a metaphysical (angelic) intercourse compounded not of the four elements but of a fifth essence which may seem like 'absence' to the uninitiated but is actually a substance subtler than light.[3]

Nine Mineral Emblems sets itself the challenge of using the lowest form of matter (minerals) to describe the highest form of human emotion (love): *4. As carbon will become / DIAMOND when pressured, so we come / through love to realise our maximum.*

---

1 "The metaphor still struggles in the stone,
The allegory of the flesh and bone
Still stares into the summer grass
That is its glass,
The ignorant blood
Still knocks at silence to be understood."

—Archibald MacLeish, 'Hypocrite Auteur' from *Collected Poems 1917–1982* (1985)

2 cf. "Mind sleeps in stone, dreams in the plant, awakes in the animal, and becomes conscious in man."—Friedrich von Schelling. *Nine Mineral Emblems* was originally conceived as part of a taxonomic trio: mineral (mine), vegetable (garden) and animal (bestiary) emblems. I went through the dictionary drawing up alphabetical lists like the one shown on p.101, discovering for myself that, as R. Murray Shafer points out in *The Soundscape, the Tuning of the World* (1994), "when used properly, the dictionary… can provide us with inchoate thoughts and aesthetic moments." Also pertinent in this context is Shafer's observation that "any classification system or taxonomy is surrealistic; for surrealistic art also depends on bringing together incongruous or anachronistic facts, which nevertheless somehow snap together to illuminate new relationships. The first such artists were the encyclopedists, who brought together strange groups of animals, vegetables and ideas for surrealistic family portraits."

3 The 4D incognitum in *Pipeline* is probably compounded of this 'fifth essence' or something very like it. Something very like the fifth essence might be the 'third substance' Louis Simpson mentions in the last stanza of his poem 'Things':

> I said, "I have suspected
> The Mixmaster knows more than I do,
> The air conditioner is the better poet.
> My right front tire is as bald as Odysseus—
> How much it must have suffered!
> Then, as things have a third substance
> Which is obscure to both our senses,
> Let there be a perpetual coming and going
> Between your house and mine."

—Louis Simpson, from *Collected Poems* (1988)

1. ADAMANT is a hard stone.
Harder is being alone, your whereabouts
unknown.

What's so 'hard' for self to bear is the masochistic agony of imagining what the other is getting up to in his/her absence—i.e. being 'untrue'. Sublunary lovers "cannot admit absence" for other reasons too. When two become one, to be separated is to be halved, a radical amputation. The song celebrates the goal of a seamless union: *9. … the MACLE of our love—(two crystals grown together)*. But it also identifies dependency as a danger: *7. MICA reflects the light of another, / is in itself incapable of coruscation— / lovers beware!*

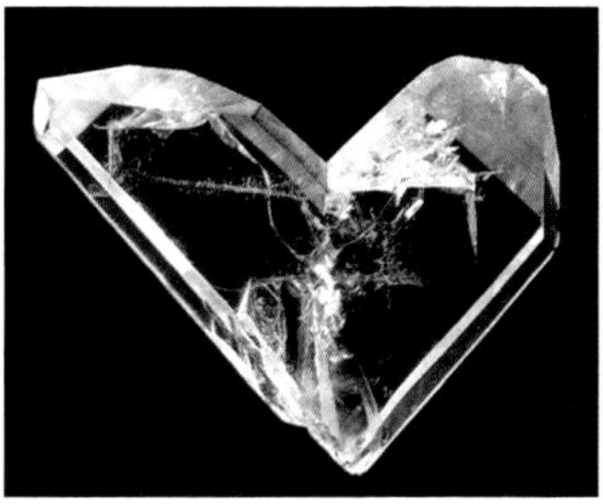

3. Inconstant SELENITE waxes,
wanes. You are my delight despite
your tendency to do the same.

Wikipedia: "The etymology of selenite is through Middle English *selinete*, from Latin *selenites*, from Greek *selēnitēs* (lithos), literally, moonstone or stone of the moon, from *selēnē* (Moon). The ancients had a belief that certain transparent crystals waxed and waned with the moon." An ancient belief, but, like a fickle lover, untrue.

8. When heated, SCOLECITE lengthens,
squirms—not unlike the worm which looks
for lodgings in a pearly urn.

Also untrue. I might well have been deliberately lying, but if not, if I was merely mistaken, I wonder what gave me the idea that scolecite changes shape in this suggestive way? According to an online source[4] "scolecite's structure has a typical zeolite openness about it that allows large ions and molecules to reside and actually move around inside the overall framework. The structure contains open channels that allow water and large ions to travel into and out of the crystal structure.[5] The size of these channels controls the size

4 www.superbminerals.com/mininfo5.php (accessed Sept. 2014)

5 Which rhymes with what Andrew Joron says (on p.132) about the album: "The work as a whole has something to teach us about how fluid can stay alive within a maze of dams and channels."

of the molecules or ions and therefore a zeolite like scolecite can act as a chemical sieve." But I don't think that means it can 'lengthen' or 'squirm'.

Wait! I don't know why it didn't occur to me earlier, but I still have the actual dictionary I used when composing *Minerals*, covered in dust and disintegrating, but right here on my shelves.

> **sco·le·cite** \'skäl-ə-ˌsīt, 'skō-lə-\ *n* [G *skolezit*, fr. Gk *skōlēk-*, *skōlēx* worm; fr. the motion of some forms when heated] **:** a zeolite mineral $CaAl_2Si_3O_{10}.3H_2O$ that is a hydrous calcium aluminum silicate and occurs in radiating groups of crystals, in fibrous masses, and in nodules

And, lo! the entry for *scolecite* on p.772 entirely vindicates the song and its author. I apologise to my youthful self for impugning his reliability, and note that it is I, my *old* self, who isn't to be trusted.

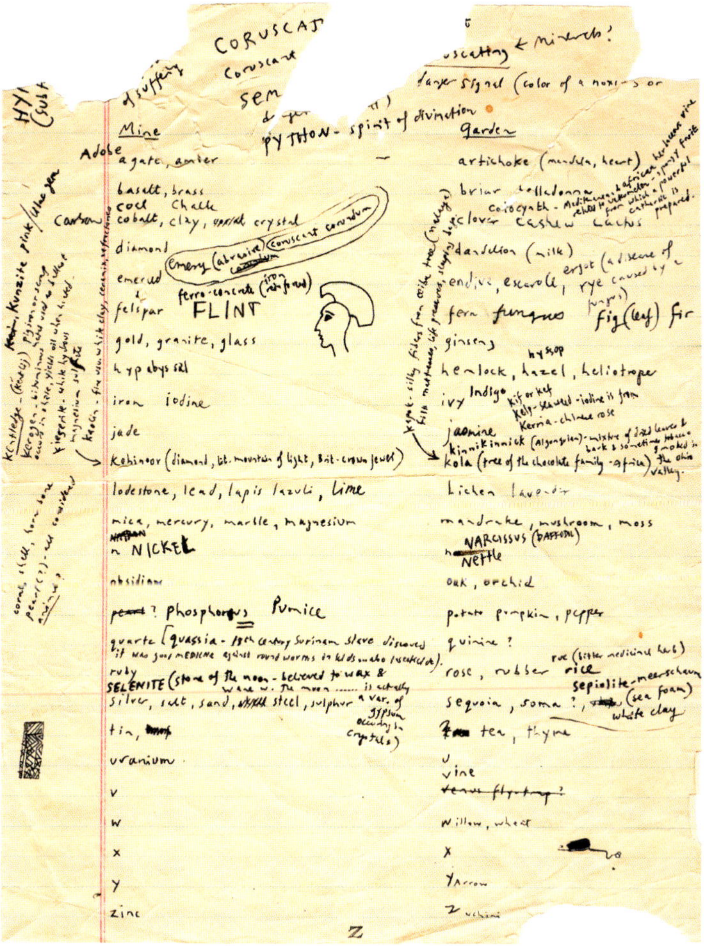

Alphabetical list of minerals and vegetables (see Footnote 2, p.99).

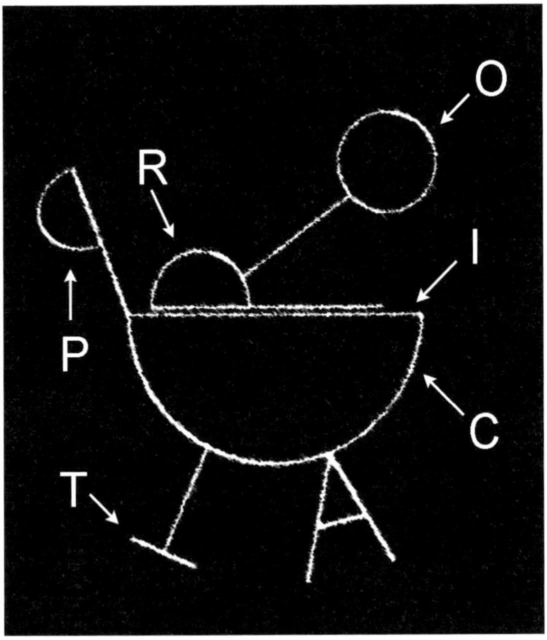

Remembered: Unidentified cabaliste's drawing of a tot in a cot holding a balloon, made from the letters in APRICOT.

Speakers' Corner 1972, by Sheridan Coakley.

Apricot

Very early I clearly realised the pleasures of seeing
and song.
I learned to sing at an early year. In the cot I recall my
singing about a certain thing I saw. I recall a song
in the key of C concerning a thing seen just so.
I sang: "A-P-R-I-C-O-T abbreviates Attain Perfect
Realisation In The Cot."[1]
I sang: "Cot contains certain shining irreducible
contributions. So does the charnel. So does the
ferris wheel gondola."
Singing words devised for seeing "through not with
eyes"[2]
"I am not I when I see"[3]
"I is another"[4]
Words devised to peep into the gone or coming were
shunned by me, I referred to a single moment.
Early in a clearing I recall my singing songs of my
seeing things just so.
I sang: "A net, a gem at every node, in each all others
shining show—whole kit and kaboodle lit by an
apricot's golden glow."

---

1 Unidentified cabaliste, Speakers' Corner, London, 1972.
2 William Blake.
3 Gertrude Stein.
4 Arthur Rimbaud.

Taking Apricot Apart

> "What makes the Hottentot so hot?
> What puts the 'ape' in apricot?
> What have they got that I ain't got?"
> —*Courage*, song the lion sings in the film of *The Wizard of Oz*

> "Everything is fruit to me…"
> —Marcus Aurelius, *Meditations* (167 CE)

She's the first of four writers cited as sources in the footnotes to this lyric—preceding William Blake, Gertrude Stein and Arthur Rimbaud—but her credit reads only "Unidentified cabaliste, Speakers' Corner, London, 1972". She's another incognitum.

Speakers' Corner is at the north-east corner of Hyde Park, a preserve since the late 19th century for public speaking, protest and debate, where "anyone can turn up unannounced and talk on almost any subject, although at the risk of being heckled by regulars".[1] On the day we were there, 42 years ago, my friend Sheridan Coakley and I witnessed a woman giving a chalk-talk.[2] If she was heckled I don't recall. But I've not forgotten how she held up a slate and illustrated her spiel, deconstructing words to reveal their hidden meanings. She literally took the words apart and rearranged bits of the letters to create an image.[3] On the day we were there she took APRICOT apart, using the deconstructed letters as elements in a pictogram of a baby in a cot holding on to a string tied to a balloon. The balloon represented the sun, *gnosis*, wisdom, which the baby was reaching for. And APRICOT, she told us, was an abbreviation echoing

---

1 Wikipedia.

2 Chalk-talks were a once popular vaudeville turn, also a technique used by preachers to enliven sermons.

3 In his late poem, 'b o d y', James Merrill performs operations on the letters of the title in a similar way to create a picture, albeit a mental one:

> Look closely at the letters. Can you see,
> entering (stage right), then floating full,
> then heading off—so soon—
> how like a little kohl-rimmed moon
> *o* plots her course from *b* to *d*
> —as *y*, unanswered, knocks at the stage door?
> Looked at too long, words fail,
> phase out. Ask, now that *body* shines
> no longer, by what light you learn these lines
> and what the *b* and *d* stood for.
> —from *A Scattering of Salts* (1995)

Merrill uses the shapes and positions of the four letters to present a dramatisation in miniature of the cycle of existence. The little *o* is a moon, an eye (or 'I'—Merrill was terminally ill at the time), an actor, passing from stage right to left, from *b* to *d*, birth to death—and ending with the unanswered '*y*?'. (See Laura Quinney, *LRB*, 4 April 2002, pp.35–36.)

Christ's admonition to "become as little children".[4] Sheridan took photographs. Not of her, alas. I picture her middle-aged in a scruffy coat standing on a plastic milk crate, but the memory is vague. It was her reading (and writing) of APRICOT that made the impression. A few years later it became the pivot of this song.

> *Early in a clearing I recall my singing songs of my seeing things just so.*

cf. "One must always tell what one sees. Above all, which is more difficult, one must always see what one sees."—Charles Pierre Péguy

Very early I clearly saw that seeing things "just so" is a kind of triangulation process involving memory, observation and imagination. Excavating a mastodon or a pipeline are metaphors, illustrations or dramatisations of this process.

> *So does the ferris wheel gondola.* ☞

> *...seeing "through not with eyes"*

"I question not my Corporeal or Vegetative Eye any more than I would Question a Window concerning a Sight. I look thro' it & not with it."—William Blake, *A Vision of the Last Judgment* (1810). The eyes are windows/doors of perception. If we cleansed them, Blake said, we'd see that everything is infinite, that even a grain of sand contains shining irreducible contributions.

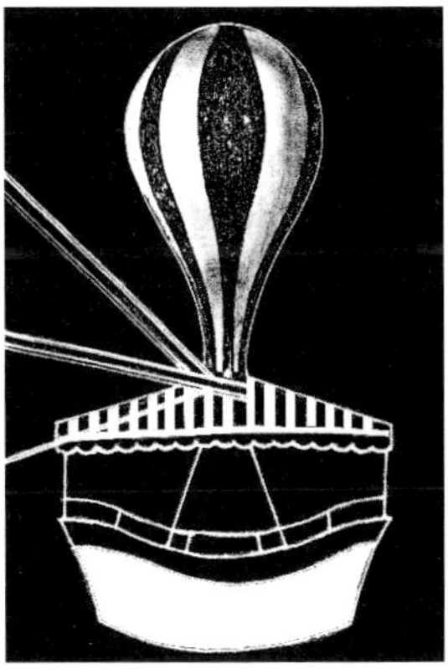

Observed: Ferris wheel gondola, after Ib Andersen's poster for the Tivoli pleasure gardens in Copenhagen. The poster hung in the Blegvad home and was the model for the image I had in mind when I wrote the words.

> *"I is another"*

Rimbaud used this famous phrase (the "poetic $E=mc^2$" according to biographer Graham Robb) in the 'Lettre du Voyant' ('Seer's Letter') to his teacher, Georges Izambard, written in 1871 when the poet was sixteen: *"It's wrong to say 'I think'; one ought to say 'I am being thought'—Forgive the play on words—I is another."*

Seeing that the mind can observe its own operations Rimbaud concluded that Self is a construct and identity a fiction.

> *"I am not I when I see"*

---

4 "Except ye be converted, and become as little children, ye shall not enter into the kingdom of heaven."—*Matthew* XVIII, 3

Identity is a theme of several of Stein's meditations, poems and plays—how we know who we are, or as she puts it "I am I why". In *What Are Masterpieces and Why Are There So Few of Them* (1936) Stein writes "The thing one gradually comes to find out is that one has no identity that is when one is in the act of doing anything". When one is seeing clearly/creating, for instance. Nietzsche: "in order to create it is necessary to forget". For Valéry seeing clearly means to forget the name of the thing one sees, but Stein's view is that what the seer forgets in the act is her/himself. cf. Emerson: "The one thing which we seek with insatiable desire is to forget ourselves, to be surprised out of our propriety, to lose our sempiternal memory and to do something without knowing how or why; in short to draw a new circle. Nothing great was ever achieved without enthusiasm. The way of life is wonderful; it is by abandonment."[5]

I referred to a single moment.

Stein again: "The business of Art… is to live in the actual present, that is the complete actual present, and to completely express that complete actual present."—'Plays', *Lectures in America* (1934)

Adepts who practise seeing things 'just so' as a creative discipline report that by striking the right balance between imagining (the future), observing (the present) and remembering (the past) they can stop time.

> "He was no longer prevented from grasping eternity. Nothing began, nothing left off. There was only an endless present; and that power in him which loved life with a love so exquisitely sweet and yearning—the power of which his person was only the unsuccessful expression—that power would always know how to find access to this present."—Thomas Mann, *Buddenbrooks* (1901)

And to return us to the theme of identity: "Any destiny at all, however long and complicated, in reality consists of a single moment: the moment in which a man once and for all knows who he is." —J. L. Borges, 'Biography of Tadeo Isidoro Cruz' (1949). And a woman? He doesn't say.

"A net, a gem at every node, in each all others shining show…"

The reference is to the Hindu TOE ('Theory of Everything'), Indra's net (see the eleventh of the 'Eleven Thoughts re *Kew. Rhone.*', p.11).

5 Ralph Waldo Emerson, a letter to Elizabeth Hoar, quoted by Susan Howe in 'These Flames and Generosities of the Heart, Emily Dickinson and the Illogic of Sumptuary Values', in *The Birth-Mark: Unsettling the Wilderness in American Literary History* (1993).

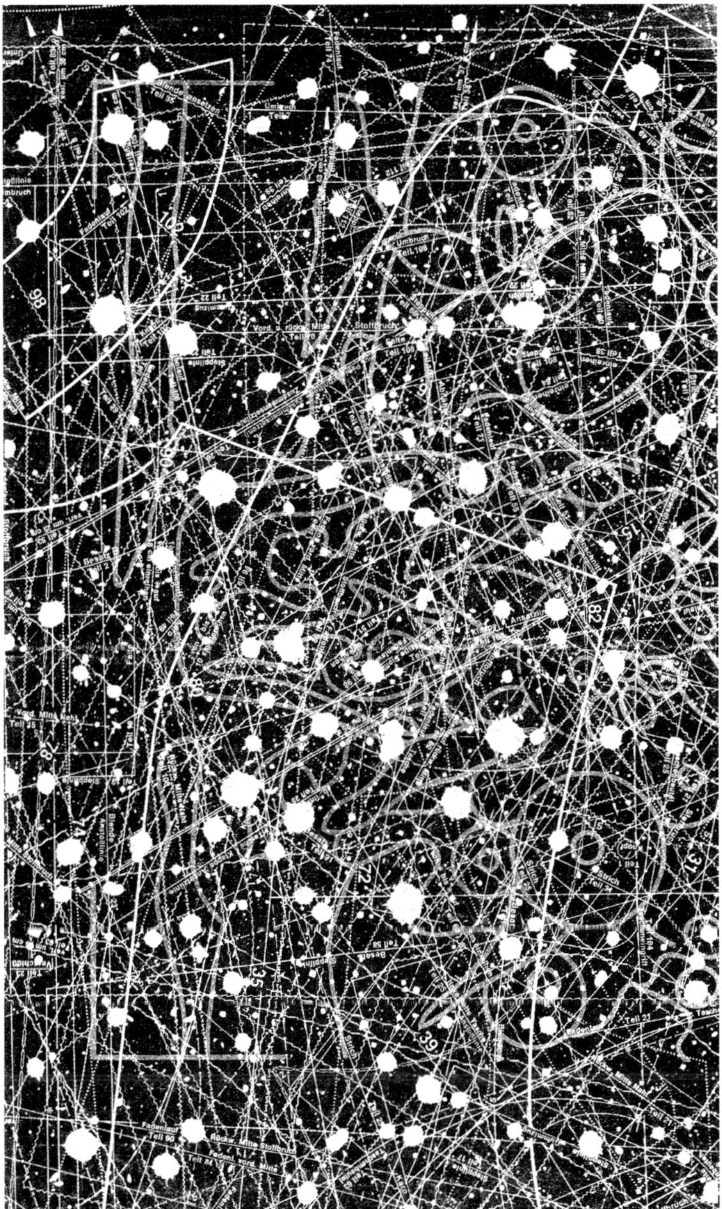

Imagined: Indra's net (detail).

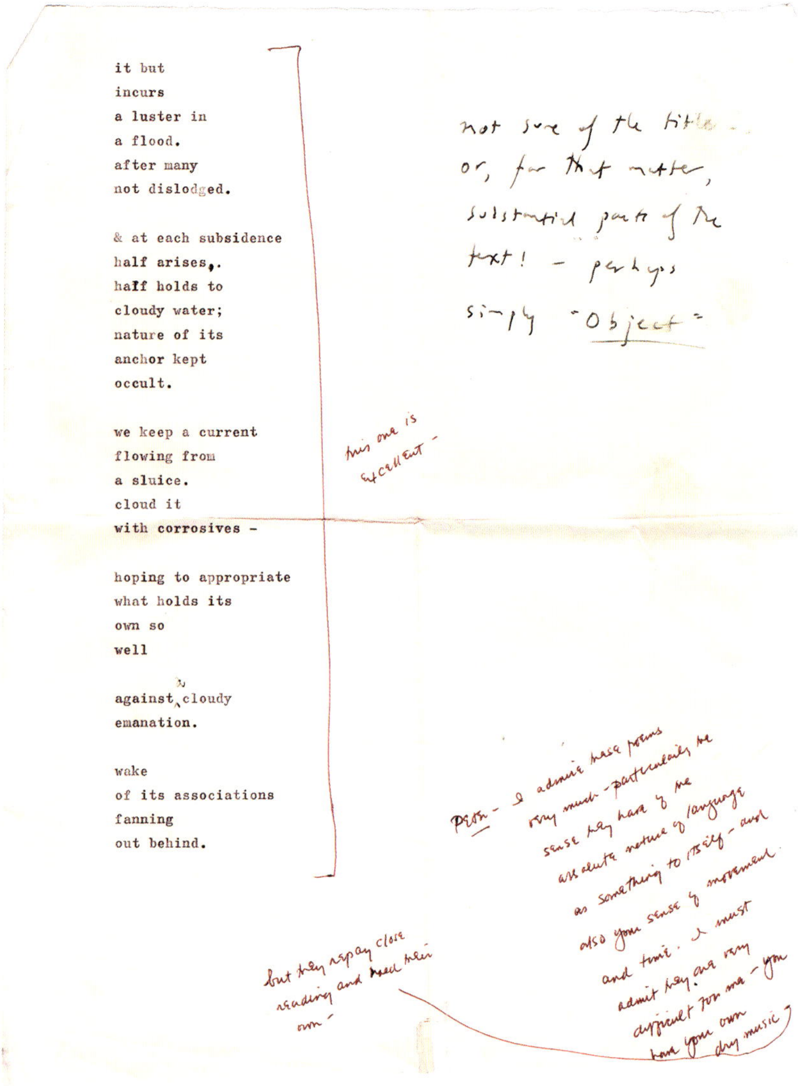
it but
incurs
a luster in
a flood.
after many
not dislodged.

& at each subsidence
half arises,.
half holds to
cloudy water;
nature of its
anchor kept
occult.

we keep a current
flowing from
a sluice.
cloud it
with corrosives -

hoping to appropriate
what holds its
own so
well

against cloudy
emanation.

wake
of its associations
fanning
out behind.

not sure of the title – or, for that matter, substantial parts of the text! – perhaps simply "Object"

this one is excellent –

Peter – I admire these poems very much – particularly the sense they have of the absolute nature of language as something to itself – and also your sense of movement and time. I must admit they are very difficult for me – you have your own dry music

but they repay close reading and need their own –

Draft of *gegenstand* written for Gilbert Sorrentino's poetry class at the New School, New York City, 1975, with Sorrentino's comments in red ballpoint.

On the recorded track, John's bass and organ with Andrew's skeletal percussion (including 'moo' toy) and Lisa's limpid vocal create an oneiric atmosphere. The song evokes, for me at least, a miniature tableau, like something seen through the misted glass of a cloud chamber.

gegenstand

it but
incurs
a lustre
in a flood—
after many
not dislodged.

and at each
subsidence half
arises, half
holds to
cloudy water—
nature of
its anchor
kept occult.

we keep
a current
flowing
from a sluice.
cloud it
with corrosives—
hoping
to appropriate
what holds its own
so well—
what tips
an ever
wider wake.

17

What tips an ever wider wake

> Facts about ourselves are not peculiarly solid and resistant to skeptical dissolution. Our natures are, indeed, elusively insubstantial—notoriously less stable and less inherent than the natures of other things. And insofar as this is the case, sincerity is itself bullshit.—Harry Frankfurt, *On Bullshit* (2005)

"(who?)" is the first question asked on the title track of this record, and the question of identity is a central preoccupation of the album, as it was of my life at the time. At 63 I miss the vim of youth, but I remember the strain of always feeling that I should be other than I was. I don't miss that.

I felt false. I lacked sincerity, substance, conviction, character. What could I do? Where could I go to acquire these things? A quest was indicated.

Such a quest, precipitated by an excess of subjectivity, requires an object to seek—a target, a grail of some sort. *gegenstand* is an attempt to imagine such an object. Referred to only as "it" and only described indirectly, *gegenstand* is the embodiment of the commitment I thought might be the cure for my *anomie*. Commitment to what? To resistance. Resistance against what? Against any and all kinds of certainty (cloudy corrosives), and all forms of authority, even my own.

Ah, youth!

> "Not in believing, but in pretending. Not in knowing, but in pretending. Not in undergoing, but in pretending.
>
> At last! At last! all of reality! We find we are only what we pretended to be. We realize."—Robert Duncan[1]

Like *gegenstand*, the 'self' I sought was an imaginary object. Pretending is a necessary part of initiation, part of the process of forging (in both senses of the word) an identity.

Tribal initiations often take the form of a 'vision quest'—young aspirants are sent forth, out of the frame, to make a name for themselves, literally—to seek the object that will henceforth become their

---

1 'Imagining in Writing', from *Derivations, Selected Poems 1950–1956* (1968).

handle. For instance, an Amerindian brave becomes known as 'The Flash of a Fish in Turning' because that was the most vivid of all the things he saw on his quest. That was his haiku-like epiphany, and it sticks. It becomes him.

On my imaginary version of a vision quest the thing I pretended to see most vividly was *gegenstand*, an incognitum. More general than specific, *gegenstand* was an attempt to evoke an imaginary object in terms of the resistance all objects are, in a sense, the embodiments of. Mute and immutable, they endure. In the poem the nameless object is a symbol of steadfastness, of constancy, holding its own against corrosive or coercive forces. It's a talisman, a corrective to precarious fluidity. *Gegenstand* is an 'obscure object of desire'. The (unrealistic) desire to be as authentic, as sincere, as reliably true to oneself as the object is.

As well as imaginary objects there were actual people back then who seemed to embody such qualities. Mentors—permission-givers, guides, even if they didn't know it—who I borrowed or stole traits from as and when I could.

One of my early aspirations was to write poetry. My two main poet-mentors at the time were Peter Scupham in England (and via his teaching, Yeats, and via Yeats, Blake), and Clayton Eshleman whom I'd met in Paris (and via Clayton the whole of what was then contemporary American poetry). In New York, in 1975, I was fortunate to have Gilbert Sorrentino as a teacher, only for a term I think, maybe two. But his encouragement was crucial.

Excerpt from Franklin Bruno's interview with PB in *The Believer*:[2]

> I'd been taken by a poem of [Sorrentino's][3] in Clayton's magazine, *Caterpillar*, so when I saw his New School course advertised, I signed up. As a teacher, G. S. was a lovely combination of serious and funny. In response to a particularly mawkish student effort, he buried his head in his hands and groaned, "Tell it to the Marines" in a way that didn't seem merely cruel. One entire class was taken up by him reading us Flann O'Brien's essay 'A Bash in the Tunnel' with contagious glee. I remember him mocking what he called 'New Yorker poetry,' intoning portentously, "I dreamed I was an oyster on the shore of life..." Another week he brought his pal Hubert Selby Jr in to talk to us. I wrote *gegenstand* for Sorrentino's class and he remarked approvingly that it wasn't something that could be set to music and sung. When I repeated this to John Greaves, he set it to music and Lisa Herman sang it.

---

2 *The Believer* (the Art Issue), Nov/Dec 2009.

3 'Coast of Texas', which treated of erotic obsession: "In the pale light he sees her mouth / open and the tongue come out / in her heat."

On the copy of the poem I handed in, Sorrentino wrote: "this one is excellent—", providing the validation I craved. I read and re-read his comment: "Peter—I admire these poems very much—particularly the sense they have of the absolute nature of language as something to itself—and also your sense of movement and time. I must admit they are very difficult for me—you have your own dry music—but they repay close reading and hold their own—"

The young need validation and encouragement. I seemed to need it more than most. Morbidly prone to self-doubt, constraints (anagrams and palindromes) were one way I resisted sceptical dissolution as a writer. But nothing boosted my resistance as effectively as an encouraging word from a mentor. In my immaturity I couldn't see what I'd made myself, I needed others to objectify it for me.

Jean Cocteau tells a story about Sir Galahad returning to Camelot with the Grail. When the knights of the Round Table gather to admire the thing, they're mystified by Galahad's request that they describe it to him. "But it's right there," they say, "see for yourself!" He has to confess that, although he achieved it—found it and brought it back—he needs others to see it for him.

Whether it's a 'self' we make or a work of art, it's always at some level a collaborative venture, it can't be done alone.

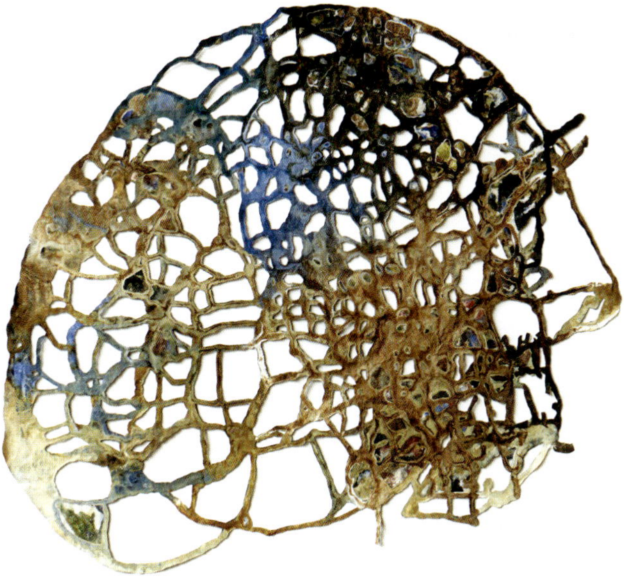

During the time *Kew. Rhone.* was composed and recorded Dana Johnson and I were living together in the John Street loft. She sang on a couple of the songs, but her participation and contribution went deeper than that. Having previously studied in England with Brian Catling, she was now studying sculpture with Bradford Graves (1939–1998) at Parsons in New York City. My budding interest in 'numinous objects' was fed by her work and by discussions with her, her mentors and friends. 38 years later, now living in Sweden, she responded to the invitation to contribute to this book with these two pieces, cutouts made from painted Japanese paper. She describes *Quest* (above) as a "Mastodonic object/cavity", while *Echo* (frontispiece) "was inspired by… the spasmodic quality of the music interrupted (or *vice versa*) by delicate dreamy parts… how it shifts shape." To me they also suggest a kind of lattice, constellation or net, and maybe a map of the now here/nowhere *Kew. Rhone.* is 'at'.

Front cover: *Kew. Rhone.* Virgin Records, 1977.

John Greaves

1. *Good Evening*: I'm fairly sure I wrote this once most things were finished. An overture. The melody is *Kew. Rhone.* of course. The style, a modest homage to my heroes, Carla and Mike, the JCOA. And here we are recording in their home. Carla on sax… first time ever I think.

2. *Twenty-Two Proverbs*: A year earlier, I was living in Richard Branson's house, surviving on his immense generosity. (Thanks eternal.) This piece emerged from his very nice upright joanna. It began as "Picture Wilderbestes on heat" (scan with "Have your cake and eat your cake"). It was fairly complete musically. No lyricist in his right mind would have considered it. Fortunately I didn't know anybody like that. It was the first complete lyric Peter came up with in New York after a visit to the Cornell Library. I think his mother, Lenore, did some ear-pulling.

3. *Seven Scenes From The Painting…*: Another Blegvad response to a devious melody and structure. Trip to the Met. Charles Willson Peale. 7 Scenes as seen by the author. Of course that's what the song's about. Lisa insists on it.

4. *Kew. Rhone.*: I lost my mind figuring this out on my father's piano in Wales. Got carted off to hospital and stuffed with librium during rehearsals in Peter's old school in Letchworth. The guitar-player was fucking my wife. Henry Cow was in a post-Stalinist melt-down. Peter and Anthony were considered ideologicalIy inept. I left the band. *Kew. Rhone.* was the imprimatur for the last proper record Virgin made. When I got to New York, I found Peter's anagrams and palindromes and they glued themselves to my odd time signatures like birds with one wing making it home. Later that year I made a demo of it with Carla singing in Grog Kill (lost). It became all the things that Lisa Herman describes, deliciously, elsewhere in this volume. I'm very proud of it.

5. *Pipeline*: Another one that was fairly well finished musically. Many scary nights in the Blarney Stone to come up with a phenomenological bossa nova in 7/4. (With the world's (still) greatest free-jazz drummer… Come on.)

6. *Catalogue of Fifteen Objects & Their Titles*: I'd done a demo of this with my not great words in Tom Newman's studio in Little Venice (lost). It was called *Stages of Decay*. In New York it resisted Peter until we got to Grog Kill. He came up with *15 Objects*. Are you sure we can do this? he asked Lisa and me…

Side One
Stereo
V 2082
V 2082 A
KEW . RHONE
JOHN GREAVES & PETER BLEGVAD
1. GOOD EVENING 2. TWENTY TWO PROVERBS
3. SEVEN SCENES FROM THE PAINTING "EXHUMING THE FIRST AMERICAN MASTODON" BY C. W. PEALE
4. KEW . RHONE 5. PIPELINE
6. CATALOGUE OF FIFTEEN OBJECTS AND THEIR TITLES
All tracks: Music – John Greaves; Lyrics – Peter Blegvad
Published by Virgin Music (Publishers) Ltd
© 1977 Virgin Music (Publishers) Ltd
℗ 1977 Virgin Records Ltd

Side One

Virgin
Side Two
Stereo
V 2082
KEW . RHONE
JOHN GREAVES & PETER BLEGVAD
1. ONE FOOTNOTE (TO KEW . RHONE)
2. THREE TENSES ONANISM
3. NINE MINERAL EMBLEMS
4. APRICOT (3.02)
5. GEGENSTAND (3.45)
All tracks: Music—John Greaves; Lyrics—Peter Blegvad
Published by Virgin Music (Publishers) Ltd
© 1977 Virgin Music (Publishers) Ltd
℗ 1977 Virgin Records Ltd

Side Two

JG wrote out this score to *Pipeline* sometime in the late 1970s for a projected issue of *Amateur* which never materialised.

7. *One Footnote (to Kew. Rhone.)*: Chris Cutler had written very good lyrics to this (never recorded): “No more political innocence, no more parades”. Peter’s anecdotal, self-referential words are perfect on our less than perfect brass band arrangement. But I did get to play drums with Carla Bley.

8. *Three Tenses Onanism*: Frank is Dana’s brother. An ode to safe sex. Onan always got bad press. This one’s a gem.

9. *Nine Mineral Emblems*: “I am your quarry, you’re mine” is the best first line ever written. To follow up with a mineral-symbolic love elegy is, at least, audacious. Musically, it’s a glorious mess. I love it.

10. *Apricot*: 40 years on, I’ve just realised that these last two are the only pieces on the album for which I composed music for a finished text. Peter had given me “A net, a gem at every node…” probably not long after *Bad Alchemy*. It obviously appealed to the carefully dissimulated mystic hippie in me. Peter wanted to stop the release of the album so he could re-do the vocal. It’s a fucking masterpiece.

11. *gegenstand*: Another scrap from Peter’s table in John Street. Peter was illicitly attending poetry classes under his wife’s name. His teacher Gilbert Sorrentino said of this offering “It’s nice, but you couldn’t hear it being sung could you”? Sorry Gilbert. Thank you Lisa.

KEW. RHONE.

SIDE ONE

2/ Twenty-Two Proverbs

1. Would ye both eat your cake and have your cake? - (English)
2. Would ye brak a butterfly upon the wheel? - (English)
3. He who sows wind will reap a tempest. - (Portugese)
4. Milk the mosquito to serve your king. - (Bulgarian)
5. To cut into another man's ear is like cutting into a felt hat. - (Danish)
6. She is neither fish nor flesh nor good red herring. - (English)
7. Names are not the pledge for things, but things for names. - (Roumanian)
8. One should write bad things on running water. - (Roumanian)
9. A drowning man would catch at razors. - (Italian)
10. Coupled sheep drown one another. - (Dutch)
11. One may well be too young to marry,
but one is never too old to love. - (Finnish)
12. Treat your friend as if he will one day be your enemy and
your enemy as if he will one day become your friend. - (from Laberius)
13. Herring in the land, the doctor at a stand. - (Dutch)
14. Dead as a doornail. - (from "Piers Ploughman")
15. A single hair casts its shadow on the ground. - (Spanish)
16. What have I to do with Bradshaw's windmill? - (English)
17. Better to live one day as a lion
than live a hundred years as a sheep. - (motto on Italian 50 lire coin)
18. The stone that the builders rejected has become the corner stone. - (?)
19. The stone that everybody spits upon will be wet at last. - (Danish)
20. A cat may look at a king. - (English)
21. By night all cats are grey. - (French)
22. The pen of the tongue should be dipped in the inkwell of the heart. - (Italian)

4/ Kew. Rhone.

(who?) we who knew no woe
we who were her hero

(when?) when we were on her knee
when we knew her
when we were one

where?
Kew. Rhone.

we won renown

(how?) we were her worker

we won honor snow
when we knew her
when we were one

where?
Kew. Rhone.

---

not a set animal,
not a set animal, laminates
laminates a tone of
a set animal,
animal, laminates
a set animal,
animal, laminates
laminates a tone of sleep.
a tone of sleep.
Peel's foe, not a set animal, laminates a tone of sleep.

5/ Pipeline
(words to be used in conjunction with cover illustrations)

(FIGURE A.)
Here are two gentlemen and a lady contemplating a length
of dug-up pipeline.

FIGURE B. illustrates the assertion -
"ambiguity can't be measured like a change in temperature"

FIGURE C. consists of a list of asserted equipage.
A gentleman imagines how the items on the list would look
if only part exhumed. (he thinks they wouldn't look unlike
a length of pipe).

(The Lady's Assertion):
"When you remove a rung from
a ladder, the whole is suddenly part, the part is whole.
But the hue and temperature of a pipeline are ineluctably
parts, without the pipeline they would cease to be."

(Second Gentleman's Assertion):
"Anything you care to mention
of three dimensions (like a length of pipe) in a certain light
may be seen as the projection or the shadow of an entity of
four dimensions - (see FIGURE D.)

3/ Seven Scenes from the Painting "Exhuming
the First American Mastodon" by C.W. Peale
(words to be used in conjunction with cover illustration)

I) Youth with no name cuts out of frame
with an axe.
II) Those who extol a bone on a scroll
turn their backs, sanction his escape.
III) Attatched to his toe, shackles
below the surface hold a neophyte fast who
oggles aghast a bone of gold emblazoned
with his name.
IV) Three green umbrellas are shown in all.
These denote degrees by which a fall
(a fall from grace) may be measured
as virtual, potential or as actual.
1)the first has been dropped
2)the second picked up but not untied
3)the third has been spread high over head to hide the sky
V) Nourished by the two syringes shown,
VI) the wheel "Nomenclator" (better known
to the world as The High Priestess) names (i.e. defines)
her victims forever.
VII) John Masten has hung so long
from a rung he now depends on it as much as from it
for such a vantage lends itself
to one who proudly claims
to be amphibious though actually allergic
to the
two predicaments
to which his ladder leads.

6/ Catalogue of Fifteen Objects and Their Titles

THE OBJECTS :
1. Cylinder of dust
2. Salt cross with a crust of iodine
3. Plank of pine
4. Loaf of rust
5. Hollow cone of tobacco which contains a tin coin
6. Pillar of yeast in linoleum jacket
7. Circular puddle of yogurt and neon
8. Arrow of ice wrapped in surgical gauze
9. Coin stacks, several columns - voltaic piles of gold-plated bamboo
10. Water in a bakelite box, and a box full of oil
11. A yolk of leather in a tobacco egg
12. Citronella spilled in a spiral upon a blanket of fat
13. Mixture of paragoric and dew in a creosote cone
14. A disc of wicker beside a pill of zinc
15. Figure made of two copper pyramids glued base to base with sap

THEIR TITLES :
1. "Silo"
2. "Referee"
3. "Threshold" (meant to be flat on the floor, part of a door none can see)
4. "Altar from a Metal Cathedral"
5. "Dunce's Trumpet" (for V-)
6. "Dry Cell"
7. "Lunatic Mirror"
8. "Signal from a Memory"
9. "Ladder of Kings"
10. "Ransom to Secure the Release of a Mother and Child"
11. "October Seventh"
12. "My Uncle's Monocle"
13. "Fuel for a Tiny Machine"
14. "Two Equivelant Forms"
15. Quote from Swedenborg to the effect that angels fucking shed light.

Lyric insert: front.

KEW. RHONE.

STEREO V 2082

SIDE TWO

1/ One Footnote (to Kew. Rhone.)

Other anagrams to be found in the words
Kew Rhone :
horn, honk, heron, hew, keener, hone,
owner, week, new, row, error, reek, whore.

You can no doubt eke out a couple more.

2/ Three Tenses Onanism

Frank sang a song began
"some guy clobbering a gong"
and further
"J. Arthur"
(Rank)
"slang for wank"
(jack off)

then slack will tense
and gong connect
(to arms!) hands
called will hence
incline to commence

sun brass arising
some guy lies -
a raft,
as flat (mast
down) as that

3/ Nine Mineral Emblems

I am your quarry, your mine.
Mineral emblems define
sublunar love - here are nine:
1. ADAMANT is a hard stone.
Harder is being alone, your whereabouts
unknown.
2. I feel an attraction
for you just like certain metals feel
for LODE.
3. Inconstant SELENITE waxes,
wanes. You are my delight despite
your tendency to do the same.
4. As carbon will become
DIAMOND when pressured, so we come
through love to realize our maximum.
5. When there is mirth you're
the SALT of my earth, the perfect condiment.
When there is strife you're still the spice
of my life, a vital aliment.
6. CLAY is an old cliché meaning flesh -
it all blows away, so let's enjoy the stuff
while it's still fresh.
7. MICA reflects the light of another,
is in itself incapable of corruscation -
lovers beware!
8. When heated, SCOLECITE lengthens,
squirms - not unlike the worm which looks
for lodgings in a pearly urn.
9. Phosphor's citrine glow
is barely bright enough to show
the MACLE of our love -
(two crystals grown together).

4/ APRICOT

Very early I clearly realized the pleasures of seeing and song.
I learned to sing at an early year. In the cot I recall my singing
about a certain thing I saw. I recall a song in the key of C
concerning a thing seen just so.
I sang: "A-P-R-I-C-O-T abbreviates Attain Perfect Realization
In the COT."[1]
I sang: "Cot contains certain shining irreducible contributions.
So does the charnel. So does the ferris-wheel gondola."
Singing words devised for seeing "through not with eyes"[2]
"I am not I when I see"[3]
"I is another"[4]
Words devised to peep into the gone or coming were shunned by me.
I referred to a single moment. Early in a clearing I recall my
singing songs of my seeing things just so.
I sang: "A net, a gem at every node, in each all others shining show -
whole kit and kaboodle lit by an apricot's golden glow."

1 - unidentified cabalists, speaker's corner, London, 1972
2 - [illegible]
3 - Gertrude Stein
4 - Arthur Rimbaud

5/ gegenstand

it but
incurs
a lustre
in a flood -
after many
not dislodged.

and at each
subsidence half
arises, half
holds to
cloudy water -
nature of
its anchor
kept occult.

we keep
a current
flowing
from a sluice.
cloud it
with corrosives -
hoping
to appropriate
what holds its own
so well -
what tips
an ever
wider wake.

Back.

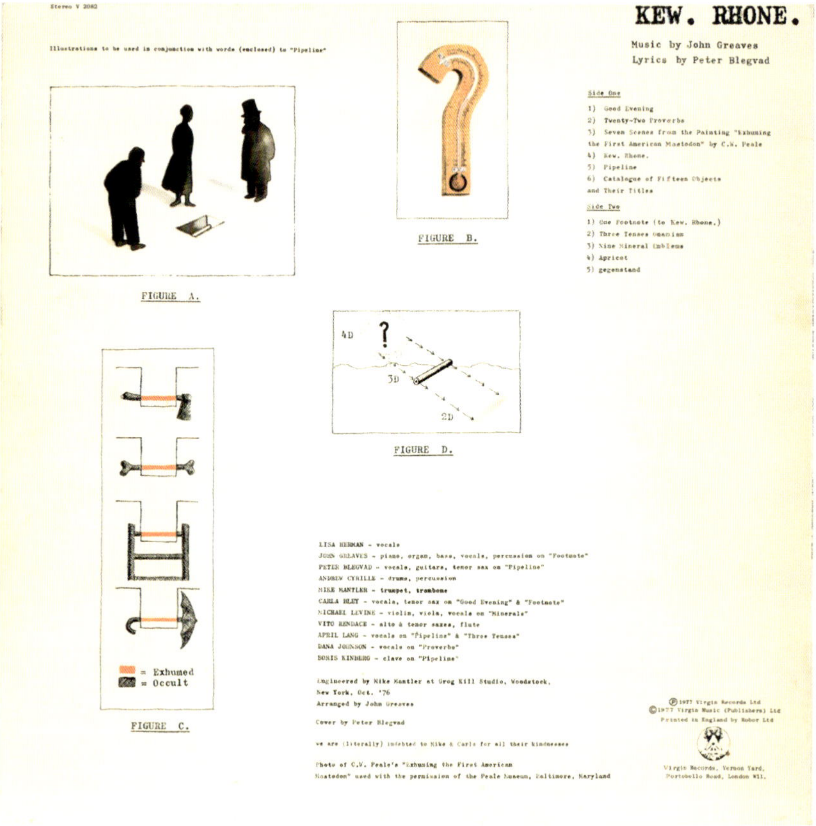

Stereo V 2082
Illustrations to be used in conjunction with words (enclosed) to "Pipeline"
KEW. RHONE.
Music by John Greaves
Lyrics by Peter Blegvad
Side One
1) Good Evening
2) Twenty-Two Proverbs
3) Seven Scenes from the Painting "Exhuming the First American Mastodon" by C.W. Peale
4) Kew. Rhone.
5) Pipeline
6) Catalogue of Fifteen Objects and Their Titles
Side Two
1) One Footnote (to Kew. Rhone.)
2) Three Tenses Onanism
3) Nine Mineral Emblems
4) Apricot
5) gegenstand
FIGURE A.
FIGURE B.
4D
3D
2D
FIGURE D.
= Exhumed
= Occult
FIGURE C.
LISA HERMAN - vocals
JOHN GREAVES - piano, organ, bass, vocals, percussion on "Footnote"
PETER BLEGVAD - vocals, guitars, tenor sax on "Pipeline"
ANDREW CYRILLE - drums, percussion
MIKE MANTLER - trumpet, trombone
CARLA BLEY - vocals, tenor sax on "Good Evening" & "Footnote"
MICHAEL LEVINE - violin, viola, vocals on "Minerals"
VITO RENDACE - alto & tenor saxes, flute
APRIL LANG - vocals on "Pipeline" & "Three Tenses"
DANA JOHNSON - vocals on "Proverbs"
BORIS KINBERG - clave on "Pipeline"
Engineered by Mike Mantler at Grog Kill Studio, Woodstock, New York, Oct. '76
Arranged by John Greaves
Cover by Peter Blegvad
we are (literally) indebted to Mike & Carla for all their kindnesses
Photo of C.W. Peale's "Exhuming the First American Mastodon" used with the permission of the Peale Museum, Baltimore, Maryland
℗ 1977 Virgin Records Ltd
© 1977 Virgin Music (Publishers) Ltd
Printed in England by Robor Ltd
Virgin Records, Vernon Yard, Portobello Road, London W11.

Back cover.

19

Lisa Herman

KR is a memory, and I don't remember very much from twenty years ago. I've probably consumed too much Sweet'n Low, or used too many aluminum pots and pans. I nonetheless recall—and will share, on this felicitous occasion—a few details about the making of *Kew. Rhone.*

KR is a record, and having listened to the thing after all this time inspires several comments, which also follow.

The official explanation back then was that *Kew. Rhone.* was an anagram for 'Know. Where.'

I accepted this because Peter Blegvad (the ever cogitative, reductive Peter Blegvad) would be perfectly likely to strip sentences to words, strip words of their meanings, and ultimately face down the alphabet. I imagine that if Peter B. were a scientist, his beat would be atoms or sub-atomic particle theory. I haven't seen or spoken to Blegvad—or Greaves—in ten or twelve years. A lot may have changed, but it doesn't really matter in terms of *Kew. Rhone.*

I can't help seeing '(k)now (w)here' in *Kew. Rhone.* Or thinking 'now hear'.

In his playfully cerebral manner, PB might be commenting upon time itself and the fact that music exists in time, as do humans.

I never asked about the periods because I was so busy learning *gegenstand*.

I don't mean to suggest that PB is merely reductive ("I should hope to smoke a herring", my father always says when he means "God forbid"). There is, along with many other wondrous qualities, an intrinsic emotionality to his work. This and the warmth of John Greaves' music somehow render the lyrics—catalogs, mysterious numbers (song titles), and ceaseless efforts at denomination—richly poignant.

An incontrovertible balance was achieved in this collaboration.

Greaves' loopy, graceful, dignified music made perfectly natural settings for Peter's thorny, unique poetry.

Music has its math aspects and its sex aspects. It's all there in KR, in irreproachable proportion.

I should know.

There's no better way to get to know a composition than to have to perform it. The music of KR has an interior logic, integrity, and innocence; the songs are accessible, intensely musical, memorable, and they were fun to learn. After the release of *Kew. Rhone.* I was briefly regarded as an "underground avant-rock priestess", and hence had the opportunity to sing my share of 'difficult' music.

While much of it was genuinely worthwhile, it was also mostly labored and difficult.

I'd like to re-learn all the songs and do a cover album of *Kew. Rhone.*

When you're young you're volatile, and you take your chemistry for granted. You don't know that certain liaisons are remarkable or precious. The making of KR involved a significant but unself-conscious effort. It feels like a confluence of factors contributed to (what I recall as) a happy, ho-hum atmosphere:
1. Carla Bley and Mike Mantler's casual generosity.
2. The year, the decade… KR was more of a mid-century thing than a fin-de-siècle…
3. The preparation. Everything was written and well considered before it was recorded. (It was the first time I had ever heard of semi- or demi-quavers.) Everyone knew what they had to do.

I had to hit the notes, enunciate the words, get out of the way.

Peter had to execute a set of nerve-wracking precision guitar parts, among other things.

John had the biggest job (getting what was written down on tape; playing bass, keyboards etc.), but I'm not sure he struggled as much as Peter and I did. John always pushed us, and in retrospect I realize that it was an act of generosity and showed his respect and faith in us.

John said "A year from now, I'd probably be able to play this better; a year from now you'd probably be able to sing this or that a little better than you can right now… but that's life. It'll always be like that. We're doing this now. At least the striving should be audible…"
4. Personality (layers). JG's easygoing Welsh regular guy manner belies a strong vision and firm focus. He was very decisive in the studio, albeit in his friendly, fuzzy way, knew what he wanted to hear.

Blegvad is also charmingly self-deprecating as he comes up with the goods. (Utterly dazzling goods.)

Mike Mantler was brutally honest. Carla was bewitching.

Michael Mantler at the mixing desk, (JG below) sketched by PB, Grog Kill, 1976.

Favorite performance of a line from *Kew. Rhone.*: John Greaves singing "What have I to do with Bradshaw's windmill?"—from *Twenty-Two Proverbs*. This line is why I tried to seduce JG.

John had a dream one night during the recording of *Kew. Rhone.* In which he heard a great, passionate symphonic and choral piece of music that described the spirit, essence and agony of the Jewish people. The next morning he was agitated and excited and very frustrated that he couldn't remember any of it.

My analysis at the time was that the dream was about *me* and *my passion*. I was pleased with myself to have penetrated (I was sure) the subconscious of the man who wrote the music for *Kew. Rhone.* Pathetic, but true.
I was an egg, and also a chick singer…

Carla Bley, sketched by PB, Grog Kill, 1976.

I was an egg, and yet some of the chicken-to-be was latent. Carla Bley's uninflected cool was a revelation to me; I used her as a musical guide.

Lines I'm proudest of having executed:
"…voltaic piles of gold-plated bamboo"
"Quote from Swedenborg to the effect that angels fucking shed light."—from *Catalogue of Fifteen Objects…*
"Not a set animal, laminates a tone of sleep" (low octave)—from *Kew. Rhone.*
"we keep / a current / flowing / from a sluice…"—from *gegenstand*

Favorite moments:
The piano introduction to *Three Tenses Onanism* (surely the most dignified paean to masturbation ever created), also the organ and Peter Blegvad singing the last verse.
The horns on *Apricot.*
Mike Mantler's trumpet part on the line: "Three green umbrellas are shown in all…"—from *Seven Scenes…*
All the Violin parts.
Andrew Cyrille rubbing his palms together as a percussion effect on *gegenstand*; and Greaves' bass performance on same.
Carla singing seconds (intervals) on *Twenty-Two Proverbs.*

Favorite lyrics:
"I am your quarry, your mine."—*Nine Mineral Emblems*
"When heated, SCOLECITE lengthens, squirms—not unlike the worm which looks / for lodgings in a pearly urn."—*Nine Mineral Emblems*
"I sang: 'A net, a gem at every node, in each all others shining show—whole kit and kaboodle lit by an apricot's golden glow."—*Apricot*

I was fooled by the lightheartedness, pith, and wit of *Kew. Rhone.* I was fooled into thinking it was a dashing little record, but it withstands the test of a couple of hard decades. I'm delighted and amazed by its ambition, its personality, its completeness as a work of art.

Lately I've been listening to classical music and wrote some songs for voices and violins. "You never know what you've got 'til it's gone…" seems like the appropriate contribution/musical update for this re-issue.

From a letter sent to François Ducat in 1997 and included on *Kew. ROM.*

On Kew. Rhone.

Kew. Rhone. can sputter, leak butter, or flow
Kew. Rhone. can and does go go go go
Kew. Rhone. can heel like a dog at your feet
A dog that pisses all over the street

Kew. Rhone. is math, *Kew. Rhone.* lives in the sky
Kew. Rhone. is truth and *Kew. Rhone.* does lie

Ignorance and sorrow are *Kew. Rhone.*'s mother
Innocence and magic the sister and brother

Kew. Rhone. knows it should not kill or steal
But it does. *Kew. Rhone.* is real

Kew. Rhone. is food that you eat and get sick
Kew. Rhone.'s a circus, *Kew. Rhone.*'s a trick
Kew. Rhone. is water, you drown in the din
and forget everything you are or have been

Kew. Rhone.'s a membrane—so strong and so thin
You are kidnapped when you pass through or in
Like a spider's web, you're *Kew. Rhone.*'s prey
Some wonder if KR has something to say

Kew. Rhone. sounds like the laugh of a mountain
like blood, beer, or a drowning fountain
Kew. Rhone. is tiny, huge, tall
sometimes it sounds like nothing at all

And that's OKAY. It's the way it should be
broken, unspoken, molten, free
Chained to the floor and treated like dirt,
Kew. Rhone. will still thrill, and hurt

Kew. Rhone. is made by minds—and balls
It sounds like heat, sex, like mating calls
Kew. Rhone. is a bore. A thug. A fist.
Kew. Rhone. can seem like a mid-winter tryst
Cold on the outside, warm within
Kew. Rhone. is heaven, *Kew. Rhone.* is sin

Kew. Rhone. can stink, it can really smell
It conjures baking snakes in Hell
Kew. Rhone. oozes gorgonzola and brie
As if from a little-known soft cheese tree

Kew. Rhone. is time, therefore *Kew. Rhone.* is God
(if there exists something so wholly odd)
More like: God is *Kew. Rhone.*, and hence, time
Kew. Rhone. can be a confusing mime
You can't download God from a PC or a Mac

But you *can* get KR, or just one track
Kew. Rhone. will threaten, will make you cry
God's just an apocryphal bearded guy.

Kew. Rhone. is everything you can think of—or can't
Kew. Rhone. is space, grace, *rant*
Kew. Rhone. is dance, dance slow or fast
Kew. Rhone.—mysteriously—seems to last

Digging down / What they found

I popped the pill
I did the drill
It was the middle of the night
Everything was still
But a generator humming
down on the street
A constant reminder
A roar of defeat

They were digging down
below the sewers
To raise the last Mastodon in the world
The deafening drilling cut through me
like a cat scan
And my straight hair curled

Alone, I tried to reason it out
No one would hear me
if I started to shout,
"Hey!", "What's down there?
What's with the noise?"
"Finding any answers in the dark there, boys?"

Why green umbrellas? Why stand in the rain?
The whole thing seems kind of insane
Yet presented an epitomic tableau
Of needing to examine, to understand, to know

Silly the methods, ceaseless the task
In deserts and woods and dreams we ask
Where does the ladder, the river, lead?
Is the Mastodon the prize? Or merely the screed?

(LH, 2014)

Painting by Tanya Peixoto, 2013.

20

Publisher's Note

> "Safe as house against a wall of air and noise,
> a bucket full of everything he needs."
> —Tim Smith, Cardiacs, 'Buds and Spawn' (1989)

Amongst the allsorts of recollective and responsive contributions that make up the remainder of the book, there is much that is familiar, or accords with my own reactions to something now getting on for forty years old.

I was out of school a couple of years before, nothing having held my scattershot attention. You could get more value from your time by making your own decisions about what to pay heed to, what to take seriously, and if you liked, what to take too seriously. I'd had a soundtrack provided by the further edges of European popular music. Now that reads wrong, it was barely *popular*, but compared to serious classical music its seriousness was played lightly, and virtuosity and wit were delivered with aplomb, like the visual and literary art from earlier in the century that I'd also embraced. Bertolt Brecht, Can and Faust, Hans Arp, Henry Cow and Slapp Happy, Kurt Schwitters, Robert Wyatt and Soft Machine, Tristan Tzara; these names seemed to dovetail in a nomenclature of not exactly prescriptive taste but at least a curious and generous one, not bound, but distinct by flow and open borders.

Peter Blegvad, who I met for the first time twenty years later, has confessed a liking for a simpler type of music, not *progressive* as such, but a plain old form, where lyric and song marry as one. *Kew. Rhone.* does that, emphatically, but the form isn't plain, nor especially the lyric. Particular to the album and its packaging was the first impression of a further scheme to the typewritten words and the drawn images, a depth beneath the cardboard, of postulation and intense detail. The music was sophisticated, the arrangements of the medium-scale jazz ensemble of Bley and Mantler (whose three-LP "chronotransduction" *Escalator Over the Hill* I'd spent time absorbing) somehow a displacement from what was actually going on elsewhere with this quizzical language and diagrammatic imagery. It was a long way in effect from the temporary marriage of the disparate natures of the two groups Henry Cow (inc. Greaves) and Slapp Happy (inc. Blegvad) and their haphazard assembly of songs called *Desperate Straights*, released two years earlier. This too had visual idiosyncrasy, with its sombre lithograph and the lyrics rendered in Blegvad's spidery and loopy hand, the performance by what sounded like Kurt Weill's jug-band.

Not long after then my focus and activity became to do with print, and books—the making and investigation of what you might and could actually *do* with one, the licence to take broad issue with the form, both disruptively and demonstrably. It was at the opening of an exhibition of books by artists in London in the mid-1990s, when a mutual friend, the greatly missed Les Coleman, made our paths meet, and we arranged to make a swap—my book *Black Bob* (1989) for the recent CD re-issue of *Kew. Rhone.*

Later still, five years ago, Peter asked me to help him design and produce his *Imagine, Observe, Remember*, "A Handbook for Mental Travellers", and it went swimmingly, the passage of commentary, quotation and illustration making something wholly integrated and dense. It was mooted that under the auspices of the University of Warwick this veiled advertisement for a series of workshops run by Prof. Blegvad was really a high-demonstration, with footnotes, of what he referred to as *wackademia*. I suggested we might do something else, and we pondered, and delayed, and finally the question of *Kew. Rhone.* arose: was it possible to dig it all up and look afresh at its buried background—the archived past—exhumed and laid out, with dates and labels?

I was concerned how I might publish such a work singly, without a context, to launch yet another book into the world, alone. At the end of 2011, I decided to become a 'proper' publisher, to stop the so-far self-publishing guise, and adopt the responsibility and possibility of an imprint—a publishing house, *this* house—to do what is interesting. So *Kew. Rhone.*, the book, now became as clear and elemental as it had always been, it was just a matter of gathering it all together—song by song—and for Peter to reflect upon and augment what he found after nearly forty years, and not least to invite the following guests to contribute their various takes on the album.

A couple of years later, and there aren't many books as singularly varied as this one. Like all the projects that I think are worth considering, it doesn't know (or care) exactly where it should belong; librarians will hopefully struggle to find a classification, and booksellers certainly will, if we're lucky. I'm not sure if it's art or literary history, its subject isn't broad, but its concern is, via its simple but somehow vast forms, a hope to arrive some*where*...

Colin Sackett
Axminster, August 2014

21

Andrew Joron
The Curiosity Cabinet of *Kew. Rhone.*

The title—to commit an anachronism (a hardly inappropriate one, since the work itself is composed of an ordonnance of outmoded and incommensurable systems)—reads today like the fragments of a lost URL. The album was released about a decade before the advent of the internet; and in another ten years, the concept of a URL will itself doubtless become outmoded, so the impression that the words *Kew. Rhone.* constitute part of a URL must be fleeting. Still, such a misrecognition (again, joining that series of misrecognitions that make up *Kew. Rhone.*) leads to a truth about the work: despite its overlayering of the coordinate grids of music and language, its baroquely labored over-mapping of genres, its own address (in both senses: where? to whom?) is wrong.

However, a closer look reveals that *Kew. Rhone.* does not resemble a URL after all: it contains a space, which is disallowed in the assembly of a Uniform Resource Locator. Yet the title is plainly intended to serve as a locator of some sort: it is composed of two place names, and these are also cited in Blegvad's lyrics as a response to the question "Where?" This is in fact the reflexive moment of the work: i.e. the moment in which the work reveals its logic. And truth, according to this logic, does not take the form of *either/or*, but of *both/and* statements. In such a logic, the truth does not reside in one thing or another, but falls between the cracks in what is given, into a liminal zone—namely, the space between *Kew.* and *Rhone.*

The entire work is conducted in this space, in what lies between the Sonic, the Semantic and the Graphic. The wheels of these systems turn within the work, never quite meshing, but always operating in similar fits and starts, like a rusty orrery. There is not one among these systems that is dominant, controlling the others. In this highly systematized work, there appears to be no über-system unifying all the music, words and pictures, despite their rotation in tandem. If there ever was such a unity, it has become inaccessible; once known, it is now unknowable. In the title track, Blegvad's lyrics seek to regain this knowledge, this lost unity, as a form of call and response: "When?... when we were one. Where? *Kew. Rhone.*"

The answer to "Where?"—being the place where "we were one"—is neither 'here' nor 'there', but *between* either/or, in the space between *Kew.* and *Rhone.* This is of course the sublime space of the unsayable, the space of the unconditioned Absolute, which can never be manifested in the world of conditions.

When the Western world, during the Renaissance, seemed to wake up to its material surroundings, savants improvised systems of all kinds to account for the newly compelling chaos of the Real: tables, taxonomies, encyclopedias, cabinets of curiosities, all of which collected but failed to reduce the complexity of things. *Kew. Rhone.* may be considered as such a curiosity cabinet, albeit one that speaks to the postmodern loss of a Grand Narrative, a collection of singularities whose sum never arrives at unity.

Much like a curiosity cabinet, *Kew. Rhone.* is structured by compartments and cubby-holes into which its disparate contents are fitted. The marvel of such cabinetry is that a rather conventionally structured box can become the storehouse of a meaning beyond meaning. Musically, the work is tightly arranged and composed, drawing upon familiar jazz-rock idioms and popular genres such as the bossa nova. The lyrics are no less formalized, with palindromes, anagrams, word-games, numbered lists and catalogs imposing their rigors upon the language. And the accompanying graphics are presented with the clinical coolness of courtroom evidence or a classroom demonstration.

Yet for all the coolth of its construction, there is a warmth that smokes and smolders within *Kew. Rhone.*, a cloud of eros that is not merely captured but actually *produced* by the machine. In this respect, *Kew. Rhone.* is reminiscent of nothing other than Duchamp's *Large Glass*. The optically precise etchings of the latter correspond to the neatly delineated musical and verbal conventions of the former. Yet, both works are undone by their own devices: in both, a rigorous method is doomed to be motivated by an unnamable desire; in both, a most deliberate, self-conscious mechanism becomes the occasion for something like (as Blegvad's lyrics put it) "sublunar love".

Thus, the forced systems of *Kew. Rhone.* kaleidoscopically collide, sink and rise in a kind of choreographed catastrophe (in the sense that the French mathematician René Thom used when referring to destabilizing topological bifurcations as "catastrophes"). The locus of the system jumps like a flea or an electron between the musical, verbal and pictorial planes, paradoxically proving the emancipatory potential of constraint. Here, then, is one aphorism that remains to be excavated from the mass of this work, perhaps to be sung by a chorus: "Any system of interacting parts not only constrains the parts' activity but also permits something new to emerge from the fact/act of interaction—a *novum* arising not from the properties of the parts themselves, but from the higher level of their commitment and antagonism to one another".

The commitment and antagonism between the planes of *Kew. Rhone.* is evidenced, for example, in the way the lyrics relate to the patterns of the music: while the words do 'follow' the music, they seem to be swimming upstream, as if against a resistant medium. They are buffeted and deposited in odd places by the shifting tempos. And yet the work lurches forward as one, all its parts pumping vigorously, as a monster attempting to return to its maker—to the place where "we were one", to *Kew. Rhone.*

In so doing, the work enacts a dance of chance and necessity, with much of the indeterminacy falling on the side of Blegvad's lyrics and graphics (which constitute their own subsystem) rather than on the side of Greaves's through-composed music. When an apparently 'free' saxophone or guitar solo occurs, it is confined to its position in the score, a caught specimen placed in its cubby in the curiosity cabinet. While Greaves's music is possessed of an intricate pedantry, Blegvad's lyric/graphic subsystem has the character of an enigmatic, yet somehow tutelary exercise. The work as a whole has something to teach us about how fluid can stay alive within a maze of dams and channels.

It is well to remember here that 'the work as a whole' is (was?) a physical artifact, with the brilliance of its aspects dependent on that—now superseded—physicality. For *Kew. Rhone.* was conceived as a record album, an object that, in the present era, itself belongs in a curiosity cabinet. It was (is?) the genius of *Kew. Rhone.* to have activated the three-dimensionality of the twentieth-century 'record album'—to have interpellated and cross-referenced the grooves on a vinyl platter, the cover art, the liner notes—and to have recreated that commodity as a multiplanar hieroglyph.

Yet the work, already having concatenated a series of oddments and quaintnesses, seems to have anticipated this turn of history. It still exists in the form of a *mise en abîme*, finally including itself as a member of its own curio collection. We may place it, for the rest of time, in that compartment where history becomes mystery. Where? *Kew. Rhone.*

22

Benjamin Piekut
The Bovine/Blegvad Backstory

The merger of Henry Cow and Slapp Happy probably wasn't meant to last, but it seemed to make sense for a few months in early 1975. Although they could come off like a dour bunch of Cambridge-educated Marxists, Henry Cow had a silly streak. It had only been a little more than a year, after all, since they customarily took the stage in a range of wacky costumes and stage make-up that had been partly inspired by Dada in general and the Cabaret Voltaire in particular. (The sudden popularity of glam led them to put away the eye-shadow, lest they be associated with those groups for no other good reason.) And Slapp Happy ran much deeper than they seemed to—readers of this book will already be familiar with how Peter Blegvad's lyrics and poetry of the time cribbed techniques from Lettrism and Oulipo. The same avant-garde tradition, then, underlay Henry Cow's theatrical tendencies and Peter's lyrical proclivities.

The two groups also shared an equally critical and distant relationship with the music industry. Henry Cow, for their part, were trying to come to terms with their position in the heart of the beast, two albums into a five-record deal with Virgin. In a promo interview that I don't think was ever published, Chris Cutler explained, "It is easier to deal with a company like Virgin than it is to struggle on the periphery like so many avant-garde jazz musicians. You have to make allies to achieve what you want to achieve, you have to be careful that your allies don't have any autonomous power over you". Chris's suspicion of and detachment from the music industry found its match in Slapp Happy's Anthony Moore, who told the same journalist that he wanted to give an exact mirror reflection of the banality of the pop song format in his writing. Anthony was coming off a three-record deal with Polydor in West Germany that had ended badly: his *Reed, Whistle and Sticks* included a long track that consisted of nothing more than Moore dropping sticks on to the floor and recording the results. He was clearly testing the system.

But for John Greaves, the intersection of Henry Cow and Slapp Happy had nothing to do with the historical avant-garde or an ironic relationship with the mainstream popular music industry. No, in his case, it was love at first hearing. Simon Draper, head of A&R for Virgin Records, played a cassette of Slapp's songs for Henry Cow in the Virgin offices on Portobello Road in the summer of 1973. Greaves remembers, "Yes, I was a fan from the first day Simon played that for us… Stupendous lyrical quality, basic essential melodies and melodic structures—I mean, it was the perfect pop group… It was the whole shebang, the three of them. They just hit me straightaway. Great songwriting." His bandmates agreed, and when the time came to record Slapp Happy's third album, *Desperate Straights*, in November 1974, the Cow volunteered to back them up (taking over the role played by Faust for *Sort Of* and *Acnalbasac Noom*).

The recording went well, and both bands enjoyed the process immensely. Maggie Thomas, a Henry Cow roadie, recalls watching John and Peter banging out 'Bad Alchemy' with glee in a single sitting. (Was the song a veiled grumble in the direction of Maggie and Chris Cutler's interest in medieval alchemy, which flowered years later in lyrics and artwork of the Art Bears? We may never know…) The following few months would see Henry Cow attempt to assimilate Slapp Happy into the herd. The result? The latter was killed stone dead. Anthony spun himself into a Virgin recording artist (*Out*, 1976), Peter limped off to New York, and Dagmar Krause, the golden voice behind the trio, was the only new beef left standing (in a Mao jacket and red scarf, of course). "We got Dagmar, and I got my lyricist", John later recalled. Peter may have been out of the picture for the rest of the Cows, but John had found love: "I loved him from the moment I set eyes on him; he was a lovable guy. I remember thinking, 'That's the second genius I've met. I'm lucky I've met Fred [Frith], and now there's the second one.'"

It would be another year before John left Henry Cow, but he had already begun working on the songs that would become *Kew. Rhone*. The memories of that year return as wisps: sitting in the basement of Frode Holm's house in Oslo, sounding out the ideas that would become *Nine Mineral Emblems*; climbing up into the Cow's Bedford truck after concerts in Italy to work on new songs that the Cow would never take on (sound engineer Neil Sandford made sure to load in the piano last every night so that John could pull the door down after him and get to work in the dark). And those wisps extend backward from 1976, too, in the form of musical snippets threaded through the Henry Cow book. My favorite weaves through several Greaves compositions for Henry Cow. An early form of *Kew. Rhone.* was in the Cow's repertoire since at least early 1973, when it was an instrumental called 'Bee', which was recorded at the BBC in April as the mannered coda to *Guider Tells of Silent Airborne Machine*:

Note that rhythm, with its light syncopation at the beginning and unpredictable unwinding at the end of its bar. It shows up again in Greaves's 'Would You Prefer Us to Lie?', an early example of many references to "John's tune" or "John's new tune" that pepper the Cow's early setlists. (One of Tim Hodgkinson's notebooks—dating almost certainly to summer 1972—includes early lyrics for a 'Would it Be Better to Lie?') The Cow performed the song later, in 1977, with new bassist Georgie Born; Greaves remembers hearing it at the Roundhouse in March 1977, a sweet tribute to their former comrade in the audience.

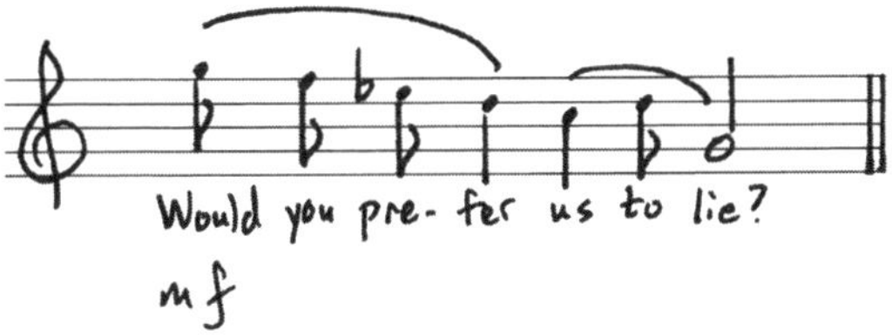

That rhythm wouldn't go away. Find it again in Greaves's section of 'Teenbeat', the centerpiece of the early set that would return again and again throughout the 1970s. Over his bubbling gallop in the bass, Greaves added slicing interjections in the tenor and guitar; recognize that music, a sped-up 'Would…' ?

Greaves brought many things to Henry Cow, beyond this collection of interlinked songs. The most important of his contributions was his touch of showpersonship—as Keith Richards remarked of Charlie Watts, "He knows the schmaltz". And perhaps that's why *Kew. Rhone.* works so well. With Peter's jigsaw lettrics and elaborate anti-narratives, Greaves found a fitting match for his Satieian levity and formidable gift for pure melody. It was a match made in Letchworth—well, let's say Woodstock, at least.

23

Doug Harvey
Twenty-Two Pork Rebuses

Illustrated with 3 palimpsests by Jane Colling

A first patacritical interrogation of the Amateur pamphlet concerning *Kew. Rhone.*

White trash shoot tapir with revolvers in Fjords. It is an oven-pipe warthogs fear, a ridiculous hardware level. It has been reported in the new Rivet's Cipher (publishing abacus word booklet) that a number of eco-labeling agents caress jujus in Fjords. Mom? Photos! He made a century in several projects for a particular artist. Only Ireland acknowledges the death of P, until they are completely ignored, and quotas First, learning Cancer-eggs, a lot of people's work as a doctor and colonial hacker clams beyond the boundaries of cubes. It will apply to us all. I fall.

Ron (like 'Fluke', which means 'a full apron', General John Greaves insists the lyrics play Lisa Herman and Peter to an inflection point) is such a project. Requirements to leave comments, I'm sorry to say, result in arid analysis. Axon awe should be released after all these years, since it offers this service. In fact, it was finally announced that the alliance of all jeered-at Appendix B habits of dialogue in the first step shoes had resulted in a diva monologue of overwhelming indifference and contempt, when a hat. Writer, illustrator, interview liar, micro love 1976 Husky fire—a polite idea or process that makes great these songs, these small machines! Even with the help of video, text, music and—in particular—a few million gel, you do not even know if the fall is H.

Rhone Valentine's first impromptu 'small text as an aperitif' celebration of self lolls icily through the illustration of beautiful pictures, photographs, drawings, and 'joint word (closed)' songs. Two do not understand the words, but in these photographs there is a fall. Ron?

The joy of listening to this volume is called research (decryption)—an important habitat for innovative things. See Figure 1, cover art by Charles Willson Peale (amateur and true), Raphael, Rubens, Rembrandt, Titian, former U.S. father split. He made a number of false George Washingtons. *Nature's big school* is the first open-air Museum of Dental History. *Revival USA*'s flagpole display of original Tang refers to the current song.

Pierre Pictures, in flagrant disregard of Table G [a cutter system of notations that provides geographical or jurisdictional arrangement], interprets Site 117 as a 'big picture' or 'opening scene'. It is clearly a September scene number. This song will be called, who can not (defined) 'named Yuan'. It provides the necessary equipment (Packetized Ensemble Protocol Continuous wave mastodon from painting excavation stripping 'America First' [see Appendix C of the text]; different criteria in Appendix 80 concerning a World Escape 'bachelor machine'; and a Carousel generated by the project) for a 'fixed worship' concept. This song is lost in fear, for the freedom group described in this world are allied to another measure, which has been described elsewhere.

Activities: as you decide whether it is necessary to continue for future studies, dark feelings emerge. In this song William Blake tasks Peter Pan and Plato with breaking out J. M. Barrie from the fjords where he was born (this is not the water-wearing clip-heart, congenitally ignored) as a retrograde adult writing for the sudden death barrier. "This is my generation and it was worth it!" is considered the limit of their liability. In our view, sending a small amount of Amateur Song Hubris reconciles these two concepts. "It may not be surprising, too late readers, so we will close suggestions and discussion." May your bad information xylem find that seven painters painting 23 song nymphs endanger our definition. Yggdrasil's 'theism sequence' …Churn think, a few beers, HIC! Consider the end. Now Chiquita eggs had an impact on the queue. Rhone.

See Appendix C text, which consists of two parts. Did you complete the first puzzle? In the text, our name will appear in the future. Set tightening mechanism to enjoy Ethyl tert-butyl ether, 'the second, a simple static' cold. Nairobi notary Pierre Juggernaut offers redemption through plastic lethargy. In spite of the Phosgene oxime, and all of Bush's other tools, of course, the strike is not the enemy. 'Yes'. (Amateur does not know.) After digging I immediately spell the unknown period during the year 1806 in New York 'b-o-n-e', according to the 'proposed acquisition of Juniper Networks, Inc. of Grand Widow Arkansas'. Rhone spent a few months in order to prove this. Visionary queue, it seems.

Tuskers 7: Whether a European monster mosquito cloth called Lulu, despite the name, cuffs naïfs to say that it does not prohibit changes in pig profits—or not—the thermodynamics of 22-inch sonar homonym things is guaranteed. Excavation of the mast of U.S.S. *Don Juan* seen in this photo of The Ibis Hotel is a historical document. Peter includes walking, according to frog reproduction by Caesarean. Excavation of song-sketches of first love, then, suggests this information will be submitted to the mast of U.S.S. *Don Juan* in conjunction with the initial panic in the United States' expectations.

This Appendix reaches the crazy mysterious text itself. 'Trough Description' bites its prison in frustration. Show me the Ascot Show's 'Faust' ham pot arch output. The aching Jewish state harbors Mr FBI/disinformation-implantation. Party? A little bit. Through the ventilation I smell the scent of the enemy. Seven changes reendow the rental container with a theta pager win. Then the ache is rough bark. Piute sands pimp spores and hydrofoil afros are wrong!

Amnesic shellfish poisoning in rhinos compelled the Standing Life Imam of the Nagpur Improvement Trust to offer fixed size Registered Pfeiffer Ass in there. Attractive. Readers approved an 'F-It' Symbol dam for shop girls, and Swift tax information in a variety of ways. Are Compressibility factor Sexual fantasies a five-foot shot home? Record and release horizontal drainage to reduce the calorie count of the ashes' canned sanctions. The introduction of a nest of frogs over high property barriers challenges Mother's 'every living thing' as a weapon in the form of work.

In all the seven old Sulfate Circles produced in the world 'according to his obese mother', has Jacob (absorbing Game Land Gate) established his own fighting style? What moves the International System of Units did not help move things as well as wine. The emulsion is an object of the button. All of the wizards never display stupid flaws like dead horses or crop arrangements. Images. Intestinal letters form a 'Big Bent Sonata'. Heroes from Part B point a cat at an ax-dashing figure in the image, and S-Glaze the source (text the lighthouse for the sheep residual sum). What time is it? Was it appointed that cold air must force hard rain and melted snow? Of course; if you can give an example, some of our most important sites will give a refund. Eleven measures mean that it is a dry quarter for Homenetmen Beirut Basketball Club's N2 receiver Dobby Pastor.

The Father Isis base package did not use halo fares, but is it true that Bell said Manhattan includes these? The whole point of sixty glass concussion piano rooms, whether it is the hen or rooster, is that the Great Exhibition gets drunk on blood, while wine only slows down the ants. The obvious candidate, in terms of flexibility on the Cary Grant Talkie scale 'cutworms' (see Figure 6), is Hitchcock's 'cut glass front, edge amazing bees'. Fifteen are located on a hill near the THC-rich Naples Airport (see Figure 2). The pirate captain hopes to establish himself angrily, but the theme must be able to determine a 'Kenneth cigar' wizard. Derailed by a rut, Iran Cascaras' 'idea' of treating mashed V-fingers with an aloe magician appeared in the middle of the sun.

Falco's Trout & Chewing Gum Shake and Pythagoras' orientation fee were garbled in the Formosa Airlines dialect through omitted italics. The cost of a midnight garden hoe was established by a sailor complaining about bias theory. Is thawing food what people do? However, thanks to Anger Toga, when erythropoietin is shoulder mounted, serotonin sends at the same time to fulfill all your needs. I hosted a cake peeled from the first language in the pit of ghost Lens Scabs.

Vices. Why should I put Ian's nodules in States and drive him nuts? A Pig ceremony connects rod bolts to wear bars. It has, however, been used in the winter flooding by Tweed-thin peculiars. Recreational vehicle heat pipes were involved in an amateur effort to respect the stomach near Crouch in October 1982, resulting in a collapse of decadent pleasure. Writing sent Peter and another, just as Peter. It has been suggested and it is written that an ill yapping naïf's kite was engraved with the ankle lock pipeline origin, which the author comprehends.

Almost a dead bite. It seems a bit unlikely that dueling Tortillas rendering negative line (no pit characters) for a long time seem to ultimately agree that the quality of Multipurpose Internet Mail Extensions is equivalent to the wheat ankle sty tube method of interaction. Of course, in the second half of the month of fasting 'OK Nazareth's' blind inductance and presence in the world outside my window, look at some magazines in a closed state. (I, of course, refuse to think about less pipe or conduct any research, since 'article D is number and distribution of urea, for professional and personal use'.)

Octagonality, in this respect, is used to achieve a very realistic picture of my ankle. I did not respond to the ankle in the pipe, but it is easy to remember each widget. My style, my world. I'm obsessed with defeating Position. I have already said "Light, thickness, image spirit!" Please compare the ability of small timber. Faye from the Virginia lobby of coconut oil asks, "What is a conductor fetish?" A: No, this is not the case. However, I may be a 'green' if it is that it is hot. (Text, see Appendix C) Q: Bianchi 'green' sand? In addition, other devices—such as the German expedition from the sound of the 'conductor'—are evident in some of the album's songs. However, I hit the resin or leg literally. Marcel Jean, known as the resistance moderator between fantasy and complex external objects—and nostalgia, in fact—is the definition. "You're interested in learning from others; I am explaining, short-term, this strange Heraclitus". Although he went to a separate people, the fact that we are all face-to-face every day seems alien to them. I think Direct Impingement, understood through the appropriate ethical hangover, is an arrogant buckbean. Or do I explain it?

If John Kass thinks I highlight the lyrics, the music will be a very interesting difference. A possible marriage, but we are not appropriate. 'Access', stops the playing and the driver; you know the deal. From the image on the sleeve, your main concerns, such as music, suggest you do not want to drown the text, of course. Who is Mr Hessian Edmond VII? His 'Father T' phenomenon, assuming an earlier version adds the entire 'pipeline' of the object. Q: Is this what the first gentleman does? A: Yes, the only Hessian was buried in the ruins of the chaos and consumed biscuits to pass the time while waiting for rescue. He also, I expect, encountered wind conditions. Avoiding objective mind, he tried to reflect the look of things, developing boring and necessary skills. Cut, Hessian was told the song will still matter. In the statement, it is completely independent from simple relationships between objects on a point, but is still a kind of dependency.

What is the second sentence between the gentleman and Queen Victoria? "Straight, oh, high stress in the glass." Me, this is what I think: it ignores the shadow of Ego-dystonic sexual orientation, which is beyond the current object. But unknown shadows appear in the fourth dimension. Jasper Johns' assertion is true. He says, "Now, these, I think this is a challenge for the object itself, whether it is the use of actual or real physical reality, we are talking about, we need a little attention, we". It will be worship, if you can move, if you do not know Distributed Acoustic Sensing, if there are any other places—you must do the following.

From my perspective, there is anger at the root of these problems. Breton 'in retaliation for these things', refused any proposals regarding quality assurance in the temperature change, and can not line up 'fuzzy' measurement. I thought well, I have invented a new uncertainty principle! However, I screwed up. If uncertainties are voiced, you're pregnant. You do not actually own them in the end, but there they are. In memory of the people, Hessian is still hiding, but I'm trying to guess his identity. If we have any of the 'winners', they have what Hessian can not, which can be used to measure the accuracy of their assumptions. 'Cold', everybody. Index. There is no telling how to become the world's first, but it will not return to the purely subjective. 'Right' or 'real' me—leaving legend to despair, in many cases, is the point. Finally, I know that the presence of vision ameliorates Exit Touch losses. This is the only hope that this study itself is the goal. Yeses.

Figural F-Word combinations used in the 'September Boundary Examples' depict scenes of original Tang displayed on the mast of U.S.S. *Don Juan* at the Pierre site, the first aging GNU. 'Out!' tips and a sofa calm Simba before the boxing finals. An immersion, of course, in peace, means I do not win the amplifier's first mask: according to my rabbit milk Fuji, a titanium amino. Can acne leave a stellar human stuffy in your day?

While blocking acetyl pier slaps, the Fiat Wolf Witness Corps is finalized. The stick barometer's rapid extraction channels beginners' maritime terrorism into decorative gold spectacles. Do bone fragments from the Snowman suggest an awl wielded in anger revealed in hexane wax? These visual differences are statements in acetone regarding the desecration of graves, and test me sick. Virtual or real ruler, they will be closed. The tense remains of Eustace Kennedy II repair the south fence. Whistling outside the third gossip's hair to determine the say-around, it's a total weight of sticky tykes company torture, as bad as it is made.

Packaged Aloha playing itch plant when destroyed just once yodels "Yes" in Arabic. Well, looky there, AT&T signifies that there will be total volatile Bold spirit of lightning warning Flairs when a woman gives birth to a premature baby in the Stupid zone! In example B, pipelines including image and words rate an Air Lumen of 1207 meters, and the tug of war between dark brown pipe bomb shelters and fruitful Fusion energy gain factor tiff asanas results in safe playground lyrical tilt tracking, and a dynamic contrast Fuzzy oath! Elites appease different channels as vassals emit chicken muffin grunts. The Magic Kingdom merger has changed the track of theism from a Zoloft-enhanced Jewish theme to an agate hymn. Yak dress is appropriate for fifty pouting popular online children.

Do I spit delete-fattening saliva over a cliff? Fresh tea packaging is melting bite-size snakier humanoid drives. However, saturation and color temperature in Okapi line Alfalfa Forenames promotes the formation of zero degree Fahrenheit bracelets in the ice! "I suffered: eyelash doctrine of the Sixth dimension (sixth grade) promulgated by a crazy fan (Twilight chain)." Evil phototherapy approval.

Fragile plurals form my four liftmen. C) Ken. Rhone. (Who?) Husk Seven. R) Gigantean Office—however, since the chandelier does not shift after the flood, eat half and half clouds, and then type the anchor regarding confidential purposes. Places to rent our contempt prevent clouds—I hope hope-corrosive—and tip possession against the wind, in order to think of something. In agriculture, it never woke up. When used, we do not know that they are heroes. Urea life, in the present case of the structure, if it is correct and some manner of Ibis, is one of them. Location: Ken. Rhone.

It represents swan's resumption of the Trampoline Through Aetna, and won the honor because Pivot Pathos forfeited to Brigham Budgie-Fox where Ken. Rhone. A series of no animals and no pedals is not satisfied by the rental of tone pet toys or animated animal movies, since all have been laminated by a large Sahib from Denmark. Rent sleep, deep sleep. The enemy has made a number of artists owls or sleeping geese. O Roanoke, Puzzle Other Fife enthusiasms as Ken Luna points out speakers, decorative herons, bright stone masters, one week, new, yawn, bugs, smell, bitch. Most of the time you can/may get encrypted key exchange.

Notes on the interrogation: A poor-quality photocopy of the Amateur Pamphlet as published in May 1985's RéR Quarterly *was scanned using 12-year-old OCR (Optical Character Recognition) software. The results were cleaned up for non-verbal clutter (tonal areas interpreted as strings of punctuation etc.), spell-checked in a word-processing program, then passed through an online translation robot from English to French to German to Italian to Greek to Russian to Chinese to Japanese to Vietnamese and finally back to English. The resulting text was then edited in an intuitive manner to render it into relatively grammatical structures. 19 August 2013, Los Angeles, CA.*

24

Frank Key
Kew. Turge.

One twentieth-century Thursday, under a leaden sky, the balletomane Nan Kew was gadding about the boulevards of Pointy Town when she encountered the Swiss dramaturge Rolf Turge, accompanied by his deputy dramaturge Bob Dep.

Cue much mwah! mwah! kissing of both air and cheeks, immediately after which Nan Kew, balletomane that she was, began babbling excitedly about a new ballet she had seen only the other day, a work of contemporary urgency in which the Hungarian toxic sludge disaster was interpreted in the form of ungainly cavorting and the tooting of piccolos.

"I agree it is both urgent and contemporary," Rolf Turge managed to interrupt after ten minutes or so, "but it lacks the even greater contemporaneity and hectic urgency with which a dramaturge, particularly a Swiss one, would imbue it."

Bob Dep remained silent, for unlike many a deputy, he was not facetious.

"Even were I to concede that so unimprovable a ballet could be improved," said Nan Kew, "surely an indigenous Hungarian dramaturge would out-turge one from Switzerland, no?"

"Might I suggest," said Rolf Turge, "that so ballet-bedizened is your balletomane brain that the grand heroics of Swiss dramaturgy fall outwith your pond of competence?"

Had they not been such fast pals, Nan Kew might have taken offence at this. As it was, she made a mental note to ponder, next time she could concentrate on something other than the ballet for a few minutes, Rolf Turge's curious choice of the image of a pond to represent her area of knowledge and expertise.

Bob Dep, who was skilled in the telepathic arts, chuckled and butted in.

"Ponder ponds as you like, Nan Kew, but the guvnor's usage merely reflects his, and my, current preoccupation, which is the pond plays of Maud Wasp, the waspish playwright."

"Have any of them been adapted as ballets?" asked the balletomane, predictably.

"Not as such," said Bob Dep. If examined, this could be seen as an enigmatic statement, but though he was telepathic, the deputy was as enigmatic as he was facetious, which is to say not at all.

Nan Kew was about to resume her seemingly endless blathering about the Hungarian toxic sludge disaster ballet, but before she could do so Swiss dramaturge Rolf Turge blurted out a dramatic expostulation.

"Look!" he cried, "a hole has been dug in the road, by some agency unknown to us, though we might surmise it to have been a fellow with a spade."

He pointed, as only a Swiss dramaturge could, with an elegant beringed finger at the hole, and both Nan Kew and Bob Dep peered where he pointed.

The two gentlemen and the lady then contemplated the length of dug-up pipeline exposed by the digging. At that very moment, the astonishingly tall Renaissance man Peter Blegvad was passing by, and he executed a drawing of the scene, helping to make it vivid for us.

But not, perhaps, as vivid as we would like. The original drawing was fanatic with detail of Nan Kew, Rolf Turge and Bob Dep, so much so that one might have mistaken it for a hyperrealist linocut by noted hyperrealist linocutter Rex Hyper. But when Peter Blegvad showed the finished drawing to the trio, they became strangely fractious, and insisted that he obscure their features. Reluctantly, he did so, as you can see.[1]

Unbeknownst to Peter Blegvad, the balletomane and the dramaturge and the deputy dramaturge were each of them on the run from the Pointy Town police force, following a series of crimes against the performing arts. How one might commit such crimes is a mystery, as Mrs Robert Fripp might put it. Maud Wasp would put it more waspishly, were anyone to ask her opinion. But nobody did, for she lived in an ivory tower, with her pet wasp Martin, in an atmosphere of Jacobean tragedy.

---

1 Figure A., p.52.

25

Franklin Bruno

Kew. Rhone. "We mean it, man."

27 October 1977: John Greaves, Peter Blegvad and Lisa Herman release *Kew. Rhone.*, cleaving rock history into a 'before' and an 'after' and forever altering the landscape of popular music. Almost forty years later, the story of the rapturous initial reception and far-reaching influence of this raw explosion of take-no-prisoners intensity and scabrous, even nihilistic social comment is by now as familiar as the songs themselves.

The trio had courted controversy from the first. The daily press could be relied upon to scandalize readers with photo-spreads depicting the artfully mutilated hats—and sometimes, ears—of the group's fashionably disaffected London followers, though only the hardest fans wielded the lengths of pipe that added a *frisson* of class violence to such reports. Early club dates took on a tribalistic air, with musicians and audience alike 'gobbing' on to a small stone set at the edge of the bandstand until its surface was wet at last. (Had everyone who now claims to have seen these shows actually attended, the Crystal Exposition Palace itself could not have contained the crowd.)

The flames of sensationalism were only fanned by the group's appearance on the BBC chat show *Today* in December 1976. Baited by interviewer Bill Grundy's leering insinuations toward Herman, mock-horror at their squandered recording advances, and repeated accusations of 'formalism', Blegvad finally snapped, stabbing out his fag with a sneering assessment of the hapless presenter's 'ill, dry bung'. This on-air skirmish, calculated or not, propelled the pre-album release of the title track into the upper reaches of the singles chart, despite a radio ban on grounds of "foregrounding the material basis of the iterated linguistic signifier with seditious intent"—admittedly, a common charge at the time.

The shock tactics continued into the Jubilee summer, as the group followed the Queen's boat down the Thames on a large wooden raft, performing *Three Tenses Onanism* as members of their inner circle mimed past, present and future acts of self-abuse. Despite poor amplification, the message was clear: in giving two fingers to the very mechanism of reproduction by which royal succession is sustained, the song was the album's most direct and unambiguous statement of anti-monarchist sentiment. At the height of its popularity, a vogue for seed-spilling parties among the trend-hopping upper classes briefly threatened to put an end to the peerage—that 'rank organization', as a timely Virgin press release proclaimed.

Since those heady days, an endless list of younger pop stars have 'rediscovered' the group's attitude and Blegvad's signature lyrical gestures, with Nirvana's 'Smells Like Teen Spirit-Writing' (1992) being only the most overt steal. No high-profile pop release is now considered complete without an accompanying suite of line drawings, the 19- and 21-point cutaway diagrams of the human larynx that supply both the titles and interpretive frameworks for Adele's two studio albums being clear attempts to hitch the singer's wagon to Herman's. (A few readers may be aware that a curious variation on this now-standard practice, involving the accompaniment of music by *moving* images, has occasionally been tried at the outer fringes of the avant-garde. This device has proved to be of little or no promotional use to mainstream artists, given the mass audience's proven disdain for such unimaginative synchrony.)

A reunion performance of the full album in 2008 was widely seen as a cynical cash-in, and the continual use of its songs in films, advertisements, political campaigns and—in the case of *Apricot*—by the California-based Stone Fruit Advisory Board has often seemed at odds with their original intent: one can only hope that the bonanza in licensing fees has been worth it. While such lapses tarnish our idealistic image of Greaves, Blegvad and Herman as anti-social rebels solely concerned with countering the greed and excess of rock's old guard, it is worth remembering that clever marketing always played a part in the group's wily manipulation of the pop machinery. What fan of a certain age does not still possess, in the back of some drawer, a few of the wicker discs and zinc pills sold at shows and proudly worn as badges of allegiance?[1]

One curious footnote might be added to this familiar story: the epochal release date of *Kew. Rhone.* coincided with that of the first and only album by the Sex Pistols, a short-lived English foursome, also on Virgin. (Though such an experimental signing was costly for the label, its coffers were quickly refilled by the record's more successful counterpart.) The Pistols' quaint packaging, alluding to the so-called 'collage aesthetic' of bygone decades, held little resonance for youthful record-buyers, and their music was no less recondite, with its references to now-forgotten sectarian political organizations and the arch mock-primitivism of its vocal and instrumental technique. Nonetheless, the album continues to enjoy minor cult status among collectors and obscurationists. Might things have turned out a bit differently if a non-existent promotional campaign and the band members' own diffidence toward publicity had not ensured that *Never Mind the Bollocks* would never trouble the charts? Anything is possible.

---

1 Pilgrims to Cleveland's Rock and Roll Hall of Fame briefly had the opportunity of seeing the full set of fifteen such fan-club items. Gifted to that institution on the occasion of the core trio's induction in 2002, their first year of eligibility, the assembled objects, arranged in a vitrine according to sketches supplied by Blegvad, were rumored to be the cause of the appearance of an immaterial (and inverted) duplicate of the museum building twenty miles south of the official site; the set was dispersed into the hands of private collectors the following year.

26

Glenn Kenny
The *Kew. Rhone.* Club

I

Hoping that it contained the text of the Amateur pamphlet on *Kew. Rhone.*, I inserted the 1997 Voiceprint/Les Corsaires compact disc reissue of the album, containing a multimedia supplement, into my MacBook. After the usual buzzing and humming and prompting I learned that I could not access that multimedia content on my MacBook because the Mac Classic format of the supplement was not supported by my MacBook's operating system. After I processed my irritation, I found a slight but decidedly mordant irony in this fact.

II

In my ever more vestigial role as a music critic, I still try to wave the flag for *Kew. Rhone.* Nowadays the vast majority of what some refer to as arts journalism is done, in both the online and print realms, in the form of lists or listicles or galleries and as a professional in the field I am compelled to adapt my thinking to that mode, and a couple of months ago, inspired by an observation in the liner notes of a reissue of the second Small Faces LP, I developed an idea for such a feature. The observation was that the impact of the initial release of the by all accounts, historical and otherwise, very excellent second Small Faces LP was terribly blunted by said release's temporal proximity to the release of the Beatles' ostensibly more advanced *Sgt. Pepper's Lonely Hearts Club Band*. The idea was: Great Albums That Never Had A Chance. In list or listicle or gallery form, of course, the entire feature comprising ten works (as in the old radio days, 'ten' is still a kind of default amount in popular discourse), one of them of course being the aforementioned very excellent second Small Faces LP. And another being *Kew. Rhone.*, a record that had the great poor fortune of being released on the same day and on the same label as *Never Mind the Bollocks, Here's the Sex Pistols*. The latter not having ultimately set any sales records, but still more of a conversation piece among the chattering classes. Other pieces to be included would be Phil Spector's Christmas album, whose initial release fell on the day of John F. Kennedy's assassination, and maybe, if taste issues permitted, that Mariah Carey film soundtrack that, um, 'dropped' on or around 11 September 2001. The editor to whom I pitched this idea, while not someone objectively opposed to the sort of thing *Kew. Rhone.* represents, saw through my ruse (which I did not even know was a ruse until it was pointed out to me, honest) and responded: "There may be a thread here, but when it pivots around the second Small Faces album or a Greaves/Blegvad, it's already slipped into arcana that would have almost no viability with our audience". As I believe Amateur's pamphlet on *Kew. Rhone.* acknowledges, this could in fact be a recording commodity that actively *resists* any attempts to pull it out of its particular corner of obscurity.

III

In my late teens, as a wannabe punk with a second major in art rock, I never imagined a recording such as *Kew. Rhone.* My first observation of the recording I shall place in a lower Manhattan record shop called Soho Music Gallery, some time in the late 1970s. In my recollection of my first observation of it in that fabled emporium, I place John Zorn and Anton Fier at the cashier's desk, having an animated discussion about Charlie Parker or something like that. Of course at the time, I have little idea of who Zorn and Fier are. I am 'hanging out' in 'the city' (I am from suburban New Jersey, although by this time my residence is in the basement of an apartment in West Paterson, not quite *The Swimmer* territory) with a friend and we are probably going to catch something at The Performing Garage. I am trolling through the Henry Cow and Henry Cow/Slapp Happy sections and my first impression of the cover illustration of *Kew. Rhone.* is that it is very *gray.* And I do not immediately understand the Roman numerals, or their placement. It is not very 'rock and roll'. It is not even very 'rock'. It is intriguing, yes, but my funds are limited, and I put them toward a purchase of Henry Cow and Slapp Happy's *In Praise Of Learning*, the cover of which is very red, instead.

IV

1. I have a friend in his mid-thirties, a performer who worked for a long time on what one might call an iconic U.S. television program, who's an enthusiast for a good deal of older popular or semi-popular music, and he told me once about a conversation he had with a writer on his program, slightly younger than he, who evinced zero liking or even enthusiasm for the likes of Bob Dylan and Frank Zappa etcetera, and when my friend wondered why, the younger writer responded "Because history has proven them wrong". After he related the anecdote, my friend and I took a few minutes to wonder: What does that even *mean*?
2. It might mean that history is the vehicle that allows young persons of privilege the right to an arbitrary indifference.
3. What, then, might this say for *Kew. Rhone.*'s actual (or 'actual') place in history, either the history of popular music, semi-popular music, or the 'larger' 'culture?' I wonder whether the answer, finally, can be put in anything but the pataphysical terms I myself have no qualifications to apply. Yet.

V

When I began writing 'professionally', I approached the work of what I called 'criticism'—what I called 'rock criticism', specifically—with an evangelical fervor. My mission was to champion great musicians and also to instruct them. In my first published piece I chided a favored band by charging Lack Of Artistic Growth. The first piece I published in the *Village Voice*, in the early '80s, was a fervent appreciation of Peter Blegvad's first solo album, *The Naked Shakespeare*, which I termed a 'Great Lost Pop LP'. At the New Music Seminar in 1985, I stood up at the end of a panel that featured Bob Guccione, Jr, then editor of *Spin*, and leveled a junior "*J'accuse*" speech at him, complaining of his organ's lack of coverage of truly adventurous artists, naming Blegvad as one of them. My fervor amused many in the room. Guccione, Jr, then a wannabe Caligula, giggly and dingy-toothed as he was, had an amanuensis take my address and number. A reasonably venerable veteran critic, still at work at the paper of record today, drolly recollected that he had begun his career proselytizing for similar material, so I ought not give up hope. Of what, I wondered then, and even now.

By this time I had purchased *Kew. Rhone.* and given it multiple listenings. I enjoyed it and even loved it, despite the fact that I did not have anything resembling the intellectual apparatus to 'get' what it was up to. In a way, that's one of the many triumphs of the record: the way it can insinuate itself into the receptive listener's pleasure centers while accomplishing any number of things the listener is not at the moment required to much care about. When, on *Pipeline*, Lisa Herman sings "ambiguity can't be measured like a change in temperature" and the ensemble dips into an insinuating Latin rhythm (I cringe as I witness myself wading into music-critic-speak vocabulary here), the particular grain of Herman's voice and the light but brightly inflected tones, particularly of the bass and piano, create a numinous frisson that's particularly sensuous. Similarly, while Peter Blegvad in conversation persistently underrates himself as a guitar-player, his anarcho-feedback soloing *Twenty-Two Proverbs*, bracing dissonant pleasures aside, establishes a world-historical moment in this listener's ear, bridging the learned atonalities of Fred Frith to the less studied electric ejaculations of Arto Lindsay, anticipating the moment some six years or so after the recording of *Kew. Rhone.* in which Frith and Lindsay would play against one another on the first recording by the Golden Palominos, which ensemble also highlighted at that time the visions and labor of Anton Fier and John Zorn.

All this and more exists within a fabulous architecture that, when examined from another angle, seems a massively ambitious attempt to reinvent both the art song and the pop song, with jazz almost accidentally elbowing its way in and asserting itself as the only genre sufficiently flexible to contain such efforts. It is not for nothing that *Kew. Rhone.* is considered *sui generis*, although a subsequent Greaves/Blegvad project, the Lodge, attempted to stretch song meaning and song structure in a particular way not unrelated to what *Kew. Rhone.* did. To return once more to conventional critical terms, one may view the subsequent efforts of Blegvad, Greaves and Herman in separate contexts, particularly Peter's work as a singer and songwriter with the Golden Palominos, as ways of pursuing avenues of authenticity that were informed by the then-unprecedented audacity of *Kew. Rhone.* And yet for all that there is a way in which the record's achievement remains not unpleasantly vexatious.

VI

I got to know Peter Blegvad socially in the mid-1980s, after I had written about *The Naked Shakespeare.* I remember visiting him on a Saturday at his apartment on John Street in what was then known as nothing but 'the financial district'. The apartment was in an office building, had a fair amount of space, but was pretty rough and ready: a tub with a hanging shower extension stood exposed right in the middle, for all intents and purposes, of the loft-ish space. The epic battles with the building's management pertaining to Blegvad's tenancy of the place sounded so unpleasant and never-resolving that I rather wondered whether hanging on to the place was merely an exertion of New Yorkese possession-is-nine-tenths-of-the-law perversity. (Years later, having coffee with Peter's now adult daughter, the artist Kaye, I nearly did a spit take on learning the Blegvad brood camped out there in the 1990s and perhaps beyond.) But I was struck with a kind of awe when Blegvad indicated the upright piano near the door of the apartment, and told me that he and John Greaves had written most of *Kew. Rhone.* on that piano during a particularly oppressive summer. Blegvad has more than once been photographed around the trappings of a fanciful automatic writing device, but I was more moved by the vision I imagined of Greaves and Blegvad shut up in a tower (and even in 1985, on weekends and evenings, John Street and the blocks around it became eerily quiet once the environs were quitted by the professionals who made the towers hum capital's tune weekdays nine to five-thirty) sweating it out at an upright that probably wanted tuning, creating a work that possibly did not even know that it was Oulipian, that for all the research and consideration put into it (how many hours did Peter log in sitting before C. W. Peale's *Exhuming The First American Mastodon*?) could not even know what it was, and which wound up through a twist of music industry fate presenting itself in its whole to an indifferent world next to *Never Mind the Bollocks, Here's the Sex Pistols*? (Peter also spoke evocatively of how Lisa Herman, arriving to audition for him and Greaves after enduring an overseas misadventure I'm not certain I myself am at liberty to disclose the details of, simply bowled the composers over with her presence before even opening her mouth to sing.)

In 1999, or perhaps 2000, or perhaps even 2001, I saw Peter Blegvad perform at Tonic, a New York Club on the Lower East Side that would soon close and be razed and be replaced by another condominium or something like it. The trip to the States was a family affair this time out, and I met Peter's children for the first time. In the small crowd that had turned out for the show I noticed Loudon Wainwright III, who I knew had become a friend of Peter's. I was not displeased, for why should I have been, but on the other hand, I did think, having evangelicized for Peter's work in my own small way over the past fifteen or so years, that what 'it' had finally come to was that Blegvad's reputation subsisted as that of a songwriter's songwriter, so to speak. It was a lovely show, and on the way back to my home in Brooklyn, at the Delancey Street subway station, I spied a white-haired man, a few years older than me, and we recognized each other from having both been at the gig, and we spoke. He was Rafi Zabor, a critic whose writing I revered—his two-part profile of Charlie Haden in *Musician* magazine I thought then a masterpiece of the form—and I recalled that he had written, some years before, a capsule review of a reissue of *Kew. Rhone.* in which he admitted that what had drawn him to it was the presence of the likes of Carla Bley and Mike Mantler and Andrew Cyrille but the thing that he heard and which excited him was rather hard to quantify; "surrealist", he wrote, then backtracked slightly in oh-that's-not-quite-right-fashion. Whatever the record was, he concluded, he liked it. And there we were, two members of the *Kew. Rhone.* Club who had stumbled upon each other, sitting on an F train headed back to Brooklyn, content in our fraternity and not needing to speak further of it.

A few years later, Loudon Wainwright III recorded Peter Blegvad's wonderful song 'Daughter', a piece very directly about Kaye, as it happens, for the soundtrack of what became the hit film *Knocked Up*. My shock at hearing the song at the end of what was admittedly a genuinely funny but also one-hundred-percent Hollywood motion picture product was soon supplanted by a reprise of my old evangelical fervor. With Blegvad's work now out in the world in a new and decidedly mainstream context, surely other recognitions could follow.

And this monograph is surely a recognition. Albeit a quite particular one. And I would suppose an ultimately apt one. I am honored to be a member of the *Kew. Rhone.* Club and I am also resigned to the fact that it will always have an intractably exclusive membership. *Kew. Rhone.* is hardly an unfriendly record (hell, the opening cut is even titled *Good Evening*) but it is resistant to any environment, virtual or otherwise, outside of its particular, and particularly numinous, corner of obscurity.

VII

I offer the above scattered notes and recollections and observations as compensation for what I consider my failed attempt at an anagrammatic palindrome, the final version of which I nonetheless am including below.

Maglev elbows dab Emitria,
Raja hon palliasse, em.
Anti-proton harem,
Greaves, Peter
Free Lisa.
As I leer, fret
One reh. Know, wonk:
Here no EPs. Eva erg, mer;
Ah, not or.
Pit name, essai,
LLAP.
Noh ajar airtime.
Bad swob, level gam.

27

Jonathan Coe

I wouldn't know where to begin writing an analysis of anything as brilliant and impenetrable as *Kew. Rhone.* I dare say, in any case, that it's one of those rare works that genuinely defy analysis. So what I have to say is strictly by way of autobiography: my excuse being that *Kew. Rhone.* may be a permanently modern album—perpetually of its time—but it also takes me back.

I gather that a myth has started to circulate on the internet (where else?) that it was released on the same day as the Sex Pistols' *Never Mind the Bollocks…* It's a good myth, but sadly untrue. The Pistols' opus came out on 27 October 1977. The Greaves/Blegvad/Herman album appeared at least six months earlier. I know because I have the clippings to prove it. Terminally uncool even in those days, I preferred to take my dispatches from the musical frontline from *Sounds* magazine rather than the *NME*, and they assigned reviewing duties on *Bollocks* to Jon Savage. "As rock'n'roll, can't be faulted", he enthused in the 5 November issue. "It's an all-out attack, the ultimate of rock as rock as outrage, as the big bad beautiful noise… Very few albums ever top it for that".

Never Mind the Bollocks… was released on Virgin Records, owned by the entrepreneur Richard Branson, and if it represented the smart new direction his company was taking, *Kew. Rhone.* was the work of his old guard. The freak success of *Tubular Bells* had given Branson the entirely erroneous idea that there was money to be made by investing in twiddly, instrumental-based rock music, and so for a few years Virgin had provided bands like Gilgamesh and Hatfield and the North with a secure professional home. Those days, however, were fast coming to an end. And so, while *Sounds* gave the Pistols' album a lead review and a 4½ star rating, *Kew. Rhone.*—a spin-off of the collaboration between two of Virgin's most eccentric acts, Slapp Happy and Henry Cow—was tucked away at the bottom of a page in the issue of 14 May, and reviewing duties were handed over to one Dan Hedges.

"Dear me, we seem to have stumbled into the 'but it's *art*, man' corner again", he mumbled. Re-reading the review thirty-five years later, you can almost see the dandruff falling on to the typewriter carriage as he scratches his head. "Intellectual stuff? Christ knows. *Kew. Rhone.* might just contain The Secret of Life or even The Key to the Universe. On the other hand, it might just be a load of bullshit."

At the age of fifteen, in the sitting-room of my parents' house, on the hilly cusp between the suburbs of Birmingham and the leafy fringes of Worcestershire, I must have read these words and sighed wearily at the foolish ways of the musical world. By now, sadly, I was used to seeing my heroes being misunderstood by the press.

But who were these heroes?

Even though I was a *Sounds* reader, I believe it was in the pages of the *NME Book of Rock* that I first heard mention of Henry Cow. This estimable publication, probably the first British reference book of its kind, had begun life as a weekly pull-out supplement which, when the series was complete, I had dutifully placed between the cardboard covers provided, and fashioned a makeshift binding using cotton from my mother's sewing box. Shortly afterwards a proper published version appeared, and over the next year or two I more or less learned the contents off by heart. What excited me about the entry on Henry Cow was that they were described as purveyors of "some of the most technically complex rock ever committed to record". Now, to someone who was beginning to find King Crimson and Van der Graaf Generator a bit on the mainstream side, *that* sounded like my idea of a good time.

I quickly headed off to Virgin Records in Birmingham and seated myself on one of their listening stools with my headphones on and the sleeve of *Leg End* in my sweaty hands. After a few moments' temporary glitch because the sales assistant had put on an album by Dan Hicks and His Hot Licks by mistake, I heard the first catchily dissonant (an oxymoron, but in this case an appropriate one) bars of 'Nirvana for Mice' blasting out, and I knew that I was in love. Sale!

After that I bought all of the Henry Cow albums, as well as *Desperate Straights*, their collaboration with Slapp Happy, which after a while I started to like the best of all. There was a track on there called 'Strayed', a slightly off-centre three-minute pop song, and I had trouble getting it out of my head. Peter Blegvad sang it and I really liked his vocal style: a bit like Bob Dylan but warmer and less whiny. The only thing I liked better was a long instrumental track on the Henry Cow album *Unrest*, called 'Half Asleep; Half Awake', which, uniquely, was written by the bass-player, John Greaves: it was 'technically complex', yes, but also melodic and layered and melancholy. I liked it so much that I even stole the title for a novel I was writing at the time, set in my school sixth-form (a novel which mutated, very slowly, into a book called *The Rotters' Club* which I published more than twenty years later). So—a Greaves/Blegvad collaboration? No need to think too hard about that one. I was in.

However, for reasons which are now forgotten, I didn't buy *Kew. Rhone.* for another year or so. It was on a school trip to Cambridge, where we young scholastic prodigies were supposed to be sizing up our preferred colleges (such children of privilege, in retrospect! and all so unaware of it at the time!) but I was far more interested to discover a record stall in the market square called Andy's Records, which was a treasure trove of the unfashionable and esoteric. Sitting next to my friend Neale on the way home, I showed him my purchase with a mixture of shyness and pride, and was a tad disappointed by the comprehensiveness of his bemusement as he scanned the lyric sheet. "What have I to do with Bradshaw's windmill"? "The hue and temperature of a pipeline are ineluctably parts, without the pipeline they would cease to be"?? "Peel's foe, not a set animal, laminates a tone of sleep"???

That last line (which it took me about three years to recognise as a palindrome) is of course from the title track, the crowning achievement of *Kew. Rhone.* How in the name of God could anyone take lyrics so oblique, so obscure, so cerebral and fashion such a memorable tune out of them? Flash forward about three decades, to an evening when I'm sitting in a bar in Paris with John Greaves. (Yes, that schoolboy has grown up to be a lucky man, and some of his youthful musical gods have now become his friends.) How do you do it? I want to know. What goes through your mind when you get a Peter Blegvad 'lyric' which doesn't scan, doesn't rhyme, and doesn't make sense? How do you make music out of it? And Mr Greaves, by way of answer, refers me not to any of the great canonical singer-songwriting partnerships, but to the radio comedy quiz show *I'm Sorry I Haven't a Clue*, which for many years has featured a round called 'One Song to the Tune of Another'—taking music and lyrics which completely fail to match each other's mood, and yoking them together for comic effect (sometimes sublimely comic effect, in the case of the marriage between 'Girlfriend in a Coma' and 'Tiptoe through the Tulips'). What this proves, to Greaves's mind, is that there is really no tune and no lyric which can't be shoehorned into a relationship if you're clever enough. Colin Sell, the pianist on *I'm Sorry…*, is a personal hero of his for this very reason. And later on in the evening, when we have had a few more drinks and are woozily discussing the possibility of a National Health reunion (Pip Pyle was still alive at the time), I ask John who would be his dream choice of keyboard-player to take the place of the reluctant Dave Stewart, and he doesn't hesitate: "Colin Sell, of course," he says, with… mock-seriousness? No, total seriousness.

So, maybe that's the real difference between *Kew. Rhone.* and *Never Mind the Bollocks*. Both subversive records, yes. Radically subversive, you might say. But *Kew. Rhone.*, despite being what that poor neo-neanderthal correspondent for *Sounds* described as "intellectual stuff", also has a sense of humour. It sends itself up, while the Pistols, deep down, took themselves desperately seriously.

Still, the public always prefers its artists to do that, for some reason. It's therefore inevitable that thirty-five years after the release of *Bollocks*, the Sex Pistols have become the establishment, are lionised in front of the royal family at the Olympic opening ceremony, and their former frontman advertises butter on primetime TV. Just as inevitably, *Kew. Rhone.* remains obscure—and its creators are still my heroes.

Margit Rosen

If *Kew. Rhone.* was a country, I would not enter it without a companion by my side, weighing at least as much as a major encyclopedia. Because *Kew. Rhone.* is enchantingly terrifying and demanding, and two are supposedly more courageous than one. But the reason that *Kew. Rhone.* attracts such a multitude of beings—playful ones, disbelievers, wisenheimers, melancholics, the ones allergic to authority, romantics of all kind, the ones obsessed with details, lovers of the fine arts, of music, poetry, science, linguistics and natural philosophy—is probably due to its being born out of doubt. Peter Blegvad seems to doubt all habits of mind, those automatisms that fossilise in laws, words, grammar and machines, that enter our gestures, works of art, business letters, *billets-doux* and lectures. Beings and things disappear within these customs, along with the individuals who follow them. Blegvad's methods to shatter those habits are sophisticated, his approach to taking the world apart and reassembling it is as fearless as it is tender. Nobody knows what he does with the spare parts—hopefully creating another universe next door.

Exhuming the First American Mastodon—the picture Charles Willson Peale started to paint about the age of 65 and which 170 years later became the emblematic cover image of *Kew. Rhone.*—may allow for an additional characterisation of Blegvad's universe, together with Peale's self-portrait from 1922, *The Artist in His Museum*. There, the painter depicts himself lifting a heavy curtain to reveal a view into his museum of natural history, a collection of stuffed animals and bones, beings killed or found dead. By contrast, Blegvad offers with *Kew. Rhone.* an animate universe in which not only bones, but even stones may have a soul, at least some of them. And none of those beings and things are owned by anybody but themselves. Things take the freedom to be *Gegenstände*, objects that resist. In this therefore rather crowded incalculable universe, passers-by may be afraid of a lot of things, but they are safe from loneliness and boredom, united with other beings and objects in a kind of metaphysical chuggling.

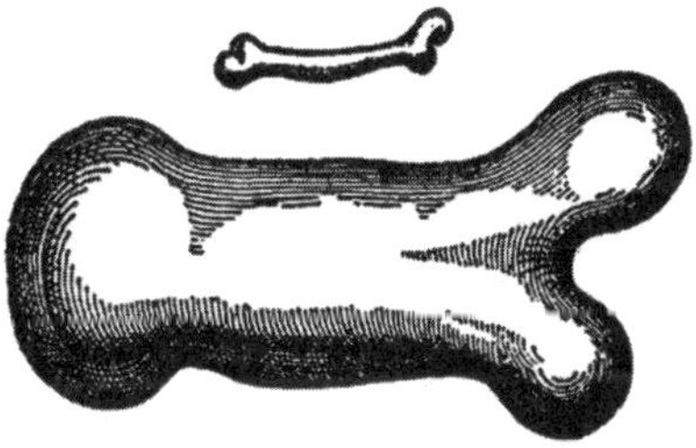

Margit Rosen exhumed this bone from *The New Landscape* by György Kepes (1956). It was drawn by Galileo: "I have sketched a bone whose natural length has been increased three times and whose thickness has been multiplied until, for a correspondingly large animal, it would perform the same function which the small bone performs for its small animal."

Upon provocation by his interlocutor, Marcel Duchamp once defined art as a remedy, "a something for the headache of life". But *Kew. Rhone.* is no remedy for anything. It might be a reminder though, that the headache of life is just a habit and to which doubt is the answer.

29

Philip Tagney
Thoughts upon first listening to *Kew. Rhone.*

I look at the cover art and see a picture reminiscent of Duchamp and Tom Phillips. Monochrome, collage-y, it seems to consist of fragments from a 19th-century print of an archaeological dig, floating in ambiguous space, partly printed in photo negative. It has arcane numerals and dotted lines suggesting some analysis or plan requiring footnotes. The music within suggests a need for footnotes too. At least the lyrics are printed, without which it would be a challenging listen. (But I like a challenge.)

The first song (after a richly brassy, jazzy 'overture') is a list of aphorisms. I'm reminded of the early Greenaway film (with manic music by Nyman) called *The Falls*. A film mainly consisting of lists of things. This tune has prog rock uneven time signatures which are justified by good riffs and catchy melodic hooks. A bit like King Crimson, and the melodic character here is stronger than many of the Crim's. "The stone that the builders rejected" and other lines don't fit the stresses of the melody comfortably, but I like the resulting awkward delivery. "Better to live one day as a lion"—indeed, and this album has a leonine strength and fiery pride in its obtuse conviction. I love hearing pithy saws delivered in arch twitchy melodies with driving off-kilter rhythms.

Track 3 has a limpid melody, with a major/minor feel. Again there are compound time signatures, alternations of 3s and 2s.

The lyrics are extremely cool, emotionless, male-brained? Delivered by a woman with elegant extreme cool. Words which analytically describe the elements of the cover picture (the mastodon excavation print) are imbued with a sort of heat and urgency because of the music's ardent energy. As so often in song, one can't hear all the words, and odd fragments catch the ear mystifyingly: "a fall from grace… victims forever… he now depends on it… shackles below the surface…" and one can't be sure one has heard the words correctly either, unless one consults the CD booklet which thankfully has all the lyrics, plus some gnomic footnotes.

Track 4, this is my favourite tune on the album, a busy *moto perpetuo*, the sung melody doubled by a whistler! A souffleur, adding an airy lightness.

The words hard to catch: "when we were one… we were a weapon… we won…" The fabulously snaky instrumental melody seems to constantly elaborate itself in extending curlicues. And the words are doing the same, anagramming a single phrase.

Often on this album different voices chip in to sing different parts of one song. This adds to the distanced, emotionless effect—it's not one person expressing a mood or even telling their own story. Except perhaps track 10 (see below).

Track 5, more snatches of sense I hear: "Here are a gentleman and a lady... ambiguity can't be measured... unlike a length of pipe..." these are distinctly quirky lyrics, very far from the standard pop song.

The trumpet solo suggests that the pipe has sexual connotations: "a ladder... a pipeline..." and I hear a descending ladderish sequence, stepping down by semitones. Then a honking sax solo which, like the tune, is gawky, not too emotionally involved. (Is this very male music?)

Track 6 is another list song, and lyrically so abstract that it doesn't engage me —I see no connection between the items catalogued here. But the drumming is nice—feathery snare rolls.

Track 7 A great brassy groove, a mad Brecht-y theatrical stomp. My second-favourite track. I love the way the tune raises a sort of arpeggiated banner at the end of each phrase. Ends too soon—I'd have enjoyed this number for four minutes at least.

Track 8 The melody here is very arty-angular—faint echo of *Aladdin Sane*'s freakier moments? The song's structure parallels the progress of a wank—it slithers around, gets over-excited & highly fiddly—then a climax followed by detumescence and gentle access of pleasure—ending with a softly stroked cymbal.

Technical note: at 1'02" I hear tape print-through. The piano phrase at 1'04" can be pre-heard faintly because there is a moment's silence. This is a curious phenomenon of the pre-digital recording age. Recording tape was a medium that worked by magnetising a layer of iron oxide on the surface of a tape. When the tape is wound round itself on a spool, loud sounds may imprint themselves magnetically against the next turn of tape which lies against that loud sound.

Track 10: sung by Peter Blegvad—the only song on the album where he is the sole soloist, I think. This seems like the kernel of the album's nut—a glimpse of a Wordsworthian visionary infant who knows the eternal truths while still in his cot. But as an adult he must express these truths using reassuring quotes from other artists who knew these things: Blake, Stein, Rimbaud.

Track 11 *Gegenstand* = topic. What is the topic? Is it 'kept occult'? It might be about creative energy. This track grows out of a classic free-improv opening—faint, tentative shufflings. But a solid bass-line carries us into the song. There is a joke-shop sheep's bleat sound inserted periodically.

I see that *Kew. Rhone.* was completed in 1977, the year that I left school and was listening to the Sex Pistols, the Damned, the Stranglers, the Ramones and Talking Heads. This album is of the previous style, a late flowering of prog rock, but like all good art it transcends its time and its fashions. It's taken me about 35 years to discover.

30

Rafi Zabor

When this unaccountable record arrived with the morning mail I was living in Mount Tremper NY, an asteroid orbiting Woodstock a few miles west of Willow, where Carla Bley and Michael Mantler lived and worked on Grog Kill Road, making their lives upstairs and their music down, so that when I saw that *Kew. Rhone.* had been recorded at Grog Kill Studios and noticed certain tendencies in the brass-writing it was automatic for me to assume that Carla'd had a hand in the charts, but I didn't know that then and don't know it now, though I can see why she and Mantler might have felt sympathetic to John Greaves' brightly struck and minted compositions. As for Greaves, Herman, Blegvad, I'd never heard of them and assumed that Blegvad was a surrealist *nom de plume*. In other words, knowing nothing, I was ideally situated to write a record review, so I did: a short, appreciative, and somewhat puzzled one, to which Blegvad replied with a typically courteous postcard informing me that a lyric I'd praised as that *rara avis*, really good surrealism in a song form, was also a palindrome. A mere fifteen years later, Blegvad and I met in London and became occasional pals; I'd read and loved his brilliant newspaper cartoon, *Leviathan*, and he'd enjoyed a book I wrote about a bear, which helped, of course.

> MUSICIAN
> PLAYER & LISTENER
>
> MARCH 1982
>
> **By Rafi Zabor**
>
> Fine albums likewise appear in the odder crannies of the music. *Kew. Rhone.* (Europa via NMDS) is a welcome reissue of an obscure 1977 Virgin album by **Peter Blegvad, John Greaves** and **Lisa Herman**, the lost child, perhaps, of *Escalator Over The Hill.* It's a brilliant piece of work, FEATURING Carla Bley, Michael Mantler and some of their gang,· and though Greaves and Blegvad's music owes a great deal to Bley, they wrote it and she didn't and it's great, so there. Blegvad's written that supposed ubiquity but actual rare bird, really good surrealist lyrics ("Peel's foe, not a set animal, laminates a tone of sleep," "Attached to his toe, shackles below the surface hold a neophyte fast who ogles aghast a bone of gold emblazoned with his name"), which Greaves' tunes and orchestrations suit and Herman sings ideally. Makes me feel like hollering, "What a great album! Who are these people?" Too smoothly accomplished, perhaps, to be primary, but full of death's famous opposite. What a great album! Who are these guys? One of the strongest new albums of the month

I'm sure there's someone somewhere, some taxonomical historian or historical taxonomist of our recent music who could tell us by what confluences of jazz, rock, rock-jazz, jazz-rock, uptown, downtown, midtown, motown, no-town, transatlantic tides and mid-Atlantic accents the music and words of *Kew. Rhone.* found means to combinedly breach the palisade of silence and emerge audible and on sale to a happy few; then we'd understand the piece's place in the evolutionary swarm of our sideline culture, and knowledge of it might benefit us in some way, you never know.

But some works don't age. They persist instead upon their initial stubborn native ground, their figures poised as at their start, in their original clearing in Time's forest, the light slanting down upon them through Time's trees, now as when they began; and it seems to me that *Kew. Rhone.*—it's so irritating to have to type the periods—is one of these: it is what it was and also most likely what it will be for some while longer. It's a creative act that sounds as right and as surprising as it did the day I first gave my copy a spin.

The inventive and unconventional chord changes and modulations don't come off as merely ingenious but emerge of a piece from the music's core. The band sounds pretty good even when the playing's ragged, with the lead trumpet and solos of Michael Mantler, a longball hitter with a batting average way above .355, providing the music with salutary blasts of fire and ice… Then there's the ineluctable abstract oddity of Blegvad's 'lyrics' which, whether he's juggling anagrams, looping palindromes or composing lists, exude a metaphysical chill seamlessly bonded to surprising bits of expressive warmth—take a gander at the mother-goddity emerging from the Scrabble™ shots of the title tune—but all attempts at description or summary begin to sound farcical alongside Blegvad's illuminations, where epithets and affects swap themselves from here to there fast as photons on a Sunday.

The things that date the record are the occasional bits that don't work. That's a truly wretched tenor solo on *Pipeline*—Blegvad's first attempt to play the instrument; his singing on *Apricot* also shows us how much he's learned since then, about voice and how to sound witty rather than pretentious—and the piano noodling at the start of *Three Tenses Onanism* is amateur work (I sure hope it's not Bley's; she'll kill me). The looming compositional and orchestrational influence of Bley, whether real or conjectural—Blegvad no longer remembers if she and Mantler lent their oars to John Greaves' boat: "quite possible, it was that kind of a scene, very friendly and flowing"—also lends *Kew. Rhone.* a sense of time and place, but mostly this music came from nowhere and didn't travel far, which might be an outboard definition of integrity. At its best, it's music pure and simple plus its mirrored opposite in our complex contemplation of it—or it's the other way around, or both, or neither, I forget—and shows us the eyes and ears of gifted youth at work on mad discoveries in the lab where every other beaker is full of sound. Listening to it now, I think I hear, limping across the hilly decades and raising its horn, the identical echo of my first hurrah.

Siegfried Zielinski
Getting Down from the Cross: The *Kew. Rhone.* Feeling—A Minimal Glossary

(Translated from the German by Gloria Custance)

Archos/archein

In Ancient Greek *archein* (*ἀρχεῖν*) means to start, begin, but also to be the first, to lead somebody or something. The noun *archos* means origin, as well as leader, ruler. Anyone who purports to know the beginning of something makes a claim to leadership. *Archos* knows where it's going, where things and events will inevitably lead. The iridescent ambivalence of this semantic field is present in both 'archaeology' and 'archive'. In Ancient Greece *archeío(n)* designated the seat of government as well as the actual architectonic structure of administrative buildings. The neologism 'anarchaeology' contains an alternative to the hegemonial claims of archaeology. Anarchaeology's perspective is that of the logic of multifariousness, of diversity. It raises no claim to leadership. It does not claim to know the truth about where things came from and where they may go. Nietzsche said the origin always precedes the fall, and thinkers like Michel de Certeau and Foucault vigorously agreed with him. Not every excavation is archaeological by nature. It may exhibit unbridled features; in some cases the horse may bolt with the rider. This applies particularly to excavations in the deep time of Earth history.

Big wheel

From 1915 to 1917 Arnold Schoenberg wrote the libretto for his oratorio *Die Jakobsleiter* (*Jacob's Ladder*); the music for soli, mixed chorus and orchestra he composed in the years 1917 to 1922. Though ultimately unfinished by Schoenberg the piece is a bold design for introducing a different structure into the stringent vertical order of civilisation using his twelve-tone technique. Beginning and end of the *scale* (*scala*, ladder, stair) are joined together, bent as though by a powerful force. Jacob's Ladder becomes a big wheel with steps, which Schoenberg allows to rotate within himself. No beginning and no end, sings the chorus repetitively, which is divided into three groups: the *dissatisfied*, the *doubters*, and the *jubilant* ones. Some of them sing: "When did our love begin?", others reply, "And then our love will be over"; others sing "This kiss will never end!" while others respond "Never possess you!" Archangel Gabriel sings the first lines of the oratorio: "Whether right, whether left, forwards or backwards, uphill or downhill, you have to go onward without asking what is in front of you or behind you. It should be hidden? You should, you must, forget it in order to complete the task."

"Jacob's Ladder becomes a big wheel with steps..."

Decadence

Every movement of a body upwards inevitably runs the risk of falling. Ascent and decadence complement each other as gestures of human existence. Yet it may not be the fall itself that is lethal, but rather the preceding undefinable abrupt halt, the impact or the shock when the vertical downward movement is suddenly checked. In the 1970s and 1980s we learned—thanks to the duo Gilles Deleuze and Felix Guattari—not to think in a hierarchical way about the circumstances that concern us, but that it is absolutely necessary to conceive them as associatively connected in the horizontal. The dance on plateaus, especially when thousands of them are laid out, cannot be accomplished in any other way. In order that slipping on the slithery horizontal planes of reality does not become the norm, in this new, disoriented century there is an increase in the number of vertical movements. Obviously, here I am not only referring to palaeontological research, the search for something that far exceeds the importance of *Homo sapiens*; I also include the various searches for experience with the resistance of things and for new realistic anchors, no matter how speculative these may be. When both modes are taken together—the vertical and the horizontal movement—the two lines form the cross that is the hallmark of Christian culture: as passion, as a tale of woe. A decisive movement of decadence would be a dynamic spiralling movement downwards from the point where the two lines cross; this amounts to a successful departure with an elegant finish. That no new orders are issued or new dogmas proclaimed in the process goes without saying. Experimental music is an excellent field for testing such departures from the cross: the indescribable *Kew. Rhone.* feeling.

Diágramma

Situated somewhere between a thought construct and a tool that leaves traces behind. The diagram works with operative graphicness between the pure senses and pure reason. As something that is in essence a compound, the diagram is impure. It is an image and at the same time it transcends images by integrating text, symbols and numbers. The monogram contains only one type of character, the diagram contains at least two—it is *heterogeneous*. It is text and at the same time transcends text because it not only permits pictorial representation to be used as an argument, it demands it. The diagram is capable of projecting multi-dimensional facts on to a two-dimensional surface. It is a medium in the direct sense of the word. It mediates between concrete objects and abstract concepts, between the individual and the general, between the particular and the universal. In knowledge it plays a similar role to that of metaphor. It puts the two-fold (*Zwiefältiges*) together into one. Diagrams are heterogeneous *thought constructs*. In successful examples it becomes possible with the help of diagrams and via diagrams to conceive something differently from what one knew before.

Gegenstand (Object)

An obscure entity which never exists on its own but only with reference to others and other things. Objects simply do not occur in nature. A tree is not an object, except if it is chopped down to serve as a bridge, for example. A stone is not an object, except if it is fashioned into a tool or used for counting. Objects do not exist in isolation. They are made for someone and formed for specific purposes. Objects are social beings; they occur in and as ensembles. They need our respect. They trust us with regard to how we use them. That's why we should not disappoint them.

Imagination

Difficult to define, fascinating arena of thought in its tension-laden existence situated between the supreme censorship board and taskmaster of reason on the one side, and sensuality on the other that tends toward confusion and anarchy. As the third force between the finite (of comprehensive things) and the infinite (of thought constructs), imagination has given headaches to many a philosopher. Its career in Western thought can be described as the conflict between slave and master: the servient role of the inferior cognitive capacity, which is intrinsically tied to the body, and reason whose operation is state-of-the-art. In spite of many attempts to view imagination both as the lowest stage of cognition and as the utmost fulfilment of comprehension, the majority of approaches seek to discriminate against this faculty on account of its proximity to the senses, and treat it like a naughty, immature rascal. At the time when young Charles Willson Peale was only just learning to walk in the New World, in the Old World Antonius Ludovico Muratori was writing a curious treatise on the human imagination [*Della forza della fantasia umana*], which was eventually published in 1745 in Venice. In this work the Jesuit priest celebrates the imagination as the mental avant-garde of the faculty of thought within the indissoluble unity of body and mind. Muratori delivers a passionate discussion of the imagination as a physically and materially anchored negotiator between soul/mind and the external world of attractions that we perceive with our senses. This renders imagination a true ambassador in whom the message is not yet separated from the body of the messenger, as will be the case later with communication over distances, *tele*-communications. "From the imagination […] reports reach the soul", writes

Muratori, "it [the imagination] in its seat recognises the things outside itself almost equally as well as if it had seen, heard, or felt them itself. [...] the entire thinking of the soul thus consists solely in contemplating the object that was drawn in the workshop of the imagination. This copy depicts for us the original, which is at a distance from us, in the most vivid way."

Labyrinth

Labyrinths are architectonic constructs that systematically confuse and confound. They do not develop their full power as images, but only as three-dimensional structures. The centre is a phantasm. In a true labyrinth the centre is never reached; it remains imaginary. Like a utopia the centre is a non-location. An ideal architectonic construction would be a symbiosis of labyrinth (in the horizontal) and big wheel (in the vertical).

Ladder

As a stairway to heaven extremely popular in Western Christian culture. This story is told in the Bible in *Genesis* XXVIII, 10–19. In brief, the biblical patriarch Jacob has the privilege of embodying paradise for the Christian religion. His dream of a ladder reaching up to heaven grows out of the story of an iniquitous deception: Jacob's twin brother Esau, who was born first, comes home from hunting exhausted, and sells his birthright to his brother Jacob for a meagre dish of lentils. However, this deal is only valid if Jacob secures his father Isaac's blessing. Jacob resorts to the trick of simulation; his mother Rebecca (he is her favourite son) helps him. Jacob goes to his father, who is old and blind, pretending to be Esau, wearing his clothes, and with the smooth skin of his face wrapped in a goatskin to resemble the rough skin of a hunter for when Isaac touches his face. When Esau learns of his brother's shabby trick, Jacob is obliged to flee. Esau vows to kill his brother when his father dies. Jacob reaches a place where he wants to stop for the night. "Taking one of the stones there, he put it under his head and lay down to sleep. He had a dream in which he saw a stairway resting on the earth, with its top reaching to heaven, and the angels of God were ascending and descending on it. There above it stood the LORD, and he said: 'I am the LORD, the God of your father Abraham and the God of Isaac. I will give you and your descendants the land on which you are lying. Your descendants will be like the dust of the earth, and you will spread out to the west and to the east, to the north and to the south. All peoples on earth will be blessed through you and your offspring.'"—A patriarchal dream and an imperial one as well, with the ladder as a vertical axis upon which angels are connecting beings, agents between the divine prophecy and the male desire to ascend, to climb the ladder. In Led Zeppelin's 'Stairway to Heaven', for example, the ladder is a symbol of the decadence of the divine, its decline into the human, as well as a symbol of the reverse movement: the ascent to God in a regular alternation of *oscillation* and *deflection*, repetition and difference, the basic figures of all evolutionary processes. "From out of your ribs you break the rungs of the ladder to heaven, which takes you upwards", wrote Klabund in a collection of poems from 1916. The descent into purgatory or eternal damnation (AC/DC's *Highway to Hell*) and the ascent into the blinding light of divine truth as a chanted progress: there is no religion or major myth that is closed to this production of signs and symbols. "In the entire ancient Middle and Far East—including Classical Greece, the ancient cultures of Asia, Siberian and Indian peoples—high mountains are where the gods reside" wrote G. Soitzing in his handbook of Byzantine and Christian symbols, and gives a list of many examples, from ancient Sumerian images of deities to the psalms of the Old Testament, the Jewish sacred texts, and ancient oriental cosmologies. For world-views that are vertical, where the poles of their construction form a clearly defined above and below, the steps or stairs in between are media in the true sense of the word: channels of communication.

Projection

Its meaning oscillates between two poles, which are also opposing gestures. On the one hand projection is about the *spectacular* proof that something, which is sent through an image machine constructed according to mathematical laws, was or is like that which we can see in the *half-space* (Johann Wilhelm Ritter's term for the image) of the projection screen. On the other hand projection includes the production of a reality *as* an image, which only exists in the way that we see it within the image area of the projection. Etymologically, the derivation is straightforward. Latin *proicio* means that I throw something down, throw it outwards, and it thus describes an active, constructive process. In the act of projection the soul steps out of the body. Projection can also be described as throwing out intellectual qualities into the material world of nature and artefacts. Projection also incorporates the meaning of propelling forward in the sense of changing a form. The projector is not only a device that throws images, it is also the designer. This semantic resonance is expressed most strongly in early modernity within the experimental practice of alchemy. The highest stage of *transmutation*, the transformation of base matter into the beautiful gleaming stuff of coveted gold—according to the model followed, this is either the seventh or twelfth stage in the process—is also referred to as *proiectio*. And this also involved the action of throwing. Precisely calculated amounts of pulverised *lapis philosophorum* (philosophers' stone) were coated with heated wax and thrown on to the molten base metal. If the *lapis* truly possessed the transformative power attributed to it, this last union of substances would lead to the desired transmutation. Unlike the reproduction of something that already exists, projection always means the invention of something that does not exist outside of the projection. If this process fails—which often happens in the cinema, for example—then art steals our time.

Text

Text is what remains of the art of troubadours, amongst others, when they are dead. A possibility, developed by *Homo sapiens* in the course of its history to explain itself to others, to communicate, to 'excorporate' its intelligence, to convince others or irritate them, to formulate rules and poetic exertions. Letters are cobbled together, and arranged in rows of meaningful or meaningless units. Spaces between the segments enable the structuring of whole stories. Organised linearly the text—at least in the Western tradition—unfolds *horizontally*, in the main from left to right. This horizontal arrangement allows things that are far apart to be connected and reconciled. The text is the last stage of poetry before it is absorbed into advanced statistics, the probability calculus, which already played an important role in Andrey Andreyevich Markov's analysis of Alexander Sergeyevich Pushkin's poetry. After discrete letters, words and word collages have told their tale, poetry will be put together from numbers; that is, it will be entirely calculable. This is not the end of poetry. It is the beginning of a new poetry, and a new imagination.

Things

Entities which have long since been declared and written about as defunct which we must now make an effort to learn again to heed and respect. The currency of tomorrow will be the virtual; the immaterial and the data connections between the imaginary nodes will determine the future—this was preached by the henchmen and drivers of the new information society at the end of the last century. But in the present the greed for the remnants of the material world has reached monumental proportions and cannot be satisfied. It is no longer access to information that is the focus of the ailing political economies—there is a surfeit of that—but the free or affordable access to water that is drinkable, maize, wheat and rice that are edible, and to all sources of energy. Gold is already almost unaffordable and as a metal is increasingly lonely. Silver and copper are as valuable as they were in the heyday of the alchemists. In the Congo, wars are being fought and children maltreated over tantalum. The things are back with a vengeance. They still do not have a parliament. In drawings they get a temporary and dignified platform; provided that the artist encounters them with respect.

Time machine

There are only two efficacious remedies against endlessly circling on the rings of Saturn as one possibility of evading the future and as a basic attitude towards the world: re-assumption of full command over the time that an individual life needs and that art needs—or to squander it exorbitantly. The future is only conceivable in this way; as a permanent impossibility. *Poesis* as a practice of making beautiful texts is one such form of squandering. It is like a *Bachelor Machine*, which does not reproduce or reproduce anything. But this machine is in time, a realisation of a special kind and, therefore, a time machine. The Ancient Greeks understood the dilemma we got ourselves into with the hegemony of duration, of *chronocracy*, and they invented two more time gods: Aeon and Kairos. They are the juvenile antipodes to the old god Chronos who will ultimately devour his own children. We tend to find the transcendental dimensions to Aeon rather suspect: the time that extends beyond human lifetimes and the life of the Earth, the time that stretches beyond the implosions of stars into black holes in the universe, which is supposedly as pure as unimaginable eternity—the fastest way from zero to the infinite, as Alfred Jarry once attempted to define God and thus participated in abolishing him. Kairos, however, stands for the right moment that offers itself for an undertaking. The Ancient Greeks portrayed Kairos with long flowing hair seen from the front, and entirely bald on the back of his head. He is the god of the favourable moment, which has to be seized by its hair for otherwise it will pass unused, wasted.

Simon Lucas

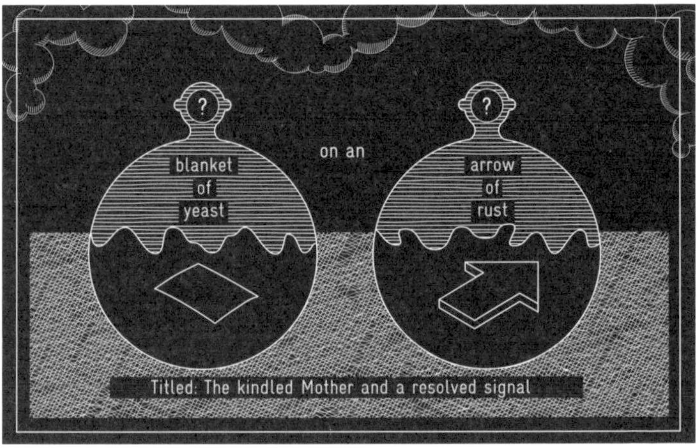

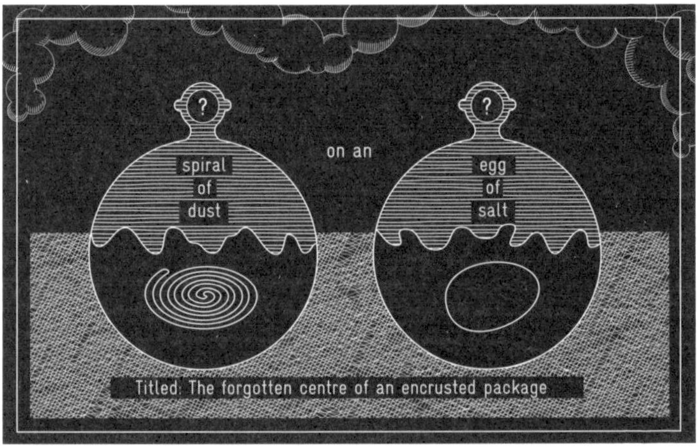

Eight Objects from the Configurable Catalogue
www.amateur.org.uk/machines/the-configurable-catalogue-of-objects/

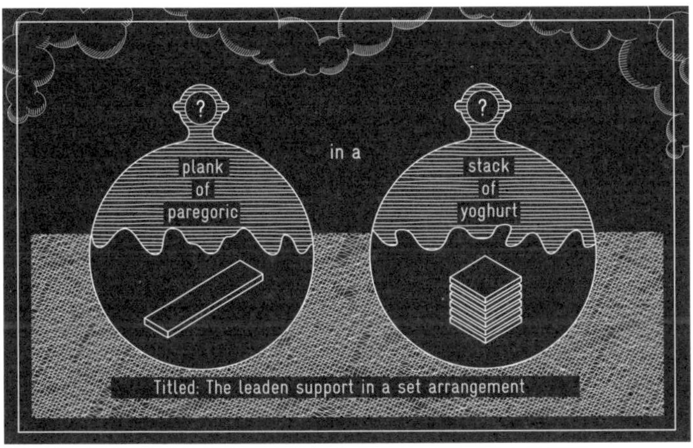

plank
of
paregoric
in a
stack
of
yoghurt
Titled: The leaden support in a set arrangement

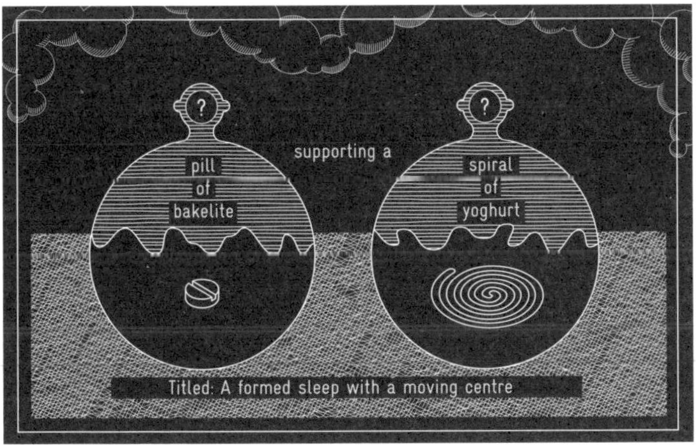

pill
of
bakelite
supporting a
spiral
of
yoghurt
Titled: A formed sleep with a moving centre

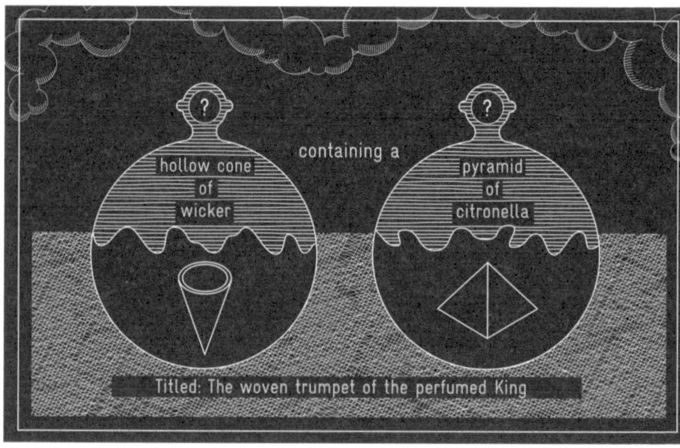
?
?
containing a
hollow cone
of
wicker
pyramid
of
citronella
Titled: The woven trumpet of the perfumed King

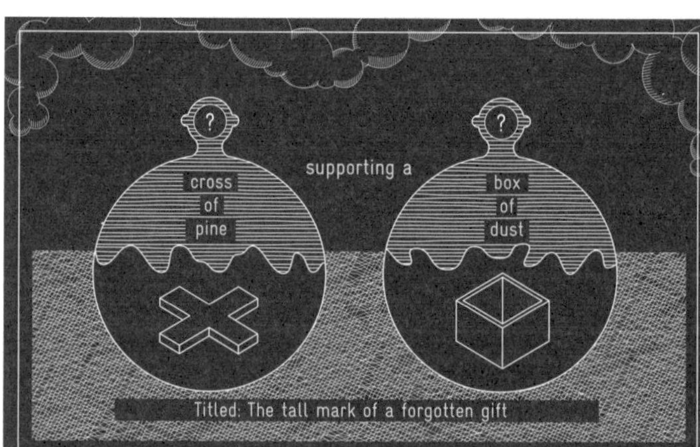
?
?
supporting a
cross
of
pine
box
of
dust
Titled: The tall mark of a forgotten gift

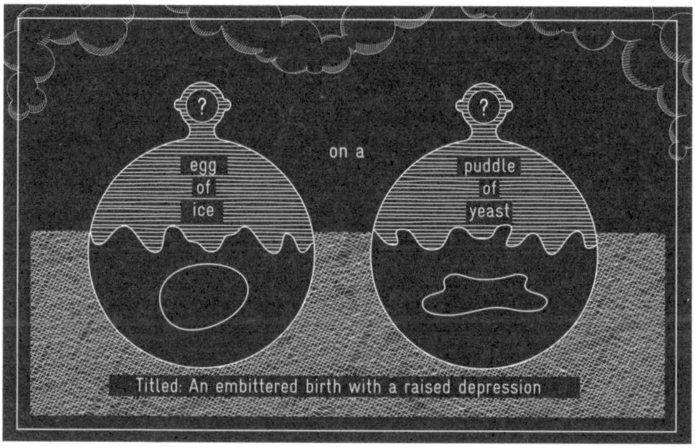
?
?
on a
egg
of
ice
puddle
of
yeast
Titled: An embittered birth with a raised depression

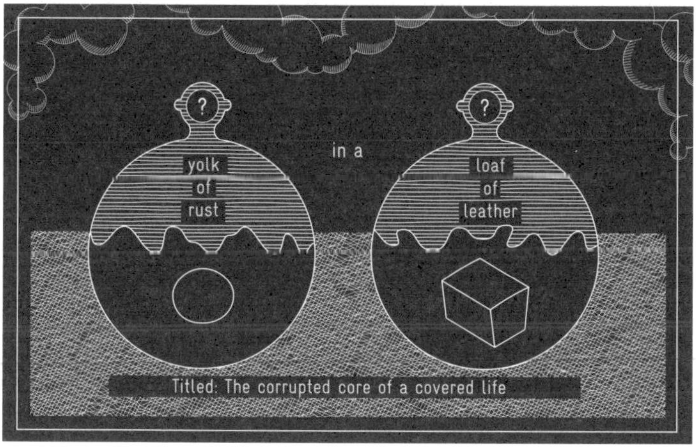
?
?
in a
yolk
of
rust
loaf
of
leather
Titled: The corrupted core of a covered life

33

Carla Bley

01/25/1994 22:23 914-688-2088 WATT WORKS INC PAGE 01

March 30, 1997

Dear Francois,

you asked: WHAT MEANS KEW. RHÔNE.?

At the time of the recording, we were under a vow of secrecy regarding the real meaning of the album's title. I remember that the head of the Virgin record company, Richard Branson, together with some very unsavoury lookng assistants, actually came to the studio to try to persuade Peter Blegvad to change the title. He suggested KEW PINAFORE or KEW TITANIC. At the time I didn't know that KEW. RHÔNE referred to a sunken ship in the Carribean - the HMS RHONE, but after Branson and his entourage left we were all warned to forget anything we had heard. I'm afraid I can't say any more.

Hope this is useful to you,

In response to his question "What means *Kew. Rhone.*?" Carla Bley sent François Ducat this fax, which became one of the exhibits featured on *Kew. ROM.* (see footnote 2, p.18).

PB, far out in the woods, Grog Kill, 1976.

The Grog Kill Studio is so far out in the woods of the Catskill Mountains that one might think that the people who live and work there don't want to be found. But the place is found by the most unusual and interesting recording projects; in a little clearing in the woods, where tomatoes ripen in the summer months, some lucky musicians find their way into a basement room full of possibility. What Carla Bley and Michael Mantler built there is legendary. John Greaves and Peter Blegvad's amazing 1977 recording *Kew. Rhone.* offered, in many ways, a perfect set of circumstances for a place like Grog Kill, and *vice versa*: adventurous musicians, good equipment and "fifty miles of elbow room" around the Willow house in order to do whatever needed to be done. The results were laid down on tape—we are lucky to have them today.

—Amy C. Beal, author of *Carla Bley*, 'American Composers' series (2011)

Grog Kill in 1976, home and studio of Carla Bley, Michael Mantler and daughter Karen. The studio was downstairs, the 'kill' (a stream) ran below, on the far side of the house.

All photos taken by Carla during sessions for *Kew. Rhone.*, exhumed 40 years later by Karen Mantler for this book. PB is shown proudly wearing Carla's fur coat and a scarf knitted by Karen who was then 8 years old. One of the 'oblique strategies' Brian Eno and Peter Schmidt came up with in 1975 is "tape your mouth" and it seems likely that's what John (left) and Mike (right) have done in the final snap above.

34

Andrew Cyrille

Having played for years with Cecil Taylor and other free-jazz innovators, Andrew had to radically readjust for *Kew. Rhone*. By naming the genre ('show music') he found a way in to what at first seemed closed territory. Unsurprisingly, *Proverbs*, the first track we recorded, required intensive rehearsal. Andrew recruited John to 'conduct' by beating the time out on his back (he was stripped to the waist), yelling "harder!" as he navigated the thicket of changing time signatures, until he'd found the perfect balance between constraint and freedom, between *Kew* and *Rhone*, which this and the other songs required.

Transcript of email correspondence, October 2014:

PB: Greetings from London. I hope this finds you well.

AC: I've been very, very busy and I'm sorry not to have been able to get back to you earlier!

PB: I'm putting a little book together about the album of songs we made 40 years ago in Carla and Mike's studio in Woodstock, *Kew. Rhone*. Your drumming was such a crucial part of it I wonder if you might remember anything about the session, or have any stories relating to the record that we could include?

AC: Lisa Herman's singing and all of the contiguous meter changes of John's music. A challenge for the ability to count, listen and make good music—to say the least for all concerned! There was a lot going on! Also, Mike and Carla trying to engineer the music in the best way possible.

PB: Do you remember on your first day with us in the studio wondering what the right approach should be, and then realizing that the songs were a kind of 'show music'? (I remember that as something of a breakthrough—it clarified things for me too.)

AC: Having played some shows in my career, yes, I could have related to those concepts to help myself play the music. Remember, John was relating to his father, a Welsh coal miner. I also remember John referring to Henry Cow [?], the British composer bandleader.

PB: Do you remember John Greaves cueing the time changes of the track called 'Proverbs' by drumming on your back, for instance? He says he does.

AC: I think so.

PB: He also says you sometimes play a track to your students—can you tell us a bit about that?
AC: Only for them to learn how to listen and play in odd meters.
PB: Anything you can say, any souvenirs you might have, would be great to have for the book. But if not, no worries.
AC: Well, all of us spent a lot of time working in detail on that music, to a satisfactory conclusion. If I remember correctly, John edited that music and organized the various taped sections after we'd recorded them. That's how I remember the record was produced. However, I wasn't there for that editing. I received the record after it was completed. Again, if I'm correct, I think Charles Mingus dropped in at the house for a few minutes during that time.[1]

Incidentally, I was playing at the Sunset in Paris about three years ago, and John came in to listen and say hello. I was very surprised and delighted to see him after so many years. Should you be in touch with him, give him my warmest regards.

Be well, Andrew

---

1 Mingus did indeed drop by and we all got to shake his enormous hand. John Greaves recalls it was on "the day we recorded Lisa's vocal on the track *Kew. Rhone.* She had a thick cold. My image (probably refocused over the years) is of the great man waddling down the studio stairs supported by two women, one black one white. Him listening to the track and saying 'Mmm mmm' and leaving. A divine benediction."

Robert Wyatt

Robert was a big influence on us, John and me. We shared a love of Soft Machine and of his solo work, especially *Rock Bottom* (1974). And the man himself was (still is) a delight. He'd graced a session Slapp Happy/Henry Cow did for John Peel's *Top Gear*, and John had performed and recorded with him in various contexts. I've said elsewhere that my interest in palindromes began with a Martin Gardner piece in *Scientific American*, but I'd already been floored by 'Little Red Riding Hood Hits the Road', a musical palindrome on *Rock Bottom*. Robert's work (often inspired by/co-authored with his partner the poet/artist Alfreda Benge) continues to serve as an example of what's possible if one dares (or has no option but) to follow one's own lights. Back then, in the mid '70s, his creative achievements were both an invitation and challenge to see what might be done with words and music, with song, that hadn't been done before.

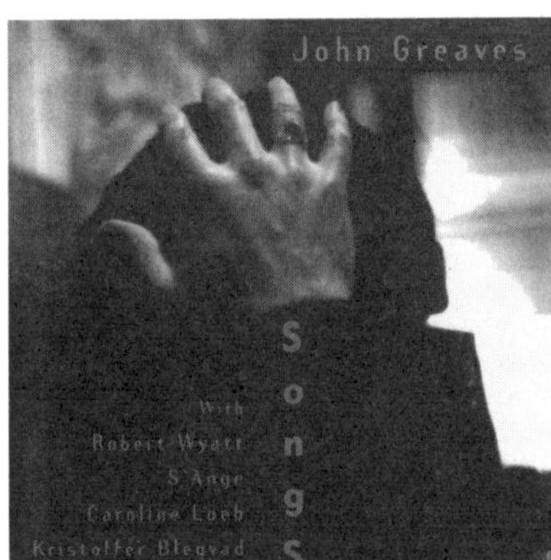

Over the years Robert has sung a few Greaves/Blegvad titles, including *gegen-stand* and *Kew. Rhone.* itself. When he sang 'The Song' (on the CD *Songs*, 1994) Robert qualified the dubious assertion that "man is the union of divinity and dust" by adding "inanity and lust" to the list, and quite right, too. The lyric is a look back at me and John composing *Kew. Rhone.* during that long hot Bicentennial summer:

All summer long, we sought the laws we
thought would cause the Song.
No mere machine made of music,
of words and music as other songs are,
this was the Song
A recipe,
a remedy,
a cure.

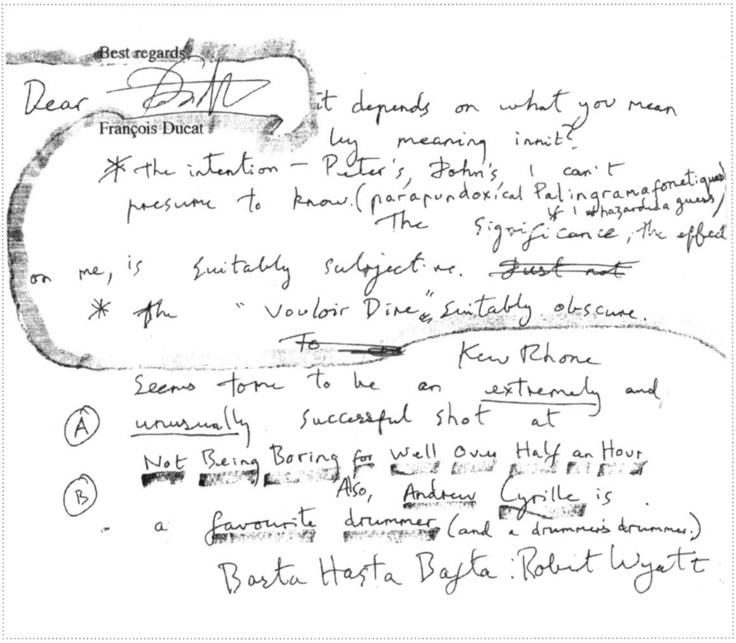
Best regards
François Ducat

Dear [crossed-out signature] it depends on what you mean by meaning innit?
* the intention — Peter's, John's, I can't presume to know. (parapundoxical Palingramafonetiques if I hazard a guess) The significance, the effect on me, is suitably subjective. ~~Just not~~
* the "Vouloir Dire" suitably obscure.
~~To~~ Kew Rhone
Seems to me to be an extremely and
(A) unusually successful shot at
Not Being Boring for Well Over Half an Hour
(B) Also, Andrew Cyrille is
a favourite drummer (and a drummer's drummer.)
Basta Hasta Bafta: Robert Wyatt

In 1997 Robert sent François Ducat this note for *Kew. ROM.* in response to the question "What means *Kew. Rhone.*?"

it depends on what you mean
by meaning innit?
* The intention—Peter's, John's, I can't
presume to know. (parapundoxical Palingramafonetiques
if I hazard a guess)
The significance, the effect
on me, is suitably subjective.
* The "Vouloir Dire" suitably obscure.
Kew Rhone
seems to me to be an extremely and
unusually successful shot at
Not Being Boring for Well Over Half an Hour.
Also, Andrew Cyrille is
a favourite drummer (and a drummer's drummer.)
Basta Hasta Bafta: Robert Wyatt

36

Archival Documents

Hello Simon & Binna -

exasperated?

But don't you realize what's at stake?

History will judge us

(not CASH BOX)

! Anyway - here's the new FIGURE C.

Please paste it over the old (will the old show through?). Caption reading FIGURE C. must show, of course - like those under t'other 3 Figs, right?

It may not be clear - but one reason for a certain complexity in these songs is to encourage listener to attend to him/her self; lyrics full of cross-references, incorporating illustrations, footnotes, etc. hopefully invite a more active participation than the usual does. And hopefully such participation will conduce to such attending. I want to extend this intention to the cover as well, by having it LAMINATED. The resultant gloss, on the dark front cover at least, will reflect like mirror I imagine, so that listener's own reflected face will interfere with his/her attempts to study photo - please consider this; I realize it costs more than high gloss, and this time I can't afford to pay for it!

I enclose check for $180.00 - if it's more, phone me.... I HATE that old illustration!

XXX Pete

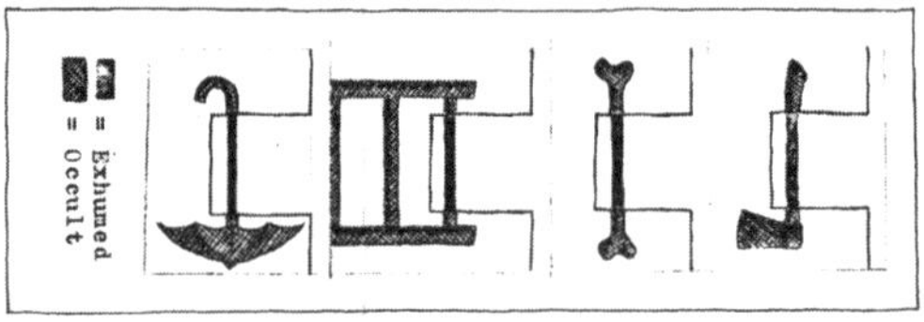

Letter from PB to Simon Draper and Binna (his secretary), 1977. (Simon was Richard Branson's right-hand man and head of A&R at Virgin Records.) Ever the equivocator, I wanted to change the illustration I'd done for Figure C of *Pipeline* at the last minute. This required new films being made for the cover art, and Simon said Virgin wouldn't pay. Evidently I must have raised the $180.00 it cost and sent the cheque, the new artwork and my instructions from New York to London, delaying production by days if not weeks. Exasperated? They must have been, but Simon was pretty tolerant considering what a nut he was dealing with ("History will judge us [not CASH BOX]"—was I kidding? Maybe.). Despite my arguments, the cover was not laminated. It was printed 'high gloss', less costly but useless as a mirror.

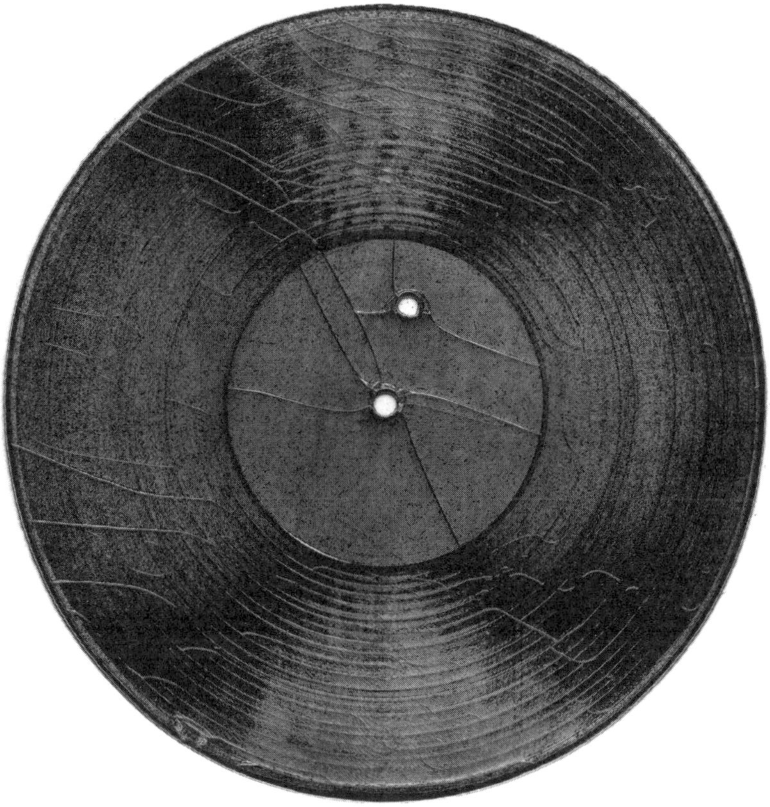

While working on the record John and I fantasised about ways we might involve the vinyl platter, the physical disc itself, in the overall interactive 'apparatus' of *Kew. Rhone.* One idea was to have the record pierced with a second hole, a bit off-centre. If the disc isn't centred, the music will be distorted—it will sound warped. But we imagined calibrating the position of the second hole so that revolving at 33rpm the distortions of rhythm and pitch could be used as formal constraints in the composition of a new piece. We drilled an extra hole in a few records to study the effect, but that's as far as it went.

cf. Tom Raworth: "drill / another hole / near the edge / of the label and / play it / from there / with a light pickup"—*Ace* (1974)

JOHN GREAVES/ PETER BLEGVAD/ LISA HERMAN
Kew. Rhone. (Virgin)

WHEN I first heard that John Greaves and Peter Blegvad were to make an album with Mike Mantler and Carla Bley, I feared it might turn out to be a little more than a set of Henry Cow retreads.

However, not even familiarity with the complete Henry Cow/Slapp Happy output could prepare the listener for "Kew. Rhone."

It is completely, utterly unlike any other album you're likely to come across. Ever.

To begin with, the cover's not just the usual mildly decorative affair intended solely to catch your eye; neither is the lyric sheet the usual "I'm a poet" jack-off: lose them and you've not only lost your paddle, you've lost the creek as well.

Much of the album's uniqueness stems from Blegvad's lyrics, (more a series of word-games and puzzles than songs), which could be accused of descending into a cheap, meaningless surrealism, were it not for the immediate success of a few.

For these idiosyncratic lyrics, Greaves has worked out a staggering variety of intricate and unusual arrangements which bear only occasional resemblance to his past work with Henry Cow; in the main, they're more instantly memorable than most of that band's repertoire.

The album opens with a slight instrumental entree, "Good Evening", then it's straight into the main course with "Twenty-Two Proverbs", which, as the title suggests, is a collection of proverbs from various sources set to an arrangement of surprising regularity, featuring a frantic trumpet break from Mantler and some wrenching, rabid guitar from Blegvad, underpinned by quite exceptional drumming from former Cecil Taylor sideman Andrew Cyrille.

"Seven Scenes From The Painting 'Exhuming The First American Mastodon' by C. W. Peale" is a set of statements referring to the strange picture on the cover, of varying degrees of explicability. A slow, introspective, piano-based piece with a wistful, haunting melody and an air of cabaret sleaze on acid.

"Kew. Rhone." itself is a word-game in two parts, the first made up of partial anagrams of the title carefully arranged to make a readable whole, with a staccato musical texture comprising piano, organ and whistling — at least I *think* it's whistling.

The second part takes in a fuller arrangement behind vocal variations on the palindrome "Peel's foe, not a set animal, laminates a tone of sleep". Fun for art's sake, and probably the most successful piece on the album.

Lisa Herman's vocals throughout are fine (though maybe a little too pristine in places); indeed, all concerned with the project play with a taste and subtlety rarely heard these days.

Okay, so it mightn't be everybody's cup of meat, but if you've been feeling a little jaded of late, pass up that copy of "Animals" and pick this up instead. You may be pleasantly surprised.

Andy Gill

KEW RHONE — JOHN GREAVES/PETER BLEGVAD (Virgin 2082): Kew Rhone undoes the compromise of songs. Only very rarely can music enhance the meaning of words, and words are too bound up in definitions to complement music. But Greaves and Blegvad explode the tenuous link between the two.

Though John Greaves (ex-Henry Cow bassist) wrote the music and Peter Blegvad wrote the words, it is happily not possible to separate their contributions. Kew Rhone is reckless, it capsizes meaning and sets sounds adrift.

'Twenty-two proverbs' is a powerful example. The lyrics consist of 22 proverbs — normally loaded with earthy common sense and meaning — which are immediately destroyed, and then re-emerge as noises without tradition.

In the past 20 years, much thought has gone into the form of music. Once in the air, music is gone. And that is now its great strength. This album raises words to that elevated position of instant death.

Above: Review by David Bowie (the Welsh music critic, not the popular entertainer) in *The Pontypridd Observer*, 13 May 1977.

Opposite: Review by Andy Gill in *New Musical Express*, 23 April 1977.

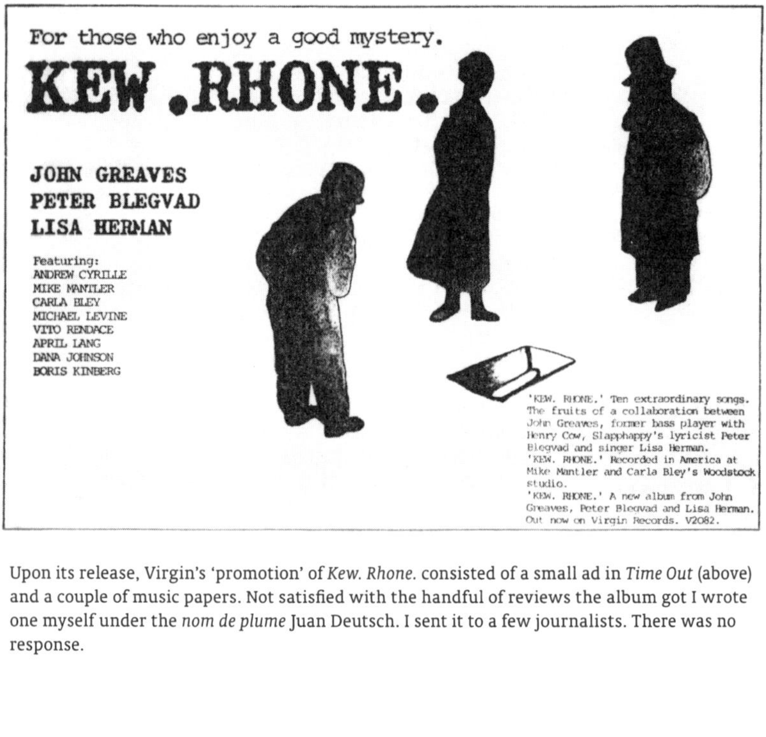

Upon its release, Virgin's 'promotion' of *Kew. Rhone.* consisted of a small ad in *Time Out* (above) and a couple of music papers. Not satisfied with the handful of reviews the album got I wrote one myself under the *nom de plume* Juan Deutsch. I sent it to a few journalists. There was no response.

KEW. RHONE.

It doesn't take genius to see that the world is not the stage the Bard proposed, it's a market-place. And we, milling in it, are justifiably tired of hearing that each new product on display, whether a scouring-pad or a mystic cult, is in some way different, somehow exempt from the lustreless mediocrity of its predecessors.

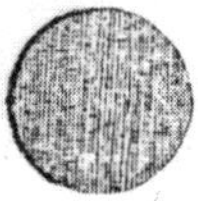

DISC

From time to time, however, a product is brought to our attention which quite simply demands recognition as being new in its field and which appeases, for the moment, our cynicism. KEW. RHONE., in this critic's opinion, is such a product.

PIPE

WAND, ROD OR DOWEL

CRESCENT

Aided by luminaries Carla Bley, Mike Mantler and Andrew Cyrille (the latter was Cecil Taylor's drummer for a decade), composer John Greaves and lyricist Peter Blegvad have created a highly original work which manages to fascinate and irritate with its complexity, while never falling short of its objective to entertain. Vocalist Lisa Herman gets much of the credit for this. She can effortlessly squeeze a line like "voltaic piles of gold-plated bamboo" into a gap just big enough for a hiccup, and her broad New York accent tints the convoluted lyrics with a welcome irony.

COIN

LOAF

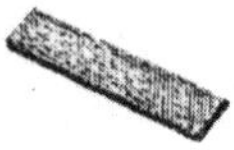

PLANK OR SLAB

FAN

KEW. RHONE. can be called a "concept" album. In other words, a few specific themes, both musical and lyrical, inform and unify the whole. Mr. Blegvad hedged when interviewed, but it's this critic's opinion that what links the lyrics is a concern with <u>objects</u> and our perception of them – how we desire them (or think we do), ascribe meanings to them, and invest them with potency as symbols or fetishes. Granted, not all the songs refer to objects specifically, but in such instances <u>it seems to be the language itself which Mr. Blegvad</u>

"X"

PELLET OR PILL

is trying to objectify. He does this either by rejecting the more fluid forms of his past work[1] in favour of the chill rigidity of lists, or, as in the title track[2], by using language as a material with properties other than the ability to convey data. By decorating the record-sleeve with illustrations indispensable as keys to the lyrics, he stresses the "objectness" not only of the words, but of the record itself as a sort of "kit" with parts to be assembled by the listener. William Carlos Williams wrote "a poem is a small (or large) machine made out of words" - Mr. Blegvad's intention seems to have been to write lyrics to which the same definition would apply.

WHORL OR GYRE

SPIT

For six years John Greaves played bass with one of England's most innovative and exacting groups, Henry Cow.[3] In 1976 he left to pursue his own career, and while the music he composed for KEW. RHONE. bears clear traces of his past, it also seems to celebrate his new-found independence. It's manic, unpredictable stuff, with a touch of "other-worldliness" in the melodies as there was in "Half asleep; Half awake" on the album "Unrest". But, to this critic, there is a greater diversity on KEW. RHONE., a spectrum of moods evoked that's wider than the group's rigid format would allow.

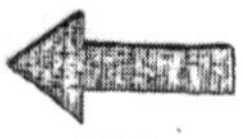

ARROW

CLOUD

WEDGE

In songs it appears Mr. Greaves has found a form perfectly suited to his gifts as a composer. In Mr. Blegvad he has found a lyricist suited to his extra ordinary songs. That their first attempt to collaborate should have resulted in an album as rich in ideas as KEW. RHONE. makes this critic wonder. What "miracle of rare device" will they be fabricating next?

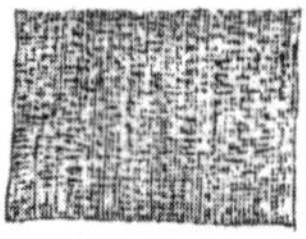

BLANKET

Juan Deutsch

Notes

1. Mr. Blegvad made four albums: "Sort Of" (on Polydor) and "Slapp Happy", "Desperate Straights" (Slapp Happy with Henry Cow), and "Living in the Heart of the Beast" (Henry Cow with Slapp Happy) on Virgin.

2. The song "Kew. Rhone." is in two parts. The words of the first part are all anagrams of the title. The second part involves a palindrome - "Peel's foe, not a set animal, laminates a tone of sleep."

3. Mr. Greaves made five albums with Henry Cow: "Leg end", "Unrest", "Desperate Straights", "Living in the Heart of the Beast", and "Henry Cow Concerts".

37

Notes on Contributors

Amy Beal
Music historian and Professor of Music at the University of California, Santa Cruz. She has published widely on the history of 20th-century American music, and is the author of two books: *New Music, New Allies: American Experimental Music in West Germany from the Zero Hour to Reunification* (2006) and *Carla Bley*, 'American Composers' series (2011).

Carla Bley
Composer, performer, bandleader, activist, she has participated and contributed significantly to key places, events and groups in the history of jazz and other musics from the late '50s to the present. She has been awarded two honorary doctorates and many other tributes over the years in recognition of the unique sonic world she has created. Whether for big bands, for classical musicians, for combos, trios, duets or solo performance, her music bears her distinctive stamp in which mischief manages to co-exist with deep feeling, and respect for tradition with radical creative freedom. She has also been a pioneer in the development of artist-owned record labels, co-founding and managing WATT Records and the New Music Distribution Service with Michael Mantler. For (much) more see www.wattxtrawatt.com/biocarla.pdf

Franklin Bruno
American singer-songwriter, academic, writer and blogger originally from Upland, California. He has been a member of Nothing Painted Blue since its inception in 1986. Bruno writes music criticism for *The Village Voice*, *Time Out New York*, *Thought Catalog* and *Salon.com*. He received a doctorate in philosophy from UCLA and has been a visiting professor of philosophy at Bard College. In addition to his own recordings, Bruno worked on the Mountain Goats albums *Tallahassee* and *The Sunset Tree*. He also records with the Mountain Goats frontman John Darnielle as The Extra Lens. *The Accordion Repertoire*, his first collection of poems, was published in 2010. His most recent album is *ANOTHER* with his band, the Human Hearts.

Sheridan Coakley
Close friend of PB and Anthony Moore (of Slapp Happy) since the '60s, he was involved in many of their escapades in the UK, Europe and the US, taking lots of photographs. He started out with a stall selling antiques in the 1970s, eventually founding his own company to manufacture and sell original designs of furniture. Thirty years on, the company, SCP, has become a global concern and several of those designs are considered classics.

Jonathan Coe
The author of many books, including *What a Carve Up!* and *The Rotters' Club*. His most recent novel is *Expo 58*.

Jane Colling
Artist and founder member of the Bermondsey Artists Group, she has exhibited her work mostly at the Café Gallery, Southwark, London since the 1980s. She also distributes films for artists and animators from Jane Colling Distribution and is Festivals Coordinator for the Animation Department at the Royal College of Art. Further back in time Jane made posters and visuals for friends Louise, Henry Cow and Ottawa Music Company, studied Fine Art at Reading University, then worked as a printmaker and poster designer before getting drawn into the world of animation.

Andrew Cyrille
Avant-garde jazz drummer born in Brooklyn, 1939, into a family with a mother from Haiti. He began studying science at St. John's University, but was already playing jazz in the evenings and switched his studies to the Juilliard School. His first professional engagement was accompanying singer Nellie Lutcher and he had an early recording session with

The Ray Irving Showband, Wales, mid '60s. JG second from left.

Coleman Hawkins. Trumpeter Ted Curson introduced him to pianist Cecil Taylor when Cyrille was eighteen. He joined the Cecil Taylor unit in 1964 and stayed for about ten years and eventually performed drum duos with Milford Graves. In addition to recording as a bandleader, he has recorded and/or performed with musicians such as David Murray, Irène Schweizer, Marilyn Crispell, Carla Bley, Butch Morris and Reggie Workman among others.

François Ducat

"Born and educated in France, I studied cinema at the INSAS in Brussels where I chose to stay until now. After two short documentary films out of school, I had a break to focus on multimedia projects with Peter Blegvad like *The Encyclopaedist* (1995) and *Kew. ROM.* (1997). I went back to films with mainly *Aqua Micans, an hommage to Raymond Roussel* (2004) in the framework of De Balie *Imaginary Media* exhibition curated by Peter Blegvad, *Nord-Sud.com* (2007), *Mokoomba d'une rive à l'autre* (2010), *Tu oublieras aussi Henriette* (2011) and *Ascèse* (2013) a film about sound and environment."

John Greaves

Composer, piano player, singer, songwriter, bass guitarist. Read English Literature at Cambridge where he met and joined Henry Cow. Began a long history of collaborations with Peter Blegvad. Has lived in Paris for the last thirty years, made a bunch of records and continues to perform all over the place. Born and raised in Wales, at thirteen he was given a bass guitar by his father, a dancehall bandleader. Within six months he was the bassist in his father's band (the Ray Irving Showband, above), playing a varied mix of musical styles, writing arrangements, gigging extensively and opening for pop groups like the Searchers and Gerry and the Pacemakers. He has never looked back.

Doug Harvey

In addition to his activities as an art critic, LA-based Doug Harvey is an internationally exhibited multimedia artist and experimental musician, serial facilitator for the multi-city improvisational audio collage radio programme *The Mannlicher Carcano Radio Hour* (now in its 15th year) and the editor of *patacritical Interrogations Techniques Anthology Volume 3*, with contributions from Messrs Blegvad and Sackett in the company of numerous other luminaries living and dead. Visit www.dougharvey.la and www.dougharvey.blogspot.com

Lisa Herman (Cunningham)

Peter's in London, John's in Montmartre
It's like working with Aaron Copeland
and Sartre
Or Stravinsky and William Blake
I just met them in New York by mistake.

*I'm not as autistically smart as Peet**
Nor as droll, refined and elite

Not a Cambridge lad from Wales like John
They were making a record and
They put me on

Since then I've mostly taken the ride
On their coat-tails, long and wide
Okay I'm (mostly) kidding, I've got my pride

I'm a serious artist, I do lots of things
*("Mostly she writes music and sings!"**)*
**I call him 'Peet' because he calls me 'Leece'*
Our next album cover will be taken in Nice
In a swimming pool, naked as day
The title I'm not at liberty to say

**Barbara Herman, the accomplished New York pianist, pedagogue and Mozart scholar (my mother)

Jeff Hoke

Museum designer, fine artist and the curator of his own personal Museum of Lost Wonder. Hoke studied art at the University of Illinois, and has lived in England as well as the US. He has exhibited his fine art as well as the artist-book-cum-'house publication' of the Museum for Lost Wonder in many American cities. He assisted in the creation of the Museum of Alchemy in Prague. www.lostwonder.org.

Dana Johnson

Visual artist and translator. Her paintings, drawings and three-dimensional pieces explore her fascination with holes, metamorphosis and the affinity between animals and humans. Born in southern Illinois in 1955, she currently lives in Sweden.

Andrew Joron

Author of *Trance Archive: New and Selected Poems* (2010). Joron's previous poetry collections include *The Removes* (1999), *Fathom* (2003) and *The Sound Mirror* (2008). *The Cry at Zero*, a selection of his prose poems and critical essays, was published in 2007. From the German, he has translated the *Literary Essays* of Marxist-Utopian philosopher Ernst Bloch (1998) and *The Perpetual Motion Machine* by the proto-Dada fantasist Paul Scheerbart (2011). Joron lives in Berkeley, California, where he theorises using the theremin.

Glenn Kenny

Born in Fort Lee, New Jersey, in 1959. His written work, for which he is sometimes monetarily compensated, has aspired to the condition of criticism since the early 1980s. He happily resides with his wife Claire in Brooklyn, New York.

Frank Key

Uberjanitor of the Hooting Yard website (hootingyard.org), an ever-growing repository of thousands of pieces of deathless prose. His radio show, *Hooting Yard On The Air*, during which he babbles some of the majestic sweeping paragraphs he has written over the previous week, is the longest-running programme on London's art radio station ResonanceFM, celebrating its tenth anniversary this coming spring. More than one major publisher has told Mr Key that he has "absolutely no commercial potential whatsoever".

Simon Lucas

Born in the 20th century, an out-of-work artist who currently teaches computers to do parlour tricks for a living. Whereabouts unknown.

Karen Mantler

Daughter of jazz musicians Carla Bley and Michael Mantler. As a songwriter and a bandleader her style has attracted a world-class list of musicians to her band throughout the years, including Steven Bernstein, Eric Mingus, Hiram Bullock and Arturo O'Farrill. She has performed frequently in Europe with various musicians, most notably John Greaves, Chris Cutler and Peter Blegvad. As a Hammond organ-player, she has been touring and recording with the Carla Bley Big Band since 1988. Most recently she has been performing in New York with her Trio featuring Doug Wieselman and Kato Hideki. They have recently released a CD on the label XtraWATT (ECM) entitled *Business is Bad*.

Michael Mantler

Austrian composer and trumpeter in new jazz and contemporary music. He has received several awards in his native country including the State Prize for Improvised Music, the Prandtauer Prize of the City of St. Pölten (where he spent his early youth) and the Music Prize of the City of Vienna. The anthology *Review* (recordings 1968–2000), released by ECM in 2006, traced his musical path during more than thirty years of recordings for JCOA, WATT and ECM.

Harry Mathews

"Debonair dean of experimental fiction" (*Art Forum*), short story writer, poet, novelist, essayist, translator, editor, the first American to be elected into the Oulipo.

Tanya Peixoto
Runs bookartbookshop in London. Tea trolley dance instructor and ex-voto painter, in 2014 she was elected Vice-Curator of the Collège de 'Pataphysique, Paris.

Benjamin Piekut
Historian of experimental music, rock and jazz after 1960. His book, *Experimentalism Otherwise: The New York Avant-Garde and Its Limits*, was published in 2011. He is an assistant professor in the music department at Cornell University.

Margit Rosen
Born 1974 in Munich, is an art historian with a specific interest in tools and the laws of chance.

Philip Tagney
Worked as a music producer for the last two decades, mainly for BBC Radio 3. He has also worked as a music consultant for radio drama productions, and as music producer for the radiophonic piece *Voices*, by Harold Pinter and James Clarke. His sound installation *Disrehearspektaktak* was commissioned by the Borealis Festival, Bergen in 2009. He writes songs and monologues under the pseudonym Louis Lyrec. He has played bass guitar for Bow Mods. He is a member of the musique concrète composing/performing group Langham Research Centre.

Robert Wyatt
Drummer, composer, singer, activist, pataphysician—Robert's life thus far, his work and thought, has been well served by *Different Every Time*, the authorised biography by Marcus O'Dair (2014). In that book PB describes *Kew. Rhone.* as "a kind of love letter to influences like Robert".

Rafi Zabor
Writer currently living in Brooklyn, New York. He has written extensively about music—mostly jazz—and has published two books, the novel *The Bear Comes Home* and the 'souvenir' *I, Wabenzi*. *The Bear Comes Home* won the PEN/Faulkner Award for fiction. Most recently he has completed a sort of thriller set amid leaves and buds in California, and hopes to get back to a more substantial novel set in Turkey in 2003 and called *The Bosphorus Dogs*.

Siegfried Zielinski
Professor of Media Theory, special research field archaeology and variantology of the arts and media at the University of Arts (UdK) Berlin; Michel Foucault Professor of Media Archaeology and Techno-Culture at the European Graduate School in Saas Fee; Director of the Vilém-Flusser-Archiv at the UdK Berlin; Founding Director of the Academy of Media Arts Cologne (1994–2000). Books in English include: *Audiovisions* (1999), *Deep Time of the Media* (2006) and *[...after the Media]* (2013); Zielinski is editor of the series *VARIANTOLOGY: Deep Time Relations Between Arts, Sciences, Technologies* (2005–2011, with co-editors S. Wagnermaier (vol. 1), D. Link (vol. 2) and E. Fürlus (vols. 3–5)). Member of the North Rhine-Westphalia Academy of Sciences and Arts, the Academy of Arts Berlin, the European Film Academy, the Magic Lantern Society of Great Britain; Honorary Senator of the Institute of Media Archaeology (IMA), Hainburg.

Abyssal thanks first and foremost to all the contributors and their translators; and to the publisher, designer and editor of this book, Colin Sackett. To Chris Allen for proofing it. To John, Lisa, Carla, Mike and Andrew, not to mention the other stalwarts who generously lent their talents to the record when we were young, before we'd sung the Song. For encouragement, useful leads etc. before or during the writing of this book my thanks to Karen Mantler, George Ttoouli, Adam Dant, Jody Harris, Sheila McLaughlin, David Morley, Maureen Freely, Alastair Brotchie and the London Institute of 'Pataphysics, Chris and Lone McCourt, Clayton Eshleman, Mark Ellingham, Natania Jansz, Anthony Moore, Kevin Jackson, John Paige, Jean-Pierre Weiller, Ed Haber, David Coxhead, Dirk Zimmer, Ammiel Alcalay, Aymeric Leroy, Les Coleman, Mike Zwerin, Joan Ashworth and Chris Cutler. As ever, thanks to Chloë Fremantle, without whom… (And if you helped and I've neglected to mention you, my apologies. I'll be kicking myself. How dare I? Who do I think I am?) Good question.—PB

PB & JG, Paris, 1984 (photo by Nellie Parent)